Dearly Beloved

LEWIS WHELCHEL

Oysterville, WA

This is a work of fiction. Names, characters, places, and incidents are products of the author's imagination or are used fictitiously. Any resemblance to actual events or persons, living or dead, is entirely coincidental.

Dearly Beloved

Copyright © 2012 by Lewis Whelchel

All rights reserved, including the right to reproduce this book, or portions thereof, in any format whatsoever. For information: P.O. Box 34, Oysterville WA 98641

ISBN: 978-1-936009-13-8

Graphic design by Ellen Pickels

Dedication

To my wife, Tracy, who continues to love me despite the many hours I spend writing. And to Debbie, who has taught me to write by her careful editing over the past years.

Thank you both!

Chapter 1

"Lizzy, I will be fine. I will recover, I promise."

"Oh, Jane, I am so worried about you, and so is Mr. Bingley. He has sent for a physician from London. He is beside himself with worry. I think he is truly in love with you, and I am so happy for you."

"Lizzy, I am sure that he is just concerned about me. And I think it is too much trouble having someone from London come to see me."

"Nevertheless, Jane, Doctor Foster will be here tomorrow, and I know that you will be kind to him and explain all that you are feeling. I am so angry with Mama for making you ride Nellie over here that day. You should never have come."

"Oh, Lizzy, it does no good to dwell on that. Mama was only doing what she thought was best for me."

"Well, it was a good scheme to be sure, and look at you now—in bed for a week and hardly able to move. I am so sorry, Jane. It is my fault for teasing Papa into saying he needed the horses at the farm."

"Lizzy, it is not your fault or Mama's fault or anybody's fault. I have a little cold—that is all—and everybody is making a fuss over it. Lizzy, I am really tired now. I think I shall sleep for a while."

Elizabeth was not as confident as Jane that it was just a "little cold." She was quite worried. Jane had never been this ill before, and she was not getting any better.

Elizabeth and Jane's acquaintance with the Netherfield party began at the Meryton assembly. Mr. Bingley had arrived comfortably late with his two sisters, Miss Caroline Bingley and Mrs. Louisa Hurst, Louisa's husband, Mr. Allen Hurst, and Mr. Bingley's dear friend Mr. Fitzwilliam Darcy. This was a great relief to some of the ladies in the room who had believed the general report that Mr. Bingley was bringing twelve ladies and seven gentlemen with him to the assembly.

Mr. Bingley was soon introduced to Miss Jane Bennet.

"Miss Bennet, if you are not otherwise engaged, may I claim the next two dances?"

"I am not engaged." She looked at him through lowered lashes as a gentle blush suffused her face.

Jane had seen handsome men before but none who sparked her interest like Mr. Bingley. At two and twenty, she had never fancied herself in love before, and she longed for the day when a passionate love would enter her life. She wanted a husband who would treat her the way her uncle treated his wife, Mrs. Gardiner—with compassion, tenderness and respect—completely unlike the example of marriage she daily witnessed. If not, she would rather end an old maid. Of course, she was so poor she would probably not marry anyway, but she would always hope—always.

When Jane recollected herself, she realized that Mr. Bingley was still standing in front of her, looking very intently into her eyes. She arched her eyebrows in the form of a question. Mr. Bingley gave a start.

"Oh! I am sorry, Miss Bennet. Please excuse me." And he turned and walked away.

"Well, Jane," laughed Elizabeth, "you have made your first conquest of the evening."

"Lizzy, please, do not say such things."

"I must Jane. I must have someone to tease. I think he is in love with you. He was out of his mind when he was staring at you. And Jane, I think you were too. Of what were you thinking, dear?"

"Of love, Lizzy—of a passionate love."

As for Mr. Bingley's sisters, they were ladies of decided fashion and elegance from the evidence of their dress and manner, and they thought themselves quite above the folks of Meryton. They spoke well, walked well and danced well, but they thought well of no one but Mr. Darcy. They nibbled on sandwiches with perfect ease and appeared born and bred with wineglasses in their hands. Nothing was beneath their notice and ridicule;

they commented that there were only three musicians, the so-called gentry were loud rather than dignified or genteel, the fashions were out of style and the assembly room was in need of dusting. How their brother came to even find Netherfield was a miracle; that he should choose to lease it was astounding, and that his sisters should be there with him was appalling. If it were not for the fact that their brother had begged them to stay with him, they would have remained in Mr. Hurst's townhouse in London.

Mr. Darcy was single, to be sure, and every female eye was upon him. What an honor it would be to be singled out by him! It was soon rumored upon his arrival at Netherfield that Mr. Darcy's estate in Derbyshire was worth ten thousand a year. He was handsome—more so than Mr. Bingley—but soon lost favor with the people in the assembly when he appeared to be above their company. He shunned introductions, danced only with Mr. Bingley's sisters, and walked around the room as though stalking prey, speaking only to members of his own party. He was decidedly proud, and his character was fixed as a result of the following exchange with Mr. Bingley.

"Come, Darcy," said he, "I must have you dance. I hate to see you standing about by yourself in this stupid manner. You had much better dance."

"I certainly shall not. You know how I detest it unless I am particularly acquainted with my partner. At such an assembly as this, it would be insupportable. Your sisters are presently engaged, and there is not another woman whom it would not be a punishment to me to stand up with."

"I would not be as fastidious as you are for a kingdom!" cried Bingley. "Upon my honor, I never met with so many pleasant girls in my life as I have this evening, and there are several of them you see uncommonly pretty."

"*You* are dancing with the only handsome girl in the room," said Mr. Darcy, looking at the eldest Miss Bennet.

"Oh! She is the most beautiful creature I ever beheld! But there is one of her sisters sitting down just behind you who is very pretty, and I dare say very agreeable. Do let me ask my partner to introduce you."

"Which do you mean?"—and turning 'round, he looked for a moment at Elizabeth till, catching her eye, he withdrew his own and coldly said—"She is tolerable but not handsome enough to tempt me, and I am in no humor at present to give consequence to young ladies who are slighted by other men. You had better return to your partner and enjoy her smiles, for you are wasting your time with me."

Mr. Bingley followed his friend's advice. Mr. Darcy walked off, and Elizabeth remained with no very cordial feelings towards him. She told the story, however, with great spirit among her friends, for she had a lively, playful disposition, which delighted in anything ridiculous. (*Pride and Prejudice, Volume I, Chapter III.*)

Mr. Bingley observed Miss Elizabeth's reaction to Mr. Darcy's statement, and he was ashamed for his friend. He had spoken so loudly that she had overheard his remark. Mr. Bingley thought her to be quite pretty—almost as much as her sister—and Miss Elizabeth must be very hurt. Later, he spoke with Miss Bennet.

"Miss Bennet, please apologize to Miss Elizabeth for me, for I fear I have caused her a great deal of mortification and embarrassment by way of my friend."

"Mr. Bingley, I do not understand. Whatever do you mean? What could have happened to distress her so?"

"I tried unsuccessfully to persuade my friend to dance and offered to obtain an introduction for him through you to Miss Elizabeth. Darcy refused outright, making a comment about not dancing with strangers and other things not worth repeating. Frankly, he was quite uncivil. I am embarrassed for him, for I believe it possible that Miss Elizabeth overheard him speaking of her."

"How could he treat Elizabeth in such a manner? She is as pretty and as kind as any young woman he could hope to meet. I am sorry for her—and for him. He is deprived of a very special young lady who would have cared nothing for his ten thousand a year. I think he very much misjudged her, but it is more his loss than hers. I see her dancing again, this time with Captain Carter, and Mr. Darcy is still standing by the wall."

"You are right." Bingley chuckled. "He is his own worst enemy. So, Miss Bennet, have you always lived at Longbourn?"

"Yes, I have. My family has never lived anywhere else. Where are you from, Mr. Bingley?"

"A small town in the far North. My father was very successful in trade and left me a large fortune. He intended to buy an estate and live the life of a gentleman, but he died just as I came of age, so he never fulfilled his dream. Now I am trying to find my place in the world. I received word that Netherfield was a worthy house near town in a pleasant neighborhood, so

Dearly Beloved

I came and looked into it. I agreed with the general report and took it for a year. And here I am." He seemed to be proud of his accomplishment of finding a home so quickly.

"I am sorry about your father. That must have come as quite a shock for you. But I am glad that you came into the neighborhood," she said with a blush. She was very glad he had come.

"Thank you. And what about your family, Miss Bennet? Please tell me about them."

"You have met most of them, I believe. I have four younger sisters, Elizabeth, Mary, Catherine and Lydia. I am very close to Elizabeth. I would say that she is my best friend. We talk about everything without reserve. I have an uncle who is a solicitor in Meryton and another in trade in Town."

"Would you care to dance while we talk, Miss Bennet? A new set is just forming."

"It would give me great pleasure, sir."

By the end of the assembly, Miss Bennet and Mr. Bingley were in a fair way to be very much in love. They had similar tempers and an excellent understanding. Of course, Jane made everyone appear to advantage because of her excellent disposition.

Jane and Mr. Bingley had common interests, a united way of feeling optimistic about the world and a general desire of thinking well of other people and looking for the good in them by overlooking the bad or explaining it away as some form of misunderstanding.

The Bennet family returned home with a happy report for Mr. Bennet on the proceedings of the assembly. He had been hoping that their expectations for Mr. Bingley would be disappointed, but he had another story to hear. In fact, he was pleased that his daughters had an enjoyable time. He only wanted their happiness, particularly that of his two eldest for whom he felt nothing but the highest esteem, and especially for his second daughter, Elizabeth, his acknowledged favorite.

When Jane and Elizabeth were alone, the former, who had been cautious in her praise of Mr. Bingley before, expressed to her sister how very much she admired him.

"He is just what a young man ought to be," said she, "sensible, good-humored, lively; and I never saw such happy manners!—so much ease, with such perfect good-breeding."

"He is also handsome," replied Elizabeth; "which a young man ought likewise to be, if he possibly can. His character is thereby complete."

"I was very much flattered by his asking me to dance a second time. I did not expect such a compliment."

"Did you not? *I* did for you. But that is one great difference between us. Compliments always take *you* by surprise and *me* never. What could be more natural than his asking you again? He could not help seeing that you were about five times as pretty as every other woman in the room. No thanks to his gallantry for that. Well, he certainly is very agreeable, and I give you leave to like him." (*Pride and Prejudice, Volume I, Chapter IV.*)

"I like him very much, Lizzy, very much indeed, and I believe he likes me as well. I look forward to our next meeting."

"Then you will be happy to know that the Lucases are having a party for all of the neighborhood tomorrow night and the Netherfield party has accepted the invitation."

"Oh, Lizzy, I did not know that! That is wonderful news! But perhaps he will not come. Maybe he will think the Lucases are below his level of society."

"Jane, Mr. Darcy may think so, but be assured that Mr. Bingley does not. In fact, it does not matter who the company is; if you are there, rest assured, Mr. Bingley will be there also."

THE BENNET FAMILY ARRIVED IN good time for the Lucases' party. All of the officers and the other neighborhood families were there except for the Netherfield party. Jane waited patiently for them to arrive. Elizabeth was no less interested in them, wanting to see how Mr. Bingley behaved towards Jane and how Mr. Darcy behaved towards everybody else. To own the truth, despite her animosity towards him for his treatment of her at the Meryton assembly, she could not deny that he was handsome and pleasing to look at, and in this way, she was attracted to him.

In the Lucases' drawing room, Elizabeth's sister Mary was at the pianoforte playing some obscure concerto to which no one was listening. Lydia and Kitty were flirting with the officers, and Elizabeth wondered whether a sensible thought ever crossed their minds. Her father thought not, and Elizabeth was starting to be of his opinion. She gradually became inured to the noise of the music and talking, for which she was thankful as it saved her from an aching head.

Then, there they were, the Netherfield party. Mr. Bingley looked very well. He glanced around the room until he saw Jane and then made his way directly towards her. He was interrupted by Sir William Lucas but quickly dispatched that inconvenience and completed his progress to Jane. He greeted her with a gentle kiss on her hand, lingering his hold longer than required. Elizabeth saw it all with pleasure and observed a slight blush on Jane's cheeks, which only made her more attractive. If she were not in love yet, she soon would be. How she could possibly resist Mr. Bingley, Elizabeth did not know. They seemed formed for one another. It was rather obvious that Bingley loved Jane already.

Elizabeth, however, never would have imagined that she was becoming the object of another's romantic inclinations. Truth be told, Mr. Darcy, who had found her to be only tolerable in appearance and had watched her throughout the Meryton assembly to verify his assumption, was now finding that perhaps there was some beauty in her form and figure; he was particularly drawn to the sparkle and vigor shown in her beautiful, dark eyes. That there should be much beauty in a country nobody was opposite to all he believed; therefore, he watched her that evening at the Lucases to verify that she had none. Unfortunately, his struggles seemed to be in vain, and he felt himself increasingly drawn towards her. He moved near her to hear the sound of her voice, and while her playful manners were so unlike women of fashion, they were attractive nonetheless.

Darcy had just terminated a meaningless conversation with Sir William when Elizabeth walked by.

"My dear Miss Eliza, why are you not dancing?" cried Sir William. "Mr. Darcy, you must allow me to present this young lady to you as a very desirable partner. You cannot refuse to dance, I am sure, when so much beauty is before you." And taking her hand, he would have given it to Mr. Darcy, who, though extremely surprised, was not unwilling to receive it, when she instantly drew back, and said with some discomposure to Sir William,

"Indeed, sir, I have not the least intention of dancing. I entreat you not to suppose that I moved this way in order to beg for a partner."

Mr. Darcy, with grave propriety, requested to be allowed the honor of her hand, but in vain. Elizabeth was determined. Nor did Sir William at all shake her purpose by his attempt at persuasion.

"You excel so much in the dance, Miss Eliza, that it is cruel to deny me the happiness of seeing you; and though this gentleman dislikes the amusement in general, he can have no objection, I am sure, to oblige us for one-half hour."

"Mr. Darcy is all politeness," said Elizabeth, smiling.

"He is indeed; but considering the inducement, my dear Miss Eliza, we cannot wonder at his complaisance—for who would object to such a partner?"

Her resistance had not injured her with the gentleman, and he was thinking of her with some complacency when thus accosted by Miss Bingley—

"I can guess the subject of your reverie."

"I should imagine not."

"You are considering how insupportable it would be to pass many evenings in this manner—in such society, and, indeed, I am quite of your opinion. I was never more annoyed! The insipidity and yet the noise—the nothingness and yet the self-importance of all these people! What would I give to hear your strictures on them!"

"Your conjecture is totally wrong, I assure you. My mind was more agreeably engaged. I have been meditating on the very great pleasure which a pair of fine eyes in the face of a pretty woman can bestow."

Miss Bingley immediately fixed her eyes on his face, and desired he would tell her what lady had the credit of inspiring such reflections. Mr. Darcy replied with great intrepidity,

"Miss Elizabeth Bennet."

"Miss Elizabeth Bennet!" repeated Miss Bingley. "I am all astonishment. How long has she been such a favorite?—and pray, when am I to wish you joy?" (*Pride and Prejudice, Volume I, Chapter VI.*)

THE BENNET FAMILY WAS INTERRUPTED at breakfast a few days after the Lucases' party by the entrance of the footman with a note for Miss Bennet. It came from Netherfield, and the servant waited for an answer. Mrs. Bennet's eyes sparkled with pleasure, and she was eagerly calling out while her daughter read,

"Well, Jane, who is it from? What is it about? What does he say? Well, Jane, make haste and tell us; make haste, my love."

"It is from Miss Bingley," said Jane, and then read it aloud.

"*My Dear Friend,*

If you are not so compassionate as to dine today with Louisa and me, we

shall be in danger of hating each other for the rest of our lives, for a whole day's tête-à-tête between two women can never end without a quarrel. Come as soon as you can upon the receipt of this. My brother and the gentlemen are to dine with the officers. Yours ever, Caroline Bingley"

"With the officers!" cried Lydia. "I wonder my aunt did not tell us of that."
"Dining out," said Mrs. Bennet. "That is very unlucky."
"Can I have the carriage?" said Jane.
"No, my dear, you had better go on horseback, because it seems likely to rain; and then you must stay all night."
"That would be a good scheme," said Elizabeth, "if you were sure they would not offer to send her home."
"Oh! But the gentleman will have Mr. Bingley's chaise to go to Meryton; and the Hursts have no horses to theirs."
"I had much rather go in the coach."
"But my dear, your father cannot spare the horses, I am sure. They are wanted in the farm, Mr. Bennet, are they not?
"They are wanted in the farm much oftener than I can get them."
"But if you have got them today," said Elizabeth, "my mother's purpose will be answered."
She did at last extort from her father an acknowledgment that the horses were engaged; Jane was therefore obliged to go on horseback, and her mother attended her to the door with many cheerful prognostics of a bad day. Her hopes were answered; Jane had not been gone long before it rained hard. Her sisters were uneasy for her, but her mother was delighted. The rain continued the whole evening without intermission; Jane certainly could not come back.
"This was a lucky idea of mine, indeed!" said Mrs. Bennet more than once, as if the credit of making it rain were all her own. Till the next morning, however, she was not aware of all the felicity of her contrivance. Breakfast was scarcely over when a servant from Netherfield brought the following note for Elizabeth:

Netherfield, Thursday, Nov 14

My Dearest Lizzy,
"I find myself very unwell this morning, which, I suppose, is to be

imputed to my getting wet through yesterday. My kind friends will not hear of my returning home till I am better. They insist also on my seeing Mr. Jones — therefore do not be alarmed if you should hear of his having been to me — and, excepting a sore throat and headache, there is not much the matter with me. Yours &c.

"Well, my dear," said Mr. Bennet, when Elizabeth had read the note aloud, "if your daughter should have a dangerous fit of illness — if she should die — it would be a comfort to know it was all in pursuit of Mr. Bingley and under your orders."

"Oh! I am not at all afraid of her dying. People do not die of little trifling colds. She will be taken good care of. As long as she stays there, it is all very well. I would go and see her if I could have the carriage."

Elizabeth, feeling really anxious, was determined to go to her, though the carriage was not to be had; and as she was no horsewoman, walking was her only alternative. (*Pride and Prejudice*, Volume I, Chapter VII.)

Elizabeth arrived at Netherfield to a room filled with people who had mixed feelings on seeing her. Her skirts were dirty at the hem, her hair disarranged, and her face glowing from the exertion of walking three miles with a purpose. They were all incredulous that she had come so far and all alone. Miss Bingley and Mrs. Hurst were all politeness, of course, but Elizabeth feared they must despise her. Mr. Darcy gave the appearance of displeasure by his stern countenance, when, in fact, he was pleased to see her though worried that her efforts were unwarranted. Mr. Hurst said nothing and thought about nothing of consequence. Only Mr. Bingley greeted her with the warmth of friendliness, expressing concern that he could not have been of service to her with his carriage, gratified that she would be willing to visit her sister and asked that she call on him for anything that might make her visit more comfortable. He did not notice her gown, or mind that she walked to Netherfield or that her hair was unkempt. She could do no wrong. She was, after all, Jane's sister, and there could be no greater recommendation in her favor.

"Mr. Bingley, I have come to visit my sister," said Elizabeth upon her arrival. "She wrote that she is unwell and that Mr. Jones has come to see her. She is rarely ill, so I determined at once to come to her. How is she?"

"I wish I could say that she is well, Miss Elizabeth, but I am afraid she reports that her head aches severely and that her throat is very sore. She is unable to eat more than a few bites of soft food and drinks only warm tea. One of the housemaids is in constant attendance on her, but I know she shall be very glad to see you. I am happy you have come. It will give me great pleasure knowing that you will provide some comfort to Ja— Miss Bennet. For your comfort and for hers, I hope that you will agree to remain with us at Netherfield until she is quite recovered enough to be moved to Longbourn. I shall immediately send a servant to inform your family and bring back clothes and anything else you may desire to make your stay comfortable."

Elizabeth was pleased at Mr. Bingley's hesitation over Jane's name, and although she was not sure in her knowledge of the nature of their relationship, she was certain of how he thought of Jane in the privacy of his own mind.

"I do not want to intrude on you, Mr. Bingley. You already have my sister on your hands."

"Nonsense!" replied Bingley. "You will do us a great favor by remaining with us, and I am certain nothing can contribute more to your sister's recovery."

"Thank you, Mr. Bingley. I should like very much to stay with poor Jane."

Elizabeth passed the chief of the night in her sister's room and in the morning had the pleasure of being able to send a tolerable answer to Mr. Bingley's inquiries. Mr. Bingley was genuinely afflicted. He was never happy when anyone was ill, but for it to be Jane—this was horrible. When he arrived home with Darcy and Hurst the evening before from the officers' quarters, he had at first been pleasantly surprised to hear that his sisters had invited Jane over for the evening, but then the weather— How could she have come at all comfortably in all of that rain? And then to discover that she had taken ill because she had ridden over on horseback and was soaked clear through by the rain. On horseback! What mother on earth would have allowed her daughter to travel on horseback on an afternoon like that? It had been obvious that it was going to rain. Was Mrs. Bennet so completely devoid of feeling for her children even to consider such a thing? Yet it was so. Here was Jane ill in his own home, under his protection, and here was her sister Miss Elizabeth come to assist in her care, all because of her mother. It was inconceivable!

In spite of Jane's slight improvement, Elizabeth requested a note be sent to Longbourn, desiring her mother to visit Jane and form her own judgment of the situation. The note was dispatched immediately, and its contents as quickly complied with.

Had she found Jane in any apparent danger, Mrs. Bennet would have been miserable., However, being satisfied on seeing her that her illness was not alarming, she had no wish of her recovering immediately as her restoration to health would probably remove her from Netherfield. She would not listen, therefore, to her daughter's proposal of being carried home; neither did the apothecary, who arrived about the same time, think it at all advisable.

Bingley met her with the hopes that Mrs. Bennet had not found Miss Bennet worse than she expected. They were sitting in the drawing room when Mrs. Bennet replied.

"Indeed I have, sir. She is a great deal too ill to be moved. Mr. Jones says we must not think of moving her. We must trespass a little longer on your kindness."

"Removed!" cried Bingley. "It must not be thought of. My sister, I am sure, will not hear of her removal."

"You may depend upon it, Madam," said Miss Bingley with cold civility, "that Miss Bennet shall receive every possible attention while she remains with us at Netherfield."

Mrs. Bennet was profuse in her acknowledgments.

"I am sure," she added, "if it was not for such good friends, I do not know what would become of her, for she is very ill indeed and suffers a vast deal, though with the greatest patience in the world, which is always the way with her, for she has, without exception, the sweetest temper ever met with. (*Pride and Prejudice, Volume I, Chapter IX.*) And thank you for putting up with the burden of Lizzy. I cannot think what possessed her to walk here in all that dirt, not that I can ever think what it is that girl will do next; she runs off in such a wild manner at all times and places. I hardly recognize her for one of my children on many occasions."

Elizabeth colored and bowed her head in shame but said not a word. She did not raise her head again until her mother went away. When she did, Elizabeth ran back up to Jane's room from where she could not be prevailed on to leave throughout the course of the evening.

Mr. Darcy, who was a witness to this conversation, was shocked. It was offensive and ill bred that one person could speak in such a manner in company, but for a mother to speak so of a daughter was incomprehensible.

Miss Elizabeth was hurt and embarrassed to be sure, but at the same time, she did not appear to act as if it were the first time she had suffered such treatment. It pained him to see it. Elizabeth Bennet seemed to him to be a kind, generous young woman, full of life and vigor, filled with love and compassion for her sister and kindness for everyone else. She had sense, wit, charm and vivacity that were rarely met with and certainly not among Bingley's sisters. Either he was misreading Miss Elizabeth's character or her mother was prejudiced against her for a particular reason. Regardless, it was amazing to him that both could come from the same family.

Jane was not privy to the conversation among her mother, her sister and the rest of the Netherfield party, but she knew something awful had happened, for not long after her mother had left her room, Elizabeth ran in with tears streaming down her face. She collapsed on the bed and said not a word. Jane knew she was crying as her body quivered from her silent sobbing. This continued for about a quarter of an hour, Jane's heart breaking all the while, when suddenly, Elizabeth sat up on the bed with dry but red and swollen eyes, announced to Jane that she was just fine, apologized for disturbing her, said she was going to take a walk and immediately left the room.

Elizabeth spent an hour in the garden, becoming invigorated by the fresh air. She pondered the cruel joke Heaven played on her to be placed in such a family with a kind but silent father and a mother who seemed to hate her. Her only comfort was Jane. She was glad to be away from Longbourn and there with Jane, and only hoped she could do enough for Jane so that she would quickly recover. The whole situation was her mother's fault. She sent Jane on horseback, knowing it was going to rain so that she would have to stay the night at Netherfield. Well, her mother got what she wanted. She always got what she wanted.

On Saturday, Jane was not feeling any better than the day before, but she decided that she needed to get up and give the appearance of improvement in order to prevail on her mother to let her return home. She felt uncomfortable imposing on Mr. Bingley for so long though he had never said an unkind word to her. In fact, he was always pleasant, and with Elizabeth's attendance, he had been able to spend an hour with her the day before and again that morning. She longed for these visits.

Bingley told Jane about a ball to be given by the officers in five days' time. He had received the invitation the day she had ridden over to spend the evening with Miss Bingley and Mrs. Hurst. The officers were a fine group of men who seemed to be a respectable lot, nothing like a person might encounter in the regulars, but for a militia regiment, one could not meet with better gentlemen. They either came from respectable families or were looking for a way to make a name for themselves and had worked hard to earn their commissions. Overall, he was very pleased with them. The ball they were to host would be given at the Meryton assembly room. The officers were delivering their remaining invitations that day, and it was expected to be a wonderful affair.

"Miss Bennet, if you are not otherwise engaged, may I claim the first two dances?" They both laughed, remembering the same manner in which he had asked for their first dance at the Meryton assembly.

"I am not engaged, sir," replied Jane. This time they both blushed at her response, since thoughts of marriage had begun to creep into their minds. They were pleasant and welcome thoughts, indeed.

"However, Miss Bennet, if you are not wholly recovered, I must insist that you defer our dancing engagement until a later date. I cannot have you up late and out of doors. I intend to have a ball at Netherfield, but it will not be arranged until you are quite well."

"You are very kind, and I appreciate your concern, but I am sure that I shall be well again and able to dance at the officers' ball."

After another half-hour of quiet conversation, he left her, concerned that she needed to rest. She thanked him for his kind attention and told him that she looked forward to seeing him again. They parted from each other with warm hearts.

"Lizzy, did you hear? He has asked me for the first two dances at the officers' ball!"

"I was trying very hard not to hear anything, Jane. Did you accept?"

"Oh, Lizzy, how can you ask such a thing? Of course, I accepted him. How could I do otherwise? Is he not a wonderful man, so kind and solicitous to everything I might require?"

"Jane, I think you are falling in love with that 'wonderful man,' and I am happy for you. You deserve each other. You are both so complying that nothing will ever be decided upon, you will never argue because you both believe the same things, and it is difficult for either of you to think ill of another human being. You are so optimistic that you both look for the sun in the middle of a rainstorm. You are perfect for each other. And I can tell you this: he is madly in love with you!"

"Do you really think so?"

"Yes, and you would too if you were not so much in love yourself. But love makes a person insecure, it makes a person feel vulnerable and fragile, so they are no longer able to see clearly on matters of the heart as they used to. Just wait. If I ever fall in love, you will know long before I do."

When the ladies moved to the drawing room after dinner, Elizabeth ran up to Jane's room to assist her downstairs. She was received very pleasantly by Mr. Bingley's sisters, who entertained them with stories of their friends and acquaintances, the latest fashions in town, and their hopes for Jane's speedy recovery. Their solicitude ended, however, when the gentlemen entered the room; Elizabeth could hardly have expected more from them. She had no opinion of them whatsoever, and counted leaving them behind at Netherfield as one of the advantages of Jane's return to health.

Mr. Hurst approached Jane and said he was glad she seemed well. In fact, he had no idea how she was. He was barely aware that she was even at Netherfield. Upon seeing Jane, Mr. Darcy said,

"Miss Bennet, may I ask if you are feeling any better?"

"Yes, sir, I am feeling a little better, I thank you," Jane lied. Actually, she did not feel well at all. Her head had started to ache again since coming downstairs, but she was determined not to complain or leave the room.

"Miss Bennet," said Mr. Bingley, "it is a pleasure to see you again. I do hope you are feeling better. In fact, I am concerned that perhaps you are over-exerting yourself and should have remained upstairs." Mr. Bingley, being the concerned lover, was ever perceptive of how she appeared and could see no amendment in her health at all, and doubted the wisdom of her joining the party downstairs. He ordered a servant to build up the fire, requested that Jane remove nearer the fire and away from the door, and sat near her for the rest of the evening in quiet conversation. Mr. Bingley appeared pleased to be with Jane, but Elizabeth could see he was worried about her.

It was Sunday morning, and Jane was frustrated. She rarely missed services, but today she must. She was not feeling any better. She was tired all the time, her head still ached if she moved around too much, and her throat still hurt, though not as badly as before, and her neck was growing stiff. *Perhaps I am sleeping in an odd position*, she thought.

"Jane, I am going to send for Mr. Jones again. You are not well, and you are not improving; I can see it in your eyes."

"Oh, Lizzy, I am so sorry. I do not want to be a burden on anybody, but I do not feel any better at all."

"I will go speak to your Mr. Bingley directly about sending for Mr. Jones."

Jane laughed. "He is not *my* Mr. Bingley."

"Oh, yes he is," Elizabeth said firmly, "just you wait and see! Is he not coming in an hour to see you?"

"Yes, Lizzy. I am so looking forward to seeing him again."

Elizabeth left Jane in search of Mr. Bingley and found him in his library. She was able to look in for a minute through the open door and saw him sitting at his desk reading a book. At least, he appeared to be reading a book. He would look down at a page and then up at the clock, then he would turn the page and look at it, and then he would look up at the clock. Elizabeth doubted he would be able to tell anyone anything about what he had read, let alone the title of the book. She knocked on the door.

"Come in."

She entered the library and approached his desk. He looked up from his book with a start. Apparently, he was not expecting to see her. He jumped to his feet and gave her a bow.

Elizabeth curtsied and said, "Mr. Bingley, I hope you were enjoying your book."

"Ah, yes, very much. I suppose I am finding ways to pass the time until I can see Miss Bennet in about a half-hour from now," he chuckled.

"Mr. Bingley, it is not my intention to alarm you, but I am concerned that my sister is not recovering, at least as I would expect her to be. Would it be an inconvenience if Mr. Jones were called to see her again?"

Responding with an alarmed look that only a lover can give, Bingley exclaimed, "Not recovering! Miss Elizabeth, I shall have him summoned at once. What think you of a physician from Town? Is it not time that we summon one for her?"

"I do not think that is yet necessary. Perhaps in a day or two if she is not any better. Frankly, Mr. Bingley, I am not prepared to face the idea that she would need to see a physician and that Mr. Jones would not be a sufficient help to her.

"Yes, of course. Perhaps I should not see her today."

"No, sir. She is counting on your visit and would be greatly disappointed if you did not come to her. Mr. Bingley, she cares for you a great deal. I hope you are sincere in your attentions to her. I could not bear to see her heart broken.

"I care for your sister very much, Miss Elizabeth, and causing her any pain is the farthest thing from my mind, I assure you. I have never met with anyone as kind, gentle and lovely as your sister. I dare not say more now. But when she is well, I intend to court her in such a manner that she will come to love me. Rest assured, madam, her heart is safe with me."

"Thank you, sir, for your assurances. Please forgive me if I caused you to say anything that may have made you uncomfortable, but I am very jealous of my sister's happiness."

"She is blessed to have such a sister as you who cares so much for her."

Chapter 2

Netherfield, Sunday, November 17
My dear Mother—
　I am exceedingly concerned for Jane's health. I have sent for Mr. Jones to see her again. She does not seem to improve at all. She did leave her room last night after the rest of us had dined, but I feel it was more because it was expected of her than that she felt well enough. Your advice would be appreciated. Yours, Elizabeth

Longbourn, Sunday, November 17
Lizzy—
　I have no intention of going out to Netherfield again. You know that at my time of life, a person takes no pleasure in visiting. I am counting on you to make sure that she returns to health and does not lose any of her bloom and beauty. She is five times as pretty as the rest of you girls and must stay that way so that Mr. Bingley will fall in love with her. I must have her well settled at Netherfield. It is your responsibility to make this happen or I shall never speak to you again. Yours, etc.

　How could her mother say such a thing? How could she be responsible for Jane getting well? Why was it up to her to make sure that Jane married Mr. Bingley? Elizabeth had no doubt that it would happen, yet she was not going to interfere any more than she had. Elizabeth felt cold and alone—abandoned with nowhere to turn.

　ON THE DAY AFTER ELIZABETH sent her letter, Mrs. Bennet unexpectedly appeared at Netherfield after all.

"Lizzy," she said, "I have come to make sure you are doing your utmost in caring for Jane, and indeed, it appears you should be doing more, because Jane is not any better than she was."

Mrs. Bennet advised that a physician from town be summoned; it was obvious that Mr. Jones did not know his business and that someone with real medical knowledge was needed.

"On the whole," cried Mrs. Bennet, "I have been ill-used by everyone. Why should my daughter be ill? Why should Elizabeth not be doing more? Why does Mr. Jones not know his business? Why was not a physician called for immediately? And why is everybody always against me?"

This speech was given in the drawing room where she was sitting for a moment with Elizabeth, Mr. Darcy, and Mr. Bingley, who replied,

"Mrs. Bennet, I shall summon a physician from town immediately if you think it necessary. I would not do anything to endanger your daughter's health. I shall send an express immediately. I know of a very capable physician, Mr. Foster, who attends my family when we are in town."

"Thank you, Mr. Bingley. I hope it will be enough to save her beauty. Illness, at her time of life, often robs a girl of her bloom and beauty, you know, and then what will become of her? Elizabeth, you must take better care of her; you must!"

And with that injunction, she called for her carriage and left.

Mr. Foster replied by return express that he would be unable to attend the patient until the next day, but he would make the trip to Netherfield and was grateful for the offer of a room at the house, agreeing to stay with Miss Bennet until her health was recovered. He was looking forward to renewing his acquaintance with Mr. Bingley, and he only wished it could be under more pleasant circumstances.

Bingley spoke to Mr. Jones. "Sir, at the insistence of Miss Bennet's mother, an express was sent to town for a physician. His name is Mr. Foster. I recommended him myself as he provides all the medical care for my family when we are in town, and I trust him implicitly. I do not want you to feel that we doubt your ability to care for her. I suppose we are all very worried. She is generally of a very healthy constitution, and it is unusual for her to remain ill for so long."

"Mr. Bingley, I am not offended and was feeling that perhaps my office as apothecary was becoming insufficient for Miss Bennet's needs. I offer any and all of my services to Mr. Foster."

"Thank you, Mr. Jones. He will arrive tomorrow and will be staying with us at Netherfield until Miss Bennet begins to show signs of improvement in her health."

Meanwhile, Jane and Elizabeth were upstairs, sharing in the following conversation:

"Dear Lizzy, I am so sorry for all the trouble I am causing everybody. I cannot understand why I am not feeling any better. I know that Mama is being cruel to you, which hurts me very much. I am trying not to complain and to bear this with patience, but it is becoming so frustrating. My head aches nearly all the time, and my neck has grown so stiff; sometimes I can hardly turn my head or look up or down."

"Jane, you have the patience of an angel. If everyone in the world were like you, there would be an end to most trouble. Do not worry for my sake and do not let her trouble you. I am sure she only means the best for you. Mama has insisted that a physician from London be sent for, and so Mr. Bingley sent a message for their family physician. He will be here tomorrow to attend you and will remain at Netherfield until you are quite well. He and Mr. Jones will attend you every day. You will be well again, Jane, and I will stay with you and nurse you and love you."

Elizabeth continued, "Do you remember when I was ten years old and was sick for several days with a bad fever? You sneaked into my room every night after Mama and Papa had gone to bed, read to me and talked to me. You would lie beside me on the bed and gently stroke my hair and make circles on my cheeks with your fingertips. Jane, I will never forget the care and love you showed for me then, ever."

"Lizzy, how could anyone do anything other than love you?"

MR. FOSTER ARRIVED EARLY WEDNESDAY afternoon with time enough remaining to examine Miss Bennet before dinner. He spent nearly an hour with her, Elizabeth attending quietly in a corner embroidering a handkerchief. He examined the skin on her arms and legs, looked into her eyes, mouth and ears and separated her hair to view her scalp for discoloration. He timed the rate of her heartbeats and breathing. He had her grasp his hands and pull against his arm as a test of her strength. He took careful notes between each exercise. Elizabeth asked about the examinations.

"I am trying to develop the basis for comparison," replied Mr. Foster. "Honestly, I do not know what afflicts your sister, but each day I will repeat this examination, and compare my findings to this first test to search for changes, be they for better or worse. This will be a clue as to whether the treatment I am pursuing is successful.

Mr. Foster was a man in his middle fifties, not quite as tall as Mr. Darcy, with gray hair and gentle hands. He held his mouth clenched in a peculiar fashion, mumbling to himself every now and again. He reported that he had no family of his own, but lived with a niece and her husband in his townhouse in London. Having no immediate connections, it was not uncommon for him to be gone for extended periods, staying at the residences of his more wealthy patients, rather than travel back and forth daily between his home and theirs. He had been trained as a surgeon in the army though he had not seen action since he had left the regulars prior to the start of the war on the continent. However, his friends in the army did not forget him and by their recommendations had eased his way into good company who were willing to pay well for his services. By this, he had achieved a respectable fortune for a man in his situation, one that would allow him comfort in his later years when he would wish to stop working and enjoy his home and niece. It was by the recommendation of one friend, Richard Fitzwilliam, who was now a colonel, that he was introduced to Charles Bingley.

"Miss Bennet, tell me about this stiffness in your neck."

"Well, sir, it has been coming on these past two days. At first I thought I had just slept in an awkward position but the discomfort has increased to the point that it is painful to move my head to the side much farther than this..." She demonstrated for him her range of motion. "...or to move my head up or down like this."

"For this ailment I would recommend frequent massaging of the muscles. They seem very tight." He paused, lost in thought for a moment. "I am going to go with Mr. Jones to his place and have his boy send over some draughts that should help with the pain in your head and neck. Miss Elizabeth, I know this is asking much of you, but I would be grateful if you would spend the whole night with your sister, to see if she is sleeping well, or is disturbed. By this I shall know whether I should offer something to help her sleep better. Rest is important for her."

JANE HAD NOT SLEPT POORLY, but then she had not slept peacefully either, was Elizabeth's report to Mr. Foster when he came in for his morning examination of Jane. He made note in his book after her remark under the date of Thursday, 21 November 1811. He made the additional comment, "The Officers' Ball."

"Miss Elizabeth," said Mr. Foster, "thank you for staying with Jane last night. I will have a sleeping draught sent over this afternoon with directions on how to give it to her. She should be more comfortable than she is."

"Thank you, Mr. Foster," replied Elizabeth. "I appreciate your care for my sister."

"Miss Elizabeth, I am growing concerned about you. You are a saint. The care you are providing for your sister is compassionate, kind and essential but also draining on you. Tonight is the officers' ball. Mr. Jones and I have already decided that we will stay close at hand and that, with the new sleeping draught and the assistance of a housemaid, there is no reason for you not to attend the ball. In fact, I insist upon it as being useful to your own health and thereby beneficial to Miss Jane's. What do you say?"

"I had not really considered it. I was planning to stay with Jane."

"I know you were, and I can hardly blame you. I can feel the love between the two of you. I cannot imagine how you are feeling, watching her suffer. I have already spoken with Mr. Bingley. He and his sister are going. He was not of a mind to go, either, but feels obliged because of his position in Hertfordshire society. He will take you in his carriage with his sister and Mr. Darcy."

"Thank you, Mr. Foster, you are kind. I am sure I do need to get out of the house a little, if only for the exercise."

"That is right, Miss Elizabeth. Please have an enjoyable evening."

The Netherfield party was one of the last to arrive. While Mr. Darcy, Miss Bingley and Elizabeth were ready in good time, it was clear that Mr. Bingley did not want to go, and therefore he was slow to get ready. Elizabeth was grateful, for this would allow her to slip in without much notice. She was eager to see her friend Charlotte Lucas and watch the dancing. She also wanted to see how Mr. Bingley behaved. She was so sorry for him, and she knew he would rather have been at home with Jane, or at least near her, but he had to be here tonight. Sometimes he was like such a little boy, Elizabeth observed. He was pacing around with a pout on his face. No wonder Jane was falling in love with him.

It did not take long to find Charlotte.

"Charlotte, how are you?" Elizabeth said, kissing her on the cheek.

"I am fine, Eliza, how are you? How is Jane?"

"She is still quite ill, Charlotte. A physician has been summoned from town and he attends to her daily. It is very frustrating. She does not seem to be getting any better, no matter what anybody does. I am very worried, but I am sure all will be well. I was not going to come tonight, but Mr. Foster said I must." She laughed.

"Well, I am glad you did. You probably did not remember that your cousin Mr. Collins came to Longbourn on Monday. He is quite desolate without the company of the two eldest Miss Bennets. I am sure you would not like him, though. He is a clergyman, about five and twenty, rather tall, but large, and he has plenty to say, though little of it worth hearing. He does enjoy speaking of his patroness, a Lady Catherine de Bourgh. I think your sister Mary likes him."

"Mary?"

"Yes, she did say that he read three pages from Fordyce's Sermons for them one evening, and that she has been quite a lost woman since."

"He is to inherit Longbourn after Papa dies. If Mary can get him, I am sure that Mama would be very pleased. I know that I should not like to marry anyone just because of an entail or a Lady Catherine."

Unbeknownst to the other, Elizabeth and Darcy's circuits of the dance floor had placed them within earshot of each other. Darcy noticed Elizabeth and Charlotte, and stopped his progress in order to hear this fascinating conversation.

"Very well, Eliza, I will encourage her all that I can. I shall visit her every day. But what about you? Why would you like to marry?"

"I will marry only for reasons of the deepest love and affection, without consideration for money, position or family. I will not consent to marry a man just for the sake of a provision. Nor will I marry a man to satisfy the desires of my mother. If I cannot love him, I shall never marry him and will spend my days in poverty before I do."

"Oh Eliza, you are so romantic. But you would never act that way, you know you would not. It is not sound. If a man came to you and said he loved you, and had five or six thousand a year, why should you say no to him? There is plenty of time to learn to love him later."

"No Charlotte. If I cannot love him, I will never, ever marry him."

Frankly, Darcy was a little surprised by this declaration. Knowing as he did the enthusiasm Mrs. Bennet had for getting her daughters married, he was filled with wonder at finding one of those daughters unwilling to play the game. In fact, he believed he had found a second one of those daughters, and she was currently ill at Netherfield. He wondered what it would be like to marry a woman who loved him for who he was without consideration for his wealth and grandeur—a woman whose passion for him would not change if she woke one day and found him stripped of everything he ever owned. Passion—a woman who married for money did not know passion. He began to consider Elizabeth Bennet in a new light—as a passionate woman—and he wondered what it would be like to be the subject of that passion. With that thought playing havoc with his mind, he continued his circuit of the room with Bingley.

The music began, and the knot of redcoats spread about the room seeking partners for the first dance. Elizabeth did not have a partner until,

"Miss Elizabeth, you look wonderful this evening."

"Thank you, Captain Carter. How are you?"

"I am very well. It is a pleasure for us to be able to have this ball for all of Meryton. Would you do me the kind honor of dancing the next two with me?"

"Thank you, sir, it would be my pleasure." He took her hand and they moved off together to form up in the set.

Elizabeth enjoyed her dance with Captain Carter. He apprised her of all the latest Meryton news. It was amazing to her that she could be gone for only one week and yet feel like a complete stranger.

Mr. Bingley walked alone towards Elizabeth. She did not know where he had left Mr. Darcy. "Miss Elizabeth, dancing with you may be the only pleasure I will enjoy this evening. May I have the honor?"

"Certainly, Mr. Bingley. I would deny you nothing."

Those standing next to them during the two dances could overhear, if they tried, the following conversation between them—

"Miss Elizabeth, I am very sorry for you. I know you are deeply concerned about your sister. The care you give her is a testament to your love and affection for her. If only I could feel the same from my sisters. You and Miss Bennet have a wonderful relationship. It must be a real pleasure being in the same household with her, and to have such a friend and confidante near you at all times."

"Mr. Bingley, you sound as if you are jealous of me." She laughed. "Seriously, I thank you for your compliments. She is the kindest person I know and is a great comfort to me."

"I am jealous of you, Miss Elizabeth. I wish that same relationship for myself with Miss Bennet. I know I am speaking rather out of turn, but I feel that I can talk to you. I have great hopes for her, and I know she returns my affections. We have already spoken of plans for the future together: How we shall live, trips we shall make to London to the townhouse so that we shall be there for the Season, perhaps purchasing an estate of our own someday. We have spoken of children, little boys and girls running under foot and climbing up the shelves in the library. I feel alive when I am with her, completely unbounded by any restraint. I feel that I can love anyone, be endlessly patient, overcome any difficulty, solve the most difficult problem, and do almost anything. Loving her has given me new life. At night, I sit in my library thinking about her lying upstairs in a strange bed. I am so grateful that you are there for her, that she is not completely alone, and I hope that she is not afraid. I want so much to go to her and hold her and make everything well again, but I know I cannot. I look forward to the day when that will be my right."

"Mr. Bingley, you are a wonderful man. I am so happy that my sister will have you to love and cherish her. You have such a delicate heart."

Elizabeth had managed to stay towards the back of the assembly room away from the table with refreshments on it, where her mother would undoubtedly be holding court, so she would not be noticed by her. So far the plan was working. While she was pondering these thoughts, Charlotte approached her.

"Eliza, I want you to know that Mary and Mr. Collins have danced the last two together. It appears that he is unpracticed in the art, but Mary does not seem to mind at all. She is all smiles. He is quite pleased with himself, and she is not walking with a limp, though I do not know how she could not, as he trampled her feet a half dozen times at least. Your mother is quite fond of him. She has reported to me that he is a very sensible young man, which

I understand to mean that he is planning to marry one of her daughters. Tell me, Eliza, other than having a sick Jane to care for at Netherfield, how do you like it there, and all its inhabitants?"

"Well, I do not have much to say. Mr. Bingley is very much in love with Jane. He is either with her or on estate business, I presume, and he is very kind to me. Mr. Darcy is a pleasant man and is probably a kind one if a person can get beyond that stern facade he presents to the world. Mr. Bingley's sisters are just what they appear to be—proud and conceited. I do not like them at all, and I am sure they consider me an intruder. They spend very little time with their dear friend Jane. Jane tries to be pleasant, tries to read, tries to engage in conversation, tries to sleep, and does all with varying degrees of success. Her head aches all the time, her neck is grown stiff, her stomach ill, but she is still gentle and cheerful. It is clear she returns Mr. Bingley's affections."

"I am very happy for her, then. She will recover from her illness, and she will be settled very happily. It will be a match of affection, advantageous for her as to fortune, and it will also give your mother something to talk of for years to come. Maybe it will throw you in the way of other men who might come to love you?"

"Perhaps you are referring to Mr. Darcy?"

"Perhaps," smiled Charlotte.

"As I told you, he is a pleasant man, but I am sure he would never care for me. He—"

"Lizzy!"

"Good evening, Miss Lucas, Miss Bennet," said Darcy. "Miss Bennet, would you please dance the next two with me?"

"Why yes, thank you, Mr. Darcy, I would be happy to."

When the music recommenced, they were not the only ones walking about the room. Mrs. Bennet had left her place at the front of the room and was walking the length of it in search of her youngest three daughters, to see what men they may have attracted. Of course, she was not expecting to see her second daughter dancing. The girl was supposed to be at Netherfield attending to every whim and desire of her eldest daughter, preserving her beauty and bloom, and seeing to it that Mr. Bingley fell in love with her. It was a duty Mrs. Bennet would rather take upon herself, but since she could not stay at Netherfield, it unhappily fell to Elizabeth. It was, therefore, with great consternation that she beheld this same and acknowledged least-favorite daughter on the arm of Mr. Darcy, proceeding towards the dance. Perhaps Mrs. Bennet liked her less just because she was the favorite of her husband, whom she did not like. For a moment, she was confused by two alternate emotions, fierce anger and amazement. Anger that Elizabeth would defy her and leave Netherfield for such a trifling reason as a ball. That she would abandon her poor sister, her favorite sister, no less, to all her ill health and misery for a night of pleasure for herself was almost beyond Mrs. Bennet's belief. Who would make Jane marry Mr. Bingley? Mrs. Bennet also felt amazement at the possibility that Elizabeth might have caught the eye and heart of the proud Mr. Darcy. They had been thrown together at Netherfield, and he was rich with a grand estate, but surely, if she were doing her duty to Jane, she would have no time for any courting of her own. This was not to be borne. Mr. Darcy or no Mr. Darcy, Elizabeth's first and only priority was Jane, and if she were not going to be attentive to these things, Mrs. Bennet would make her attentive.

Mrs. Bennet, whose active mind and imagination by this point were beyond the reach of reason, rushed rather rudely through the crowd of onlookers up to Darcy and Elizabeth. As she reached the couple, she pulled Elizabeth's arm off Darcy's and shrieked,

"Miss Elizabeth Bennet, what are you doing here? Do you not belong at Netherfield with your poor sister?"

"Mother, release me. Please, recollect yourself; do not speak thus. What is the matter?"

Darcy was speechless. Mrs. Bennet never ceased to amaze him—accosting Elizabeth in such a way in front of all those people. If she were a man, he would have to call her out immediately, let her choose whatever weapons she may, wherever and whenever. Publicly humiliating her own daughter! Darcy wondered how much cruelty a person could inflict in one lifetime and not fall victim to the justice of divine intervention.

Elizabeth was nearly overcome with embarrassment—for herself, of course, but more so for Mr. Darcy. That he should witness such a display was intolerable. That her mother should have the audacity even to touch him as she ripped her daughter's hand off his arm was unthinkable.

"Mr. Darcy, would you please excuse us," was all Elizabeth could utter before her mother started again.

Darcy moved two steps away. He was not going to leave Elizabeth in the grips of that insane creature. He meant to be of use to her, and he would witness what happened and make sure that she knew he was there for her.

"Elizabeth, I am your mother and am entitled to speak to you however I will, and obviously I need to speak to you in a way that you will clearly understand your duty, which you are neglecting."

Her mother was still screaming. The room had grown quiet. It seemed that all of Meryton would now know Elizabeth's shame. "Your duty is to your sister. She is quite ill if you have not noticed, and now she is alone at Netherfield. It is your duty to nurse her and make her well again, to return her to beauty and good humor. It would be better if I was there, but then who would look after the younger girls? Certainly not you! You always think you are too good for the rest of us — lazing about in your father's study or taking your long walks away from the house. You owe me this, Elizabeth Bennet, and you will do it. If Jane cannot be dancing with Mr. Bingley, you have no right to be dancing yourself."

"Mother, Jane is with Mr. Jones and Mr. Foster. They particularly recommended that I come tonight because of the amount of time I have been spending with Jane. I was up all of last night at Mr. Foster's request to measure her sleeping. You are not aware of all I do for her, and there is not one thing I would not do for her," Elizabeth replied quietly, tears forming on her cheeks, her body quivering.

"Elizabeth, who knows better: a couple of strange men or her mother. Now mind what you are told. You are a selfish girl and have been your whole life, undeserving—"

At this point in Mrs. Bennet's speech, Elizabeth could endure it no longer and fled through the crowd to the door and out of the assembly room. She stumbled her way down the stairs, beyond the knot of postilions, past the carriages and began running towards Netherfield until she could run no more. She stopped her progress, turned towards the moon and looking upwards screamed as loud as she could, "MOTHER!" She slowly moved again towards Jane, not knowing she was being followed.

Mr. Darcy had felt certain that no good could come from Mrs. Bennet's attack on Elizabeth. She was proud — not in a conceited way — but accusations of that type would not sit well with her, and she would not long endure them or the shame of having them repeated before such a crowd.

Dearly Beloved

Anticipating what might happen, he had moved towards the door of the room. Suddenly he heard the sounds of skirts moving briskly behind him, and he had just time to look to his side and see Elizabeth fly by him. His heart caught in his throat. He quickened his pace and was able to see her as she went down the stairs. *Thank Heaven she did not fall.* He took the stairs two at a time and went to the carriages.

"Rossiter!"

"Yes, sir, Mr. Darcy, I am over here."

"Prepare the carriage at once."

"Yes, sir."

Darcy strode off into the darkness towards Netherfield. He was searching in the moonlight for her, and he walked quickly until he heard a scream: "Mother!" His blood went cold. What could that mean? He started to run.

Elizabeth was all confusion. What did her mother mean by accusing her of such things? Mr. Foster was taking care of Jane that night. He told her to go to the ball, and she had been thinking about Jane the whole time. It was not fair. Elizabeth felt trapped between reality and her mother. She was becoming cold and a little frightened and disoriented. *Am I going to get lost?* Maybe she should not have run out of the assembly room. But how could she stay there another moment with her mother? *Wait! What was that noise?*

Darcy found her nearly frozen to the ground, shaking from cold and fear. She looked at him with relief and collapsed into his arms, where he held her quietly for a few minutes. He felt all the impropriety of their situation but decided that, if he had to choose, he would choose taking care of Elizabeth's needs and comforts over the cares of the world. She was more important. He felt her begin to support her own weight, so he took off his jacket and wrapped it around her shoulders. She looked up at him and smiled a 'thank you.' He put his arm around her waist and led her back towards the assembly room. When they were near but not close enough to be seen, he asked her to wait, walked to the carriages and found Bingley's equipage.

"Rossiter, please follow me up the road towards Netherfield."

"Yes, sir."

They proceeded back to where Darcy had left Elizabeth. He pulled down the step of the carriage and handed her in. Before climbing in himself, he had a word with Rossiter,

"I am counting on your discretion tonight to preserve Miss Elizabeth's honor. She had a terrible argument with her mother and fled the assembly room. I went after her."

"I have heard the story, Mr. Darcy. I feel nothing but the greatest respect for the young lady and would do or say nothing to hurt her or yourself, sir."

"Thank you, Rossiter. Please take us to Netherfield and then return for Mr. and Miss Bingley.

"Yes, sir."

Darcy stepped into the carriage and sat opposite Elizabeth. He took one of her hands, tracing circles on her palm. She was so distracted by the events of the evening that she missed the feeling of his hands or the intense look of love and passion in his eyes. For Mr. Darcy, the danger from Elizabeth was over. He knew he would ask her to marry him for her stated reasons: that of the deepest love and affection. Now, he had to discover how she felt.

At Netherfield, he escorted her to her bedchamber and called her maid. She quietly thanked him for his help and company. She was very touched by his help. Indeed, she did not know what she would have done without him. She slipped into bed that night still not certain at all of her mother's meaning or the reason for her attack. She was too tired even to cry.

On Friday morning, Mr. Foster again examined his patient and could see no improvement in her. If anything, she was growing worse, and she was now experiencing periods of drowsiness and sleep in the afternoons that were wholly unlike her.

Elizabeth knew she could not expect any help from her mother, so she wrote to her father, asking that he come to Netherfield to visit Jane and give his opinion regarding her health and the course of treatment. What Elizabeth did not say was that she was looking for some encouragement from him as to her efforts at nursing Jane. Elizabeth could not believe that she was failing her sister as her mother thought, and she hoped her father would realize it.

Mr. Bennet came in good time after receiving Elizabeth's note. Elizabeth often wondered why her family never came to visit Jane, but that thought only made her unhappy, so she chose not to dwell on it for now.

"Elizabeth, I am come to visit Jane—and you, of course."

"Thank you, Papa. I will take you to her now." She led him up to Jane's room, announcing his presence before they went in.

"Oh, Papa, thank you for coming," said Jane. "But you need not have troubled yourself."

"Jane, I should have been here long ago. Please tell me, honestly, how you are feeling?" inquired Mr. Bennet.

"I have a headache all the time, my neck is stiff and I find myself growing more and more tired. Lizzy stayed all night with me once to see whether I was sleeping properly. I was not, so Mr. Foster has been giving me some sleeping draughts."

"Jane, it is a beautiful day outside. Why do you not have the curtains drawn? I shall open them for you."

"Please do not, sir. The sun brightens the room more than usual and the extra light is very uncomfortable."

"I see." He paused. "Are you able to eat or drink?"

"A little. If I eat too much I feel ill. I try to drink a lot of water, but even that makes my stomach hurt."

"I am very sorry for you, Jane. You are a good girl and certainly do not deserve to be ill like this. You are receiving the very best attention from Mr. Foster and Mr. Jones, and I am sure Lizzy is a great comfort to you."

"She is, Papa. I do not know what I would do without her."

"Well, good-bye, Jane. Come along, Lizzy. Let us visit our host."

When she and Mr. Bennet were safely away from Jane's room, she noticed tears falling from Mr. Bennet's eyes.

"Papa, whatever is wrong? You told Jane she would be well!"

"What can I say to the girl? I know many people who have had her symptoms who have died — the weariness, the stiff neck, the sunlight. And, Elizabeth, I believe that Jane will be one of them." He began to sob. She took him in her arms and let him cry into her shoulder, unable to comprehend what he had told her. Jane was to die?! Unbelievable! Jane, her only friend and comfort, would leave her alone in the world! *'Tis too much — too, too much.* A tear rolled down Elizabeth's flushed cheek, but until she heard from Mr. Foster, she would hold herself together. She had to. And even then, for Jane's sake, she had to keep her composure. Someone had to be strong for Jane, and that would be her. Nobody else would. Elizabeth knew her mother would blame her, but she no longer cared what her mother thought. She would request that her remaining belongings be brought to Netherfield. If Jane were to die, Elizabeth decided she would stay at Netherfield until she could find a place as a governess. She never would go home again.

Her grief could no longer remain inside her. She fled the house as if it were on fire, ran to the edge of the park, and sat at the base of a tree. Her tears were salty and bitter. How would she face Jane or Mr. Bingley knowing what her father said? In her heart, she knew it to be true. Jane was not getting better. She was getting much worse. None of Mr. Foster's remedies was working. Life was slowly seeping from Jane right before Elizabeth's eyes.

Mr. Bennet watched her run to the tree and quietly left Netherfield. It was a sad ride back to Longbourn. Mr. Darcy also watched Elizabeth leave the house. His heart was full of her. Since the night of the officers' ball, he had come to realize that he loved her. Her pain had become his pain, and he could hardly endure her suffering. Darcy decided to follow her from a discreet distance.

Elizabeth did not know how long she sat beneath the tree. She noticed that it had grown chilly, but she did not care. Somehow, it seemed like a natural punishment to her, though she did not know what she had done to deserve such treatment. Suddenly, a pair of strong, warm hands seized her shoulders and she felt herself being lifted to her feet and cradled in those arms. It felt so good to be protected and held, not to have to be the strong one, even for just a moment. She cried into his shoulder. He stroked her hair lovingly and told her that she was not alone and that she should trust him.

"But Jane is going to die."

"But you are not."

"How can I face her again? How can I face Mr. Bingley? You must know they are in love."

"Yes, they are very much in love, and what a tragedy it is for them. I cannot say enough of the pain I feel for them and for you. Poor Bingley, to have finally found the love of his life and then have to watch her slip away from his grasp. It is not fair to either of them."

She had not left his arms, so it was easy for her to turn into his chest and sob some more. This time she cried for herself. Why must she find comfort in a man who was nearly a stranger?

"Thank you for finding me, Mr. Darcy. I am ready to go back to the house now."

"Let us take the shorter way, though, through here." And he led her back to the house, both of them quiet and deep in thought. Their feelings were quite similar. Both were thinking of Jane and Bingley, but mostly of each other — the conversation they just shared and how they hoped they could have more conversations in such an intimate manner but under more pleasant circumstances in the future. Elizabeth was unsure of her heart, for she had Jane on her mind. Mr. Darcy, however, was very sure of his; he had nothing to do but think of Elizabeth.

MR. BENNET ARRIVED EARLY AT Netherfield so that he could consult with Mr. Foster under less emotional circumstances. Elizabeth joined their conference.

Mr. Foster began, "Mr. Bennet, Miss Elizabeth, good morning to you."

"Good morning, Mr. Foster."

"Well, you are probably not interested in pleasantries, so let us get to the point. Miss Bennet has somehow contracted a peculiar form of influenza, though that is not really a good word for it. It is not a common ailment, and we really have no specific treatment for it. We had hoped that by making her more comfortable, her body would become stronger, but in your daughter's case, Mr. Jones and I have been unable to develop any draughts to loosen the muscles in her neck, allowing her more freedom of motion, and she is almost continually suffering from a headache."

"Mr. Foster," said Mr. Bennet, "Jane told me she did not want the curtains opened because the light was too strong for her eyes and that eating or drinking made her stomach ill. Tell me the truth; what is going on with her?"

"Mr. Bennet, as I said, this is a rare case of a type of influenza. Fortunately, it is not very contagious. All of the symptoms you described occur in the later stages of this illness."

"Later stages?"

"Yes, Mr. Bennet. Later stages. I do not believe your daughter will be alive one week from now."

"Jane dead in less than a week? How can that be? I agree she is ill, but she does not look that sick."

"Nevertheless, she already reports periods of drowsiness and difficulty in awakening. These periods will increase over the next three or four days until she lapses into a coma from which she will not awaken. She will be unable, in the next day or so, to keep any food down at all. This will only contribute to her weakness. I am sorry, Mr. Bennet. I wish there was something I could say or do, but she is in the hands of Providence now."

"This is her mother's fault. I blame her mother for this!"

"Oh Papa! Please do not! Cannot we all overcome our immediate differences and console each other now? We need each other. Please help! Why do not you go back to Longbourn and arrange for the family to come today and see Jane while she can still enjoy them. Send word by way of a servant when you are to come so I can have Jane ready to receive you. That is the best thing for now. Do not tell my sisters of Jane's condition. My mother should know, but tell her privately and insist she hold her tongue before my sisters, the servants and the neighborhood. The last thing we need is all of Meryton involved in our lives right now."

Elizabeth had to stop; a sob choked in her throat. "Papa, should we tell Jane?"

"Yes, Lizzy, I think we must. This is her life we are discussing. She deserves to know what Mr. Foster thinks. She may have things she wants to say or to do that cannot be put off and must be done while she has the strength."

"I will tell her, Papa. I will go to her now, as soon as you leave for Longbourn. Please let me hear from you as soon as possible.

Chapter 3

Elizabeth turned from her father and walked slowly towards the staircase. The unanswerable question lingered on her mind. *How do I face Jane?* Elizabeth halted her progress towards Jane's room in front a picture of a former inhabitant of Netherfield Park: a long dead, beautiful woman in her late thirties, perhaps. *What would she think*, thought Elizabeth, *knowing her descendants did not believe Netherfield worthy of inhabiting any longer and had let it to the lowly children of a tradesman? What would she think, knowing that they had not taken her picture with them, that no one spared a thought for her, that only the housekeeper knew her name or kept the dust off the bottom of the frame?* Elizabeth had to laugh. Was it not the ultimate form of arrogance to have a likeness taken, to assume that anyone who did not know you would really care who you were, that two generations from now your place on the wall would not be better taken up by a pier table and pier glass? From ashes to ashes and dust to dust, memories take up much less room, and they are gone after only one generation. Who would paint Jane's likeness? And where would it hang now that it was all too late?

Elizabeth trusted Jane's memories with no one but herself. Indeed, no one but herself knew Jane — certainly not her mother. All she did was shop Jane about looking for the highest bidder — or any bidder, really. She did not hear. All cries to her were in vain, be they happy or sad. Mr. Bennet appeared to care when it was convenient, but when it came time to be serious, when there was a real hurt to mend, a heart to heal, a hope to dream on, or a future to wish for, he had not the strength of emotion. His heart was not available for more than a few moments at a time, before he felt he had to conceal himself.

It seemed as if his love had been strangled by his wife. Only bits and pieces were left struggling for air, and what was left to share with Jane or Elizabeth could only last for a few minutes before dying. Mary probably had a heart with which to care if she had only been taught to use it. By the time she was born, her parents were expecting a son. When a daughter was born to them, Mr. and Mrs. Bennet had little time or attention for an inconvenience. Mary was neither loved nor hated; she was ignored. Jane had a heart. No one without a heart could know Jane. Mary could never know Jane; her parents had seen to that. Then there were Kitty and Lydia—where Mary had been ignored for having been born a daughter, they were emotionally abandoned. To survive in such a large family they knew only themselves and perhaps each other. They had no concept of anyone else. If Jane were to survive in anyone's memory, it would be Elizabeth's, and now Elizabeth had to tell Jane that she would die within the week.

With a sigh, Elizabeth entered her sister's room.

Jane was propped up on her bed with pillows, trying to read a book. A glance at the cover showed it to be *Camilla*, by Fanny Burney. It was apparent to Elizabeth that Jane was focusing with difficulty on the words, yet she was persistent in trying, moving the book closer and farther from her eyes as she moved down the page, moving her head from left to right as she followed each sentence. She had not yet noticed Elizabeth. The longer Elizabeth watched her, the more difficult it was for her to retain her composure. Her eyes were welling with tears eager to be spent. How could she face Jane?

"Jane, I..."

Jane looked up. "Lizzy, what is wrong? Please come here."

Elizabeth broke down sobbing, collapsed on the floor next to Jane's bed, and laid her head in Jane's lap. She cried and cried as she had never cried before. Jane grasped her hand and stroked her hair in silence; she knew not what to say to her but felt a sense of dread in Elizabeth's manner. They remained thus for ten minutes, until Elizabeth's body gradually stilled.

"Papa and I just spoke with Mr. Foster about your health. Oh Jane!" Elizabeth started to cry again.

"Lizzy, what did he say? Please tell me. You are so distressed; you should not have to carry the weight of this knowledge alone."

"Jane, you are too good, and I have never loved you enough. Jane, Mr. Foster... Mr. Foster says—believes—that your illness is going to progress, and that you might... you possibly might die. Oh Jane!"

Jane was shocked into silence for a moment as she searched her feelings. No, she was not getting any better; the symptoms were getting worse. Was she actually to die? *But I am so young. I have not had a life. Mr. Bingley and I are to marry when I am recovered. Poor Mama. She will move on to try and marry Lydia off, Papa will continue in his study, Mary will philosophize, Kitty and Lydia will ask for my things, only Lizzy and Mr. Bingley will really care. They are the ones who really love me. I cannot believe this is happening to me.* Jane started to cry as she had never cried in her life.

When Elizabeth saw Jane cry, she knew it was time for her to be strong and save her tears for private moments. She dried her eyes, slid up on the bed, took Jane in her arms, and held and rocked her like an infant. She would never again cry in front of Jane. She would be the strong one for her sister. Jane settled down and fell asleep, so she left her in the bed and went in search of Mr. Darcy, the man she could trust.

MR. DARCY WAS IN THE Netherfield library conducting estate business when a footman brought in a letter on a tray. He recognized the handwriting with a smile, having no expectation of what it might contain. He waited just a moment before opening it while he reflected on his encounter with Elizabeth that afternoon. In his mind, she was no longer Miss Bennet or Miss Elizabeth, she was just Elizabeth, and he intended to win her love and make her *his* Elizabeth. He opened the letter and read:

Dear Mr. Darcy –

Thank you for your kind attention to me this afternoon while in my state of distress. I cannot thank you enough for the comfort of your attention to me.

I am taking this bold step in writing you in response to something you told me today. You said I should trust you. I need to trust you now, and I need your help. Mr. Foster has said that Jane will die within the week. I believe him, as does my father. I just spoke with Jane, who did not take the news well, as can be understood. I have left her asleep in her room.

My present concern is for Mr. Bingley. It is my belief that he and Jane are very closely attached and that this news will strike him forcibly. I am prepared to break the news to him, but I would appreciate your presence. Would you please arrange a gathering of the three of us if you are willing to engage in the task of assisting me, of which I have little doubt. I await word from you in the drawing room.

EB

DARCY CERTAINLY HAD MIXED FEELINGS about the note. That Elizabeth thought with kindness on his actions that afternoon and stated that they gave her comfort put him in the highest of spirits. However, he was horrified about the rest of her note—that poor Miss Bennet would actually die, and Elizabeth was concerned about Bingley. There was nothing to be done but to ease Elizabeth's mind further by not putting anything off. He asked the servant, "Pray, have you seen Mr. Bingley?"

"Yes, sir, he was walking towards the stables just a moment ago."

"Thank you."

Darcy ran towards the stables, hoping to catch Bingley before he left on a ride. He had to settle this now for Elizabeth's sake, but what would he say to Bingley?

"Bingley, where are you going?"

"Ah, Darcy, I was just going to take a tour of the park. Why not join me?"

"There is a pressing matter of business in the study that needs my attention, and I was hoping to have your advice on it. It should not take too long, and then you could take your ride. Would you please come?"

"Darcy, you never ask for help with estate business. Just what is this pressing matter?"

"Please, Bingley!"

"Of course."

As they were heading into the study, Darcy stopped a footman and asked him to go into the drawing room and summon Miss Elizabeth to the study.

"Bingley, can I get you something to drink?"

"I thank you, no."

"Are you sure?"

"Yes, Darcy, I am sure. Will not you tell me what this is about?"

Elizabeth chose that moment to enter the room. "Miss Elizabeth," Darcy said, "Thank you for coming. Please have a seat by the fire. Come, Bingley, let us sit with Miss Elizabeth."

Bingley noticed that Miss Elizabeth did not look well at all and, for the first time, began to worry that perhaps this little meeting had something to do with Jane.

"Miss Elizabeth, you do not look well. May I get you something? Perhaps a glass of wine? Should you retire to your room? Shall I call for Mr. Jones and Mr. Foster?" asked Bingley as he grew quite agitated.

"No, I thank you for your concern, Mr. Bingley, but I am quite well. It is just that I have had some dreadful news from Mr. Foster and..." Elizabeth broke down in tears and could say no more. The men looked on helplessly. Mr. Darcy wanted to take her into his arms, and Mr. Bingley wanted to leave the room and go to Jane. Something was wrong with her — very wrong, indeed.

"I am sorry. Please forgive me. I am not myself today. As I was saying, I have had bad news from Mr. Foster. He expects that Jane's symptoms are a type of influenza and" — she paused, not knowing how to tell Jane's lover the truth — "that she may die within the week." There was another long pause while Bingley's face turned white. "I am very sorry, sir. I know the depth of your attachment to her."

"NO!" Bingley cried, "You must be mistaken, Miss Elizabeth; this cannot be true. We have made plans together. We have dreams and hopes. Mr. Foster cannot take them away from us." Bingley started to pace the room, tears welling in his eyes. If not for Darcy's presence, he would have been crying by now.

"Mr. Bingley, please, it is not Mr. Foster who is doing this. It is Jane's illness. Mr. Foster is doing all he can to save her life. I left Jane asleep a few minutes ago after telling her this same news. Go to her, sir, and be strong for her. I know you love each other. Continue to love her. Go to her, Mr. Bingley — go to her."

Mr. Bingley was dumbfounded. What could he say to Jane? *Oh, the hurt.* Was the day his mother died to be repeated, but worse? Maybe he need not say anything to Jane. At that point, they both knew. Maybe all he needed to do was hold her. He could do that. How could it be that his Jane was going to die? Of all the people in the world, she was the kindest, gentlest, sweetest, most loving, and most beautiful creature of all. What kind of joke was nature playing? *Joke, nothing — it is that mother of hers. I would have married her regardless; she need not have forced her to ride through the rain. I already knew who she was, where she lived, and who her father was. We would have had opportunities to be together without her having to kill Jane to make it happen. What a mother! What a family!*

Bingley made his way to Jane's room in a sad, solemn sort of way, pausing for a moment below the picture of the long-lost relation of someone who used to inhabit Netherfield. *I wonder who she was? I suppose it does not really matter now.*

Elizabeth received a note from her father that her family would be coming to Netherfield the next morning after Sunday services.

"Good morning, Mr. Bennet, Miss Mary, Miss Catherine and Miss Lydia," said Mr. Darcy. "I presume you are all come to see your sister. She is upstairs with Mr. Bingley and Miss Elizabeth. If you will follow me..."

Darcy led them to Jane's room. She had just barely woken up even though it was late morning. It became more difficult to wake her each day, and she still seemed drowsy. On seeing Jane's family, Bingley slipped out of the room.

"Hello Mary, Kitty, and Lydia; it is very nice of you to come and visit me. As you can see, my kind friends will not hear of my leaving until I am well again," Jane lied, fighting back tears.

"Well," said Lydia, "we know you are going to be well enough, but Papa insisted that we come anyway, even though we did not want to. We were supposed to go into town to see if Denny and Chamberlayne were there. We are hoping that Papa will stop and let us out on the way back to Longbourn."

What could Jane do other than smile? She was not going to tell them the truth about her condition. Her sisters never would understand. They would learn soon enough anyway.

Elizabeth looked determinedly at her father. He met her gaze and suggested that the two of them meet in the hall for a moment while the girls continued talking.

"Papa, where is my mother?"

"She is unwell this morning, Lizzy, and was unable to join us."

"Papa—"

"Lizzy, she said she had no intention of coming over here. She did not believe a word I told her about Mr. Foster's statements. She said that Jane would be just fine in a couple of days and back at Longbourn in no time, and that she will see Jane then. She also added that you have been a very ungrateful and undeserving daughter in your treatment of her because of the poor care you have given Jane, which has caused her to be ill so long, and the disrespect this shows her because she specifically told you to take care of Jane and to see that she got well again."

"Father, what am I supposed to do? I have no control over Jane's illness. I would make her well in a heartbeat, and I would trade places with her if I could. She has a bright future ahead of her. Mr. Bingley loves her, and they were to be married when she recovered; I have nothing. The wrong Bennet daughter is to die, Papa."

"Elizabeth Bennet, do not say such a thing. You are loved and respected wherever you go. This is an accident of nature, and you are not responsible for it. In time, your mother will see that I am correct. I know you have done all you can. And you do not look well, so I would imagine you spend more time with her than you ought, though I know there would be no persuading you otherwise."

"What would it be like with Mama if I were to return home now? How would I endure it?"

"It would not be a pleasant experience for you, Elizabeth. It would not be pleasant at all."

"Well then, sir, I will not be going home. I will not go where I am not wanted. When Jane dies, I am dead too."

Mr. Bennet returned home shortly after his exchange with Elizabeth. Somehow, he knew that in the carriage with him were his last three remaining daughters, and when or if he saw the other two again was entirely beyond his control.

Later that afternoon, two servants from Netherfield arrived to obtain the remaining items from Elizabeth's bedchamber at Longbourn. Mr. Bennet helped them load the trunks. Miss Elizabeth Bennet had moved out. He cried softly as the wagon drove away.

EXCEPT FOR A FEW HOURS in the afternoon, Jane did not wake up that day. Bingley stayed with her, alternately crying over her when she was asleep and talking with her when she was awake. Darcy did his best to look after things at Netherfield. Bingley had completely abandoned any efforts at running the estate. All he cared for was Jane. Elizabeth spent the chief of the day in Jane's room, sitting in the corner watching Bingley and Jane. She was a little jealous of the time Bingley spent with Jane, but it made Jane happy, and she knew if she were talking to Jane, they would ultimately approach subjects that would make them both unhappy. So Elizabeth sat quietly, attending her embroidery as best as she could. Fortunately, this handkerchief would not be a gift. Perhaps it would be a keepsake memory of Jane.

Elizabeth sent word to her father and mother separately, updating them on Jane's condition and begging her mother to come. She received no response from either. She sent a note by express to the Gardiners, explaining Jane's current condition and praying that somebody at Longbourn had let them know earlier of her illness. She felt the responsibility of the whole world on her shoulders, and she wished for Mr. Darcy to hold her and comfort her again. But it is not sensible to like a man in such a vulnerable time as that of mourning and grief. Elizabeth would be on her guard; however, she was going to trust him once again. She wanted to stay at Netherfield with Mr. Bingley and his sisters, and she wanted Mr. Darcy to make the request.

She went to a writing table in the drawing room and penned the following -

Dear Sir –

I once again beg your assistance. You may have overheard conversations that have indicated tension between my mother and me regarding what she considers deficient care on my part and that, should Jane not recover, it would be my fault. As Jane's condition deteriorates, I have found myself completely estranged from my family, and my father cannot or will not intervene. I am pleading for your help in asking Mr. Bingley if I might remain as part of his household throughout the year of mourning, at the end of which time, I will find employment and no longer be a burden to him.

Sincerely,
Elizabeth Bennet

Mr. Darcy was shocked to receive Elizabeth's note. That her family should actually cast her off was unthinkable. What kind of mother would do such a thing? Well, Mrs. Bennet was just such a mother. Darcy knew that he wanted Elizabeth whether the Bennets did or not. He would speak to Bingley immediately and have Elizabeth installed at Netherfield for the duration of Bingley's stay. He would also gain an invitation for Georgiana to come to Netherfield as well. When Bingley left Netherfield, Elizabeth would join Georgiana and be under his protection as a part of the Darcy household. They would return to Pemberley where Mrs. Annesley was waiting, and things would be proper in appearance and in fact, and Elizabeth could finish her mourning taking walks around the beautiful Pemberley grounds. When her mourning period was complete, he would ask her to marry him, and if he were fortunate, she would say yes. He would even intervene with her family to strive for reconciliation. Perhaps during her year of mourning, Mrs. Bennet's heart would soften, and she would realize she had lost two daughters, not one. Maybe he could help her understand that she could have one of those daughters back again, but only if Elizabeth agreed. Elizabeth came first. There was only Elizabeth.

THAT AFTERNOON, MR. DARCY HAD several matters of business to settle. He sent a letter by express to Georgiana, requesting her to come to Netherfield as soon as possible. He sent another letter by post to Pemberley's housekeeper, requesting that a family apartment be made up and kept available for a young lady who would be accompanying the Darcys when they next came home. Finally, a letter was sent by post to Mr. Darcy's steward at Pemberley, directing that all his correspondence and estate business be forwarded to him at Netherfield for the near future, as his stay there would be of an unknown duration. That same afternoon, Elizabeth moved from a guest room to one of the larger family apartments at Netherfield.

ON TUESDAY, JANE DID NOT wake up at all, and Mr. Foster said she was in a coma. There was a constant vigil by her bedside, comprised of Mr. Bingley holding one hand, and Elizabeth holding her other. Mr. Darcy sat in a chair in the corner, and occasionally Mr. Bingley's sisters came in and out of the room. Elizabeth had sent a note to both her parents that morning informing them of Jane's condition and that she was not expected to live. Quite to her surprise, her father came later in the morning.

"Elizabeth."

"Papa, you came. Thank you. Jane has been unconscious all day. Mr. Foster does not believe she will revive. All we can do is hope and pray."

"I do not know what to do for her, Elizabeth."

Elizabeth took his hand and held it to her cheek. "Cannot you look at her, hold her hand, and talk to her? Papa, she is your daughter. Oh, Father!"

"May I speak to you in the hall please, Elizabeth?"

"Yes, Papa," she said in a disappointed tone of voice.

"I bring you a note from your mother." He gave her the note. "She has instructed me that you read it in my presence."

"Very well." She opened the note and read:

Longbourn, Tuesday, November 26

Elizabeth—

You have failed me in every way. You have been a disappointment to me your entire life. Why your father thinks so highly of you, I will never know. But now you have gone too far. You have let Jane die, and I will not forgive you for this. You are not welcome back at Longbourn. You are disinherited from any portion of the money that was settled on me at my marriage. You are not to try to speak or write to me or to Mary, Kitty, or Lydia. I cannot prevent you from trying to contact your father, but I if get the post first on the day a letter arrives for him, I will destroy it before he ever sees it. Your name is not to be spoken in my presence ever again. I have dismissed without recommendation the upper maid who waited on you and Jane. Anything remaining in this house that is yours will be burnt. You are worthless and unwanted. Do not ever come back. FB

Elizabeth stood shocked, and her mouth gaped open.

"I am sorry, Lizzy; there is nothing I can do. I will assume you are staying at Netherfield for the present, but I will instruct the servants to give me all letters in case you should write me. Give me new directions if you should leave. I will send you your allowance as you direct."

She closed her mouth. He obviously knew what the letter contained and had nothing to say against it. Mr. Bennet took her hand, kissed it gently, took one last parting look at her and left her standing in the hall. Her whole life passed before her eyes, and she wondered what she had done to deserve this.

Elizabeth had to decide whether to feel for herself or for Jane. It only took a moment to decide on Jane. She set the note down on a table in the hall and went back into Jane's room, taking her place by her side. Mr. Foster and Mr. Jones stood against a wall, whispering to each other. Darcy was standing at the foot of the bed. Bingley was holding Jane's hand in both of his and silently crying, tears pouring down his cheeks. Jane was dead. Not only had her mother taken Elizabeth's own life away, she had caused her to miss the last few minutes of Jane's life as well.

There was no longer a need to ignore all the embarrassing moments her mother had caused her because of her ill-spoken words and deeds. Elizabeth's life had been a continual stream of abuse. There was no reason to pretend in the name of keeping peace and a semblance of love in the family that the embarrassments caused by her mother never happened. Elizabeth no longer had a family. All she had now was nearly one and twenty years of pain. She wept for the loss of Jane, for everything that Jane lost, for Mr. Bingley, and for herself. She was inconsolable. Why could not somebody love her and take away this pain?

Darcy, standing at the foot of the bed, watched her with a lump in his throat. He thought how beautiful she was even at the worst moment of her life. How he longed to touch her and hold her. *I love you*, he said to himself.

Darcy could bear it no longer. He left the room. As he passed through the hall, he noticed an opened letter resting on a table. It was addressed to Elizabeth from her mother. It was very improper of him, but knowing the troubles in that family, he decided to read the letter. When he finished reading it, he realized he had not been that angry since Ramsgate.

Dinner at Netherfield that night was a subdued affair. It had taken enormous persuasion on Darcy's part for Bingley to join them. Having succeeded in that, he then left Bingley alone to persuade Miss Elizabeth to leave Jane. Darcy laughed grimly to himself. *Miss Elizabeth*, he thought, *by all that was right they should be calling her Miss Bennet. What else would change for her with the passing of a few heartbeats?*

Nobody said much at dinner. Bingley and Elizabeth were lost in thought and had no appetite. Neither wanted to be there, but Bingley was there because Darcy told him it was the right thing for him to do, and Bingley always wanted to do the right thing. Elizabeth came down because Bingley had told her she needed a respite from her sister's room and also needed some nourishment. Only compassion for Bingley had motivated Elizabeth, and perhaps she had been wrong. Miss Bingley and Mrs. Hurst where chattering away as though nothing had happened, commenting on how delighted they were with this or that dish that Cook had provided.

"Miss Bennet, I am very sorry about your sister," added Miss Bingley rather coolly after a mouthful of Florentine rabbit. "I am sure you will miss her very much. It must be a comfort to you to know that you will be able to return to your own home and family very shortly."

"Thank you, Miss Bingley."

Miss Bingley had been expecting a little more from Elizabeth, hoping to find out when she would be leaving, and she was about to press further when Mr. Bingley said,

"Caroline, Miss Bennet will be remaining with us at Netherfield until we return to town in February." Bingley gave his sister a pointed look. "I think we are finished here; please lead the way to the music room."

And with that pronouncement, Miss Bingley discovered she was to be hostess to Elizabeth Bennet for the foreseeable future.

GROWING UP WITH FOUR SISTERS and a loud mother never made Elizabeth sorry for the times she could be alone. Indeed, she sought time alone and, by so doing, had become an excellent walker. She had explored secluded places in the woods surrounding Longbourn and Meryton that seemed almost private to her, for she never saw a soul when she walked there. She had become comfortable enough to take off her bonnet, let her hair down and sing into the breeze, enjoying the sun on her skin, the birds in the air and the solitude. That night, however, was different. She was in her bed in her room next door to Jane's, and the isolation was eating at her. She did not want to be with anybody, yet she did not want to be alone. She was inside a home where people lived and servants moved about, almost at all hours, yet she felt forgotten. *Oh Jane, how could you do this to me? I was never alone, knowing that you were there for me. You always understood me and never judged me ill. You were always so happy and wore a smile for everybody. No one could have been more pleasant than you. See? I should know better; you would not have left me on purpose. I hope it was not anything I did. I hope Mama is not right that I somehow made you ill and you died from it. I should not deserve to live myself. What will it be like to live without you? There is no one who really loves me anymore. Mama and Papa made that quite clear. I cannot even go home. If you would just talk to me, you could tell me what to do, what to say, where I should go. But I know you cannot. You are gone. And now I am truly alone.* Elizabeth curled up on her bed and wept until she fell asleep.

BINGLEY WAS ANNOYED WITH HIS sister. *How could she be so insensitive towards Miss Elizabeth? She is in mourning now, and Caroline is not going to make things harder for her—or for me. She was not my sister, my betrothed or my wife, but I will be mourning just the same. How shall I ever love again? This is not fair. It is just not fair. Her mother killed her, and because that was not enough for her, she decided she would try to kill Miss Elizabeth as well. Well, I shall take care of her for the rest of her life. I do not think I will be able to, though. That job will be Darcy's. Oh Jane, Jane, Jane. You were so beautiful, so gentle, so delicate. We would have been so happy, snuggled in here at Netherfield. I would love to have seen your children. They would have been angels. We could have gone out riding for picnics, taken trips into town, traveled north to Pemberley and beyond. The happiest part of all for me would have been the delighted sparkle in your eyes as you took in all the new sights, smells and sounds. You were too good, Jane; yes, Death triumphed when he took you away from this world, and I will be left with nothing but memories that will gradually fade over time.* He looked again at Jane, left her room and went to his library where he poured himself some brandy, which did not last long, and then he poured himself some more. He fell asleep that night at his desk, joined by a half-full glass of brandy, an empty bottle, and a letter from his steward stained with tears.

"Good morning, Miss Elizabeth."

"Good morning, Mr. Bingley. Good morning, Miss Bingley."

"Miss Bennet, as much as it pains me to say so," said Miss Bingley, "I know you are in need of clothes and other things with which to properly observe your mourning. My brother and I would like to escort you into Meryton this morning in the carriage so that you can make your purchases and not have to walk or be alone."

Miss Bingley was quite impressed with the sweetness of her address to Miss Eliza. She did pity her. She knew she was attached to her sister and was not a stranger to the events between Eliza and her mother at the officers' ball. It really was the most interesting part of the ball, which otherwise was a rather boring affair, for who could possibly care about a collection of redcoats anyway. The colonel was married to an infant girl, and none of the others had a suitable fortune, so a good family argument was more than welcome.

The party left soon after breakfast and visited a milliner's shop where Elizabeth bought some black crepe, black gloves, several black bonnets and shawls and several different styles of black fabric to take to the modiste for new gowns. She had brought several petticoats with her so the modiste could also sew crepe along the bottom hem just in case they should show. They went to the shoe seller where she bought black slippers and ordered a pair of black half boots. Elizabeth had expected to see her family during her time in the village, but from what she heard from the shopkeepers at each of her three stops in the village, her family had not yet made any purchases.

Elizabeth was grateful to be able to show such respect to her sister and her memory by being in mourning for her. She only hoped it could proceed without conflict with her family. She knew they wanted nothing to do with her. She wished she could be far away from them, but she was at the mercy of others for a year at least. She did not mind it. She no longer felt unwelcome at Netherfield. Mr. Bingley was a gentleman and was always kind to her, and Mr. Darcy had changed considerably towards her. She liked him very well and was always happy to be with him. He was careful and gentle with her; he almost seemed protective of her, and in her fragile state of mind, his attentions were not unwelcome, especially as he made no attempt to smother her. Mr. Bingley made sure that his sisters were at least considerate and civil, and Mr. Hurst was happy with sport or drink.

When the shoppers returned to Netherfield, there was a note for Elizabeth from her father. She went to a corner seat in the drawing room to read it in private.

Longbourn, Wednesday, November 27

Elizabeth,

I have arranged with the rector at Longbourn church to have Jane's funeral service there Monday at noon. She will be buried under the floor of the small chapel aside the church where the Bennets have been buried since coming to Longbourn during the reign of Charles I. Your mother and Mary are arranging for all the flowers for the church and the chapel. It will be a small service, befitting what I would imagine would be Jane's desire. I will invite Mr. Bingley, Mr. Darcy, and Mr. Hurst, of course. They can tell you how it went along. A jeweler from Meryton will be by today for some of Jane's hair with which he will make mourning rings. Additionally, I am having him make a special ring and locket for you. There is no arguing that you two were the closest of any in our family, and I consider the loss on your part to be the greatest. In light of recent events involving your mother, I have judged it inappropriate for us to call at Netherfield, visit with you and see Jane for a last time.

I have contracted by express mail with Mr. William Wade of Leadenhall Street, London, to arrange the funeral. He will arrive at Netherfield before noon Friday with Jane's coffin and shroud. Miss Dawson from Longbourn parish will arrive Friday afternoon to assist you in dressing Jane. On Monday morning around 10 o'clock, Mr. Wade will close the coffin with the help of some men. They will then transport it by horse and wagon to the church at Longbourn village.

Lizzy, I am very sorry for the sad business that is going on in our family. I would do anything to change it, but I feel powerless. I miss you very much, my love. Your Father.

AFTER DINNER THAT EVENING, MR. Bingley approached Elizabeth saying, "Miss Elizabeth, I cannot tell you again how very sorry I am for you. I know how much you loved your sister, and I know how you cared for her and nursed her while you were here. I hope you know that I did everything I could for her. If only I had sent for Mr. Foster sooner, or perhaps a second physician may have helped. And this situation with your family, the injustice of it, is all too horrible. How you are able to endure such hardship I do not know. I could not begin to be able to teach you patience, or any virtue for that matter."

"I feel for your loss as well, Mr. Bingley. It was impossible for me to expect always to be with her. She would eventually be taken from me, and I wished it could have been by you. You would have spent far more years together than she and I would have. So in some ways, sir, your loss is greater than mine. I know that you loved her. I know that she loved you, as well. And there is not anything so precious as love. Somehow when two souls are joined, there is a completeness of being that cannot be measured, and once achieved, they are almost unable to live without. Take one away, and the other loses half their life. And having just lost my most beloved sister and my family, I believe I feel as if almost my whole life is lost."

"I do not know whether or not I have loved her long enough to say that my life is half lost, but I feel her parting immensely," said Mr. Bingley. "It has been years since I have known the tears that have been my company this past day or so. All of my carefully laid plans for the future are gone. I feel adrift. I have no purpose, no direction, nothing to motivate me, nothing to smile at, no reason to be happy. I suppose I did live for her. Maybe I was wrong to wrap my life up so wholly in another person, but it could not be helped. She was irresistible. Who would want to resist her? Loving her was my only option."

"You will rally again, Mr. Bingley. If Jane were here right now, she would tell you to be happy and to love again, if not for your sake, then for hers. You know I am right. There was not a sad bone in her body, and she would suffer to see you so miserable. Take your time. Your heart will heal, but you will never forget her." Elizabeth started to cry. "Oh, Mr. Bingley, I would change things for you if I could, and I would gladly change places with her if I could. She so deserved to live. Indeed she did. And I feel that I deserve nothing. Please do not forget her. Let your heart heal. And please, someday, love again for her sake." And with that, she ran from the room.

MR. WADE ARRIVED AS PLANNED by noon on Friday. He described Jane's coffin as a 'triple case' coffin with recessed cover, suitable for burial in a double brick grave under the floor of a chapel. It was made of one and a half-inch oak board, surrounded by a lead shell of five pounds weight per square foot that was formed and welded at the corners and seams. The shell was covered by an outer wooden case of one and a half-inch oak board, covered on the outside in scarlet Genoese velvet. There were four pairs of gilt grips on the sides, and an oval shaped 'depositum' on the top, a plate that would have Jane's name engraved on it before her burial. The cover would be bolted on before burial, and small velvet patches placed over the bolt heads. He also described it as a 'single break' coffin: narrow at the head, growing wider at the shoulders and then gradually getting narrower towards the feet. Inside, the coffin was covered in cambric with 'soft furnishings' of white linings on the cover and sides, a pillow, padding and a flannel shroud.

The white flannel shroud was woven specifically for use in burials. It originally started as a piece of cloth about twelve feet long and a shoulder width's wide, sewn down one length, making it about six feet long. This was placed over Jane, covering her feet first, after holes for her arms were slit in the sides of the shroud. Straight sleeves of flannel, without gussets, were sewn onto the sleeve holes. Black strips of cloth were used to gather the shroud at different places along her legs and at her ankles. Before the shroud had been placed over her, a small strip of cloth had been used to tie her big toes together to keep her legs straight. The shroud was tied and gathered at her wrists. Her arms were laid out straight against the side of her body. At her waist, the shroud gathering included her wrists, to keep her arms in place. The shroud was also gathered around her neck. A cap of the same material was placed on her head.

All the work of dressing Jane was done by Elizabeth and a woman from the Longbourn parish who traditionally helped prepare the dead for funerals. Miss Dawson, an old spinster, spoke very quietly as she instructed Elizabeth in the proper way to dress Jane. These arrangements took place in the room where Jane died. The coffin would remain there until Monday morning, and neighbors would be calling with their condolences. They would view Jane throughout Friday evening and all day Saturday and Sunday.

It was very special for Elizabeth to be with Jane this last time. Although Jane's body was cold, Elizabeth could feel her warmth in the memories they shared as she tied the shroud to her wrists. Miss Dawson was working on Jane's legs. It was impossible for Elizabeth to work without tears escaping her eyes. As she leaned over Jane, a teardrop landed on Jane's cheek, and for just a moment it looked as though Jane were also crying. It was more than Elizabeth could bear, and she collapsed on the bed and sobbed, unable to comfort herself. Miss Dawson was unmoved as she completed the work in silence. It was not that she was unsympathetic, but being often in the company of death, she was inured to tears and heartbreak. She smiled kindly on Elizabeth as she walked from the room. Her work there was finished. She would go to Mr. Bennet at Longbourn, collect her money and wait for the next death in the parish that would cause her to stir from her small home and warm fire.

Chapter 4

After breakfast on Saturday morning, Elizabeth prepared herself for the trials of the day. She knew she would be receiving calls from people in the neighborhood wishing to give their condolences and to see Jane. All of this was appropriate, and it was her place to be strong, but it was going to be difficult. She wished to be alone with Jane and her thoughts.

The first to arrive was Mrs. Long and her two nieces. Elizabeth had always considered them to be pretty, if not a little rude, but her mother had always considered them plain. After seeing Jane, the eldest niece said, "I am so sorry, Eliza that your sister has passed away, but I suppose that things like this will happen from time to time."

Elizabeth said nothing.

The younger girl continued, "Jane was the prettiest girl in the country. She does not look quite as well now, though, you must admit. I am very glad I will not be able to see myself when I am dead. I would be mortified." She laughed at what she thought was a clever joke.

Elizabeth could hardly retain her composure. "Well, for my part, I still consider Jane to be the prettiest girl in the country."

The nieces gave her a strange look. Mrs. Long sneered at her and said, "I am very sorry, Miss Bennet. We must be going. Come along, girls." And with that, they left the room and Netherfield. Elizabeth decided her mother was right after all. Any beauty they had was diminished by their vulgar behavior.

The next visitors were from the regiment and included Colonel and Mrs. Forster, Captain Carter and Lieutenant Denny. Elizabeth was very glad to see them, as she considered them her friends.

"Miss Bennet," said Colonel Forster. "You cannot imagine how deeply moved I am by your loss. I have seen young men die in battle in my lifetime, which is tragic enough, but to see a beautiful young woman struck down at the height of her beauty and bloom is the most horrible scene I can behold. I am truly sorry. On behalf of the whole regiment, we express our deepest concern for you and your family and offer our services in any way that would be of use to you. I know it could not make up for the loss of your dear sister and may be just useless words to you, but it is consolation to our own hearts that we can offer our services to you."

Elizabeth was very moved by his words and had tears burning her eyes by the time he had finished.

"My dear Colonel, thank you so much for your kind words. You and your officers have always treated me with kindness and respect, and your coming to visit means a great deal to me. I know Jane would be grateful as well. I promise if there is any need that can be satisfied by you and your men, I will send a servant to you immediately. Indeed, I may need your assistance when it comes time to move Jane to the chapel on Monday.

"We are at your service, Miss Bennet."

Captain Carter added, "Please let me add my own words to what my Colonel said. We are truly grieved. *I* am truly grieved. You have cared for her very well. She still looks as beautiful as she ever was, Miss Bennet. We have all been invited to the funeral by your father and are grateful for the opportunity to pay our respects. Please allow us the opportunity to serve you in any way you deem possible."

"Thank you all very much." *Captain Carter must have been in love with her, too*, thought Elizabeth. These welcome guests then left her.

Elizabeth did not know what the regiment ever could do for her. She had chosen to rely on Mr. Bingley and Mr. Darcy, but it was still gratifying to know that she had such good friends. It was sad to think she was not quite as aware of their friendship before Jane died.

Several other families in the neighborhood also called. Although no one had much to say, everyone was kind. It was pleasing to hear Jane spoken of with such respect. She had touched the lives of so many people with her love, patience and kindness. Truly, Jane was too good. Elizabeth knelt next to Jane's coffin and began to weep for the loss of Jane and everything that was good.

On Sunday, Elizabeth felt too ill to attend services. She was too weak emotionally to be in company beyond Netherfield, and she was always too close to tears. It was the first day of December. Jane's birthday was that month, but there would be no celebration.

The Lucases called after morning services. Sir William and Lady Lucas looked at Jane for a few minutes and made some comments to Elizabeth about how sorry they were. The younger Lucases and Maria said nothing at all and soon left with their parents. Only Charlotte remained behind. She sat with Elizabeth in Jane's room when they were alone.

"Eliza, you do not look well."

"I am fine, Charlotte."

"No, you are not. I can tell by looking in your eyes that you are ill and drained. You have been crying too much. This must be an awful time for you. I was with my mother when Mrs. Bennet called to tell us that Jane had died. She also said that you had been disinherited from the family for not having taken care of Jane and for contributing to her death, and that your name was not to be spoken in her presence ever again. I am sure it must pain you to hear this, but I wanted you to know what she is saying about you to the neighborhood. I do not believe a word of it regarding Jane. I know you must have attended her with every bit of strength you had. I know how much you loved her. You would have done anything for your sister."

"Mama sent me a letter by way of my father on the day Jane died, telling me the same thing, Charlotte. I do not know what I have done to deserve such treatment. I spent nearly every waking moment with Jane the whole time she was at Netherfield with the exception of the officers' ball when I was ordered by Mr. Foster, the physician from London, to get out for the evening as he was concerned for my health. He, Mr. Jones and a housemaid stayed with Jane that evening until I returned. My mother was cruel to me that night; I am embarrassed to say how much so. Mr. Darcy found me on the road to Netherfield. I think I was lost. I was crying, nearly out of control of myself, and I was so cold. Maybe I would have died. He brought me back in Mr. Bingley's carriage and made sure I went to bed. I was in a horrible state of mind, but I felt much better the next morning."

"Mr. Darcy seems to care very much for you."

"He and Mr. Bingley have been very kind to me. I am to remain with them, Miss Bingley and Mr. and Mrs. Hurst for my year of mourning. I will then take a position as a governess and earn my own bread."

"Oh Eliza, is there no other way? Must you become a servant?"

"Charlotte, I will not live in this world dependent on someone else. I will earn my own way. My portion is too small for marriage to be an option. Indeed, my mother cut off what small dowry I had. I have been completely disinherited by my family. I am alone in the world, left to shift for myself."

"Oh, Eliza, if only there was something I could do for you."

"There is nothing, Charlotte, so do not trouble yourself by wishing for something that is not possible. I am comfortable right now and grateful to Mr. Bingley for his hospitality. He and Miss Bingley took me into Meryton the day after Jane died so that I could order mourning gowns and buy bonnets and gloves. They have been very kind to me, and Mr. Darcy has been very kind, as well. I do not expect the situation with my family to change. The sooner I learn to give up hope the happier I will be. So you see Charlotte, I am doing the best I can," Elizabeth finished with a weak smile.

Charlotte rose to take her leave. The friends hugged and kissed each other as they mixed their tears on each other's cheeks and said their good-byes. Elizabeth walked Charlotte towards the door.

"Be happy for me, Charlotte. I am sure all will be well somehow."

"Yes, Eliza." With that, Charlotte descended the steps and returned to Lucas Lodge. Elizabeth, tears on her cheeks, watched her leave as she stood at the open door, not at all sure that all would be well. She slowly returned to Jane's room to ready herself against the arrival of the next mourners.

JANE WAS GONE. AT THAT moment, the funeral service was being conducted at Longbourn church. It seemed to Elizabeth a lifetime since she had even been in that church. Perhaps it would not be until the end of her life that she would enter it again. There would be no one to go to *her* funeral. Papa would be gone and so would her Uncle Gardiner and Uncle Philips; and Mr. Bingley and Mr. Darcy would have forgotten about her long ago. Death was a convenient way to gain new connections. If a person did not have any close friends or relatives and just died, somebody was bound to come out of the paneling and say nice words. It was just too bad they did not do that when the person was alive. But when they were alive, there was no property to be disbursed, nothing to get. So, apparently there *was* more value in death than in life.

Netherfield felt empty and cold. Miss Bingley and Mrs. Hurst did not say much, and they acted as though it were just an ordinary day. They would talk to each other in the drawing room near the fire, making plans for this party or that ball to which they would undoubtedly receive invitations that Season in town. They were so looking forward to it. Mr. Hurst had dispensed with all propriety and decency and refused the invitation to the funeral, nearly an unheard-of action. He was out with his man and a couple of dogs, a-shooting. He said that funerals were too sad for him and that he was not in the mood to cry in front of other men — that, of course, Miss Bennet would understand and not think ill of him for his not going. "Of course not," she lied. From that moment on, she despised him. Before, she only disliked him.

Elizabeth wondered about her mother and sisters and what they might be doing at that moment. How would Lydia and Kitty calm themselves for a year of mourning: no dances, no concerts, no chasing after officers, with only private dinner parties of small numbers probably in their own home? Elizabeth was sure that this was not how they imagined life at their age. They were impatient, reckless girls with no time for anybody or anything but themselves. Hill almost required a separate housemaid just to follow them around and clean up after their little hobbies in the still-room and in the dining parlor when they decided to rip apart bonnets and then quit halfway through repairing them, leaving ribbons and thread strewn everywhere. Mary spent her whole life in mourning, so all it meant for her was new gowns and things; she might even enjoy it.

Jane seemed to be the common connection for the whole family. Jane love everybody and was loved in return, so in some strange way, with Jane alive the family was complete. Now, that common bond was gone. Mrs. Bennet no longer had to be patient with her second daughter. She had completely disowned her and barred her from her home. With Jane's death, Kitty and Lydia would grow wilder than ever, being cooped up in mourning with no outlet for the animal spirits they were allowed to develop. This could only worsen their temperaments. Mary would withdraw even more into the fantasy world of imaginary human morality, where everyone acts perfectly in every imperfect situation. With Jane gone and now Elizabeth at Netherfield, Mr. Bennet would have no inducement to exercise himself in the role of a parent. He cared little for the younger girls other than to laugh at them. Jane was the only hope the Bennet family had, and that hope was gone forever.

Elizabeth sat down on a settee near a window in the drawing room. She was now alone. Outside, it was sunny though chilly. *How odd*, she thought. *It should be rainy and cold. How could nature be anything other than sad on the day of Jane's funeral?* She leaned her head against the arm of the settee and began to cry. She felt like all she did was cry. But there was no Jane to comfort her, so how would she ever be able to stop?

On Tuesday, a carriage was heard driving up the paddock. One servant went out to assist the occupants in descending from the carriage and another proceeded to announce the arrival of the carriage to the ladies and gentlemen who were spending the afternoon in the music room. They all repaired instantly to the entryway where Darcy saw Georgiana descending from the carriage and hurried out to greet her.

"Oh, Brother, it is so good to see you. What is so urgent, that I should come so quickly to Netherfield? Is something wrong?"

"Georgiana, I am so glad to see you again. Is all well in town, I hope?"

"Everyone is well at the townhouse, I suppose. Miss Langhourne's niece just had a son. She is the new cook, if you remember."

"Yes, I do remember Miss Langhourne. Please come in, and then we can have a serious talk." They moved together into the house.

"Miss Bennet, this is my sister, Georgiana. Georgiana, Miss Elizabeth Bennet." Elizabeth's eyes swept over Miss Darcy. She was young, but her figure was well formed. She was lovely with beautiful, golden hair, just the opposite of her brother's dark hair although she shared his dark eyes. Her skin was pale, and if she held still enough, she looked like a china doll. She had an air of innocence about her that was charming. The curl at the corner of her lip suggested she was more inclined to laughter and lightheartedness than was her brother. Unfortunately, she appeared to be no match for Miss Bingley. It was hoped that Mr. Bingley would take mercy on her and keep his sister at bay.

"I am pleased to make your acquaintance, Miss Bennet."

"And I you, Miss Darcy."

"Dear Georgiana, welcome to Netherfield," added Miss Bingley.

"Thank you, Miss Bingley." It was clear Georgiana was not comfortable around Miss Bingley. She was far older than Georgiana and seemed too condescending, as though she were trying to gain something. Miss Bingley always addressed Georgiana by her Christian name, which seemed improper as she had never given her permission to do so. However, for her brother's sake, Georgiana would be patient with Miss Bingley. He was a great friend of Mr. Bingley, so there would be no escaping the acquaintance. Besides, who would want to escape Mr. Bingley?

"Miss Darcy, welcome to Netherfield," said Bingley with a bow. "I wish you were here under happier circumstances, but indeed it is a pleasure to see you anytime. Please, just call on me for anything you may require so that your stay here will be comfortable and enjoyable. I am sure you have much to talk about with your brother, so I will leave you two to yourselves. The library is available for your privacy if you wish."

"Thank you, Bingley. Come along, Georgiana. I have much to tell you."

The Darcy siblings retreated to the library, leaving the others to scatter through the house in search of their own amusements until dinner called them together. In the library, the conversation went something like this:

"What is wrong, Fitzwilliam?"

"Miss Bennet's sister Jane has died since I last wrote you. I mentioned that she was here and quite ill."

"I ventured to guess that something had happened; Miss Bennet is in mourning."

"Yes, it was not pleasant, though I suppose it could never be expected to be so. She appeared to die without pain. The most awful part of the business is that Elizabeth's family, her mother most particularly, accuses her of having facilitated Jane's death by not properly caring for her. That is absolute nonsense, of course, but her mother is the most foolish, disagreeable woman with whom I have ever been acquainted. Elizabeth was with her sister night and day since she arrived here and fell ill more than two weeks ago. Her mother actually sent Miss Jane here on horseback in the rain to answer an invitation sent by Caroline and Louisa."

"That is shocking! But what of Miss Elizabeth?"

"She has been cast off by her family and has sought and received Bingley's protection while he remains at Netherfield and for the year of her mourning. She intends to find employment as a governess after that. Georgiana, I have asked you to come here to be her friend. I think very highly of her, and I am hoping that at some point we can persuade her to come to Pemberley with us."

"I noticed, Brother, that you called her 'Elizabeth.'"

"Yes, well, at the end of her mourning, I intend to ask her to be my wife."

"Oh, Fitzwilliam, I am so happy for you. I am sure she will love you."

"I do not know her feelings. I have only recently become acquainted with my own. I do not intend to do or say anything that will intrude on her time of mourning, nothing that will disturb her peace, interrupt her healing, or affect her in any negative way. She is in no way prepared to hear anything now, nor will she be for many months, I would imagine, but I have great hopes. She is kind and generous. It is a horror that she could be treated thus by her family, and it is my intention to replace, with all that is in my power, the loss of love and home from which she is suffering. They have never known her if they choose to treat her in such a way."

"Fitzwilliam, I will try. I will to do everything I can, but you know my reserve with strangers, especially those who are older. I am only sixteen, you know."

"She is nearly one and twenty, but I have heard that her dearest friend in Meryton is nearly six years her elder. Age does not make a difference to her. And you, Georgiana, are one of the sweetest young women in the world, so I know that she will love you as I do. You need not worry. All will be well."

It was the middle of December, and Christmas was approaching. The snow falling that morning reminded Elizabeth of that happy family holiday. The Gardiners used to come to Longbourn, but there would be no celebrations that season. There would perhaps be some sweet things, but the parties away and at home would not happen, and all the gay times of singing and laughter would be dispensed with in favor of black gloves and solemn faces. It would be weeks yet before her family would visit outside their home. It had been weeks since she had been inside her home, and according to both her parents, she would never be inside it again. If only she had died and not Jane, none of this would be happening. Yes, her family would observe a mourning time for her, but the discord in her family never would have occurred. Jane would have been there to love them all through it. She would have been able to talk sensibly to Papa, calm Mama, and encourage and love the younger girls with gentle and infinite patience. Why must she live with the pain of her own death without the blessing of death's insensibility? There would be no celebration that year or in any year to come. Jane had taken that with her to the grave.

CHRISTMAS DAY WAS AN AWKWARD affair at Netherfield. Bingley wanted to put on a happy face, for he loved this time of year with its gifts, family, and good cheer. *Nothing better than a cold evening spent near a large fire in conversation after a filling dinner*, he thought. And even though his Jane was gone, he wanted it to be a pleasant time for Darcy and his sister. They were a family and had every right to happiness while under his roof. Then there was Miss Bennet. She was in mourning, and it was necessary to make proper allowances for her and to be respectful to her. Indeed, he thought more of her than of anyone else, for she alone could understand what he felt. By now, he and Jane would have been formally engaged, and all the Bennets would have been his guests that evening, laughing and dancing. He would have borne with ease Mrs. Bennet's voice and manners. Until the day Jane came to Netherfield, he had thought she was only looking out for the interests of her daughters, although in a rather crude way. Now, he could not say what he thought, even though the edge had come off the pain somewhat. At least he did not cry as he used to do, though this was no comfort to him. In some ways, he felt unfaithful to Jane by not shedding a tear every time he thought of her, and he thought of her nearly all of the time.

IT HAD BEEN OVER A month since Jane had died. If a woman could be allowed to look beautiful in mourning attire, Darcy believed Elizabeth did. He also thought it was not an advantage to Elizabeth for her to remain so close to her family. She could not be prevailed upon to go into the park or walk anywhere beyond the pleasure gardens of Netherfield. She would not go into the countryside around Meryton at all and, in fact, had not been to Meryton once since the day she returned to pick up her new mourning gowns. In all of this, Darcy saw a concerted effort to avoid any possible meeting with her family, and he felt that she considered herself a prisoner at Netherfield. He was determined to speak to Bingley about it. Elizabeth should be invited somewhere else where she would have the freedom to move about and yet retain her privacy — and that place was Pemberley. He decided to speak with Bingley directly.

Darcy knew he could find Bingley near the billiard table at that time of day, so he went there first in search of him. He was there, and Darcy closed the door behind him as he entered the room.

"Bingley, I would like to extend an invitation to you to come to Pemberley."

"Thank you, Darcy; I did not know you had any thoughts of returning to Pemberley so soon."

"Honestly, I did not until very recently, but I do now. And the reason I do is Elizabeth — I mean, Miss Bennet."

"So it is Elizabeth, is it?"

"It is for me, Bingley. I do not know how she feels, and certainly it will be many months before that question can be asked." Darcy stopped speaking. He had revealed more about his feelings for Elizabeth than he had intended. "But I am very worried about her. Though she is in mourning, one would expect her spirits to be recovering at least in some measure. She will not walk beyond the pleasure gardens, yet she used to walk all over the countryside. I do not think she is getting enough exercise. I think she stays so close and does so little in an effort to avoid her family. If she were away from them, away from the source of the pain and bad memories, I think she would have a chance to heal. And Bingley, I might say the same for you."

"And so you think that getting her to Pemberley would be the right thing for her? Is this your thought for her or do you think this would be her thought for herself?"

"Personally, I do not think she would express an opinion either way. And so I would like to extend an invitation to the whole party, including her, and have us all away to Pemberley with her joining us as a matter of course. If you do not care to join us, I will speak to her myself about coming with Georgiana and me. She can stay there comfortably with Georgiana and Mrs. Annesley, and she will be free to walk about the park and grounds as much as she wishes. When her time of deep mourning is over, Georgiana will take her into Lambton and Bakewell and will gradually introduce her into society there. Perhaps we will travel to town later in the year. I intend to court her as much as propriety will allow. Towards the end of her year, in September, perhaps, I will ask her to be my wife and pray that she accepts me."

"Well, Darcy, you seem to have this all figured out. And what does Miss Elizabeth have to say about this?"

"I told you, she has said nothing, and it is inappropriate for me to say anything. I do not wish, nor could I ever, say or do anything to hurt or offend her. I am asking for your help in removing her from her family and taking her to Pemberley, that is all. I should be asking for your opinion. Do you believe that this is the correct thing for me to do?"

"What, the great Darcy asking advice from me?"

Darcy looked at him awkwardly and with not a little hurt in his expression.

Bingley paused for a moment and let the feeling of guilt torture his mind before he apologized. "I am sorry, Darcy. I am very envious of you. And I am missing Jane very much. I loved her, you know, just as you love Miss Elizabeth. I will not presume to know what is best for either of you, but I do agree that remaining at Netherfield is odious. I had intended to leave for London, but I may as well go to Pemberley. I have decided to give up the lease immediately. There is nothing for me here except memories. I cannot imagine remaining now without Jane."

ELIZABETH RECEIVED A VISITOR THE Monday after Christmas when her father suddenly appeared at Netherfield. Her maid came to her private sitting room, where she had been reading, to let her know that a gentleman was waiting for her in the drawing room. When questioned as to the identity of the gentleman, she replied, "Mr. Thomas Bennet of Longbourn, ma'am."

Elizabeth did not immediately go down. She had not seen her father since the day Jane had died. In the way she viewed her life, the day Jane died represented a huge wall. There was her life before Jane died on one side of that wall and her life after Jane died on the other. And no matter what she did, there was no way over that wall. She was irrevocably changed—and for the worse, she thought. The last conversation she had with her father had been on the far side of that wall when she was banished from her home. What place did this man have in her life now? Did he come to apologize, to accept her back? Of what use was she to him now other than an embarrassment? Obviously, her mother thought Elizabeth a disgrace to the family, and Mr. Bennet did nothing about it. Elizabeth began to grow angry and decided she would rather face him in anger than any other way. The only thing her family left her was her pride. According to her mother, they were going to burn everything else.

She rose with a determined air, prayed for patience, and moved for the stairway.

MR. BENNET WAS GLAD TO be at Netherfield. He loved Elizabeth very much, and he felt nothing but guilt and anguish over his behavior. He had been forced to make a decision—his wife and three younger daughters or Elizabeth. He would much rather have Elizabeth, but the scandal that would be caused by his wife publicly denouncing him as an adulterer would forever ruin the prospects of all his daughters. He had been faithful to Mrs. Bennet—he had felt no temptation on that score—but she had caught him in what could be construed as a compromising position with one of Mrs. Long's nieces. What a fool he had been! No matter what he did, he would hurt Elizabeth, and she would hate him forever. At least her reputation would not be tarnished by the indiscretions of a foolish father and an even more foolish mother. He loved her too much, and he would not ruin Elizabeth's future for the gratification of his pride in justifying his actions to her. Some day he might be able to tell his daughter the truth but not until she was settled and forgotten by her mother, and by then it might be too late for him. In fact, he intended to find a bright, young solicitor to hold a letter of explanation for Elizabeth to be sent to her upon his death. Perhaps then, the secret could be revealed. Today, he was on an errand and hoped—just hoped—her sorrow for Jane had not been replaced by anger for him.

ELIZABETH ENTERED THE DRAWING ROOM cautiously.

"Hello, Papa."

"Elizabeth," he said walking towards her. He took her hand and kissed it gently, too timid to give her a hug or kiss her cheek. Her skin looked flushed. She was angry.

"I have brought the mourning jewelry I promised you."

"Thank you, Papa. I am sure I will like it very much."

Elizabeth felt tears stinging her eyes. She walked right up next to her father, raised her chin to his face and cried, "Why, Papa, why?! What have I done?!" She was screaming at him. Elizabeth began to sob and beat his chest with her fists until her knees gave way and she nearly collapsed to the floor. He caught her and gently laid her down on a sofa. Between her cries he heard her asking, "Why, why, why?"

Mr. Bennet leaned down and kissed her forehead. He stood up with tears in his own eyes. How was he ever to forgive himself for the pain he was causing his daughter? How would she ever forgive him? Somehow, he would recover from Jane's death. With Elizabeth, he was losing her afresh each day.

Elizabeth was not aware that he had kissed her or of the thoughts on which he was meditating. She was trying to understand why he left Netherfield without her.

When Elizabeth awoke, she was dressed in her nightclothes and in her bed. The curtains in the room were drawn back, and the sun was pouring in. Sitting next to her, holding her hand, was Georgiana Darcy, an uncertain smile on her face and the doleful appearance one gets from having been awake all night.

"Good morning, Miss Bennet, how are you feeling?"

"I have an awful headache, Miss Darcy, and I am very tired. How did I get dressed like this?" said Elizabeth, pointing to her nightclothes.

"I am very sorry, Miss Bennet, but none of us could help but overhear your conversation with your father nor witness its outcome on you. It was just too horrible." Georgiana choked back a sob. "I am so sorry," she whispered.

"Please, do not cry for me."

"You were crying so hard, we could not calm you. We were so worried about you, Miss Bennet. We sent for Mr. Jones almost immediately. By the time he got here, you were not crying as hard, but he gave you enough laudanum for you to sleep the rest of the night. He is coming this morning to check on you. You are not to leave your bed until he advises it. I stayed here with you last night because I felt so sorry for you, and I was not going to leave you alone. I remember how I felt when my father died — the feeling of complete loss and abandonment. I am sure you feel something like that."

"Oh, Miss Darcy, you should not have done that. You should not risk your own health for such a silly reason as my wellbeing. Please go to bed now and get some rest. You look so tired; how you must be suffering."

"I will not leave you until I have heard what Mr. Jones has to say and I know that you are following his advice."

"You are too good to me."

"I do nothing for you that you do not deserve." Georgiana remembered the two packages Mr. Bennet had brought for Elizabeth. "I put the packages your father brought for you in your dressing room. I hope you do not mind."

Elizabeth did not mind. Nor did she mind being told by Mr. Jones that she should remain in bed the rest of that day. He said she needed rest, to which she agreed. When Georgiana was convinced that Elizabeth was going to remain in bed, she removed to her own room for some much-needed sleep but not before reporting, along with Mr. Jones, on the condition of the patient. Darcy and Bingley had been exceedingly worried about Elizabeth. They had never witnessed such an outburst before, and knowing Elizabeth as they did, it was a statement of how disturbed she was regarding her family and the death of her sister. They had had no idea she suffered so severely. Darcy and Bingley agreed that, if they had not already decided to go to Pemberley, they certainly would be going now.

The next morning, after Mr. Jones had come to give Elizabeth his permission to leave her bed and carefully resume her normal activities, she went into her dressing room, curious to see the contents of the packages her father had brought for her. She knew they were mourning jewelry, but she did not know what style he had chosen.

The first package contained a beautiful gold and black enameled locket, with a lock of Jane's hair curled behind glass. On the enamel were the words: "IN MEMORY OF." On the back was the inscription: "Jane Bennet, 26 Nov 1811." The locket opened from the bottom with enough room for a small piece of paper or other such relic to be placed, or perhaps more hair. On the front between the glass that covered the hair and the black enamel, was a circle of gold in a twisted pattern. On the outside edge, gold was stamped with 'O's all the way around. There was a ring at the top through which a chain could fit. It was beautiful. Jane's golden hair set against the gold and black enamel of the locket made a striking contrast. This was truly a treasure. Her father had done well.

The second package contained a ring. It had a round face with gold on white enamel worked to form a weeping willow tree traveling up the left side of the ring over the top and down the right side. In the center was an urn in an oval. The main stem of the tree was made from pieces of Jane's hair. The whole face of the ring was covered in glass. The shank of the ring was engraved with, "Jane Bennet, 26 Nov 1811." The ring itself was made of gold. Elizabeth tried the ring on her right ring finger. It fit perfectly. While she was in deep mourning, she could not wear the jewelry, but she would be glad for it when her mourning ended. She was pleased to have pieces of Jane's hair, something of hers that would be lasting. Hair lasts forever.

Lewis Whelchel

Netherfield, Monday, January 6

Dear Father,
 This note is to let you know that I will be leaving Netherfield today and traveling to Pemberley, where my stay will be of indefinite duration. Mr. Darcy tells me that Pemberley is a grand estate with a large park of many paths for me to wander and lose my way in. I will be grateful for the privacy. I have not walked far while at Netherfield for fear of an accidental meeting with a member of my family. I fear I suffer from the lack of exercise. We leave today without plans for returning. Mr. Bingley is to give up the lease on Netherfield. He wants nothing more to do with it. All it provides for him are fond memories of Jane, which, he says, are almost too overpowering to live with and yet remain happy.
 I remain your affectionate daughter, EB

The Netherfield party, now the Pemberley party, arrived home the first Tuesday in January after spending one night on the road. Miss Bingley, after a tense conversation with her brother, persuaded Mr. and Mrs. Hurst to return to London to Mr. Hurst's townhouse. Even with Jane dead, Caroline could not abide the remaining eldest Bennet girl a moment longer, and as she appeared permanently installed in the family and held what seemed to be a position of greater import than herself, she would no longer remain with them. Mr. Darcy must not be the man she thought he was if he could be charmed by a woman in mourning.

To Elizabeth, who had never traveled beyond London to her Aunt Gardiner's, it was an exciting adventure. She and Georgiana shared a room at the inn. They had such fun together, talking about their childhood, the friends they had and the pranks they had played. Georgiana was particularly entertained by Elizabeth who was a rather precocious child and got into perhaps a little more trouble than she ought. It was a night of more giggles than sleeping, though this alteration in nighttime behavior may have been healthier for both of them. Elizabeth, or rather, Lizzy, as Georgiana now called her, had not had such a relaxing time since Jane died, and Georgie finally had a friend.

Darcy had arranged the seating in the carriage the young ladies were sharing so that Elizabeth sat on the left side, facing forward. This would give her the best view of Pemberley's prospect as they progressed through Pemberley Woods and came down the valley opposite the house. Elizabeth was in awe of the beauty. Even though the trees were bare at that time of year, she could feel the grandeur of the place and knew that to be the mistress of Pemberley would be something magnificent indeed. She wondered whether she would ever meet her.

Darcy had the carriages stop when they drew over the hill and the house came into view. He wanted Elizabeth to have time to take it all in. For her, it was a breathtaking view. The sun was low in the sky, and the light reflected a golden glow off the windows of the stately Jacobean building. The grounds had been landscaped by Lancelot "Capability" Brown, so there was no ornamentation or false adornment to ruin the natural beauty of a stream that grew into a body of more significance towards the far end of the house. It was all tastefully done, and Elizabeth had never seen a place she liked as well. This, she thought, was to be her home, perhaps until December when she would find employment as a governess and no longer be a burden to anyone but herself.

Chapter 5

About a week after they arrived at Pemberley, it began to snow. It was a gentle snowfall with only a small accumulation blanketing the grounds in white. From an upper window, Elizabeth could see the tracks of deer and rabbits in the snow as they made their way across the park. The next day, Georgiana came to Elizabeth's sitting room for a visit.

"Lizzy, how would you feel about a walk in the snow?"

"Georgie, you are daring. What would your brother say?"

"I do not intend to tell him. If he does ask, I will say it was your fault," she teased.

"Trying to get me in trouble and we have not been here two weeks. I would love a walk in the snow."

The ladies bundled up and went out the door. Darcy was working in his study with his steward, and they were able to slip past him unnoticed.

"Lizzy, how do you like it here at Pemberley?"

"I like it very well. It is a beautiful home—and so large. I am afraid I will lose my way in all the passages. The grounds are beautiful. I eagerly await spring when I can walk about them more comfortably. I am also glad to be away from my family. I felt so inhibited, so confined at Netherfield. Are you able to spend much time here, Georgie?"

"I am glad you like it, Lizzy. I am here about half the year. I would say that my primary residence is in London. A piano master comes to the townhouse almost daily to supervise my education on the pianoforte, and Mrs. Annesley is a much stricter schoolmaster while in Town. I do enjoy the break, though. I am very pleased that you are here, Lizzy. My brother is very kind, almost like a father to me, but it is not the same as having a young woman with whom to spend time talking."

"Your brother loves you very much. That must be a great comfort to you."

"He takes such good care of me. I imagine the pressure of managing Pemberley and caring for a younger sister must be a great weight on his shoulders, his being such a young man. I love him dearly for it. I am convinced that there is nothing he would not do for me. He is so kind — too kind, sometimes — more than I deserve."

"I am sure you do deserve it. He is an ideal elder brother, then. I am jealous, for I have no brothers, just four sisters."

"I should have liked to have had a sister." Georgiana paused for a moment, wondering how she would ever get along without Elizabeth. "I am so glad you are here, Lizzy."

As this was spoken, their short circuit was complete, and they returned to the house.

It seemed to be a long night. Georgiana could not sleep. Every time she started to drift off, she saw George Wickham in her mind's eye, and she was overcome by the feelings associated with him, but she was determined not to spend the night like that. Instead, she put on her robe and went to the library in search of a book to read. She was not quite sure what. Perhaps it did not matter.

Elizabeth was similarly disturbed. While she was tired and managed to fall asleep easily, she was constantly awakened by images of Jane dying, which roused all the feelings she had at the time. Elizabeth sobbed and knew she could not endure another night like that again. It was late, so she decided it would be quiet in the house. She would go to the library in search of something to keep her mind off her troubles. She hardly knew what that would be, but perhaps something might catch her eye.

Mr. Darcy was working late in his study. It was a frustrating night when he had more estate business than he wanted, and he was distracted from it because of Elizabeth. He was so glad she was there. The thought of not seeing her every day would be insupportable, 'not to be borne,' as his Aunt Catherine might say. He had written to his aunt telling her that Elizabeth was there. Lady Catherine had become so furious, assuming he was going to marry Elizabeth, that she told him all connection between them was severed until he got rid of that "country hussy" and married Anne as he had been born and bred to do. The library was not far from his study, and he thought he heard voices coming from it but was not sure, so he paid it no attention.

"Lizzy!" Georgiana was startled by Elizabeth's entrance into the room. "Oh my, you scared me! I thought I was quite alone here."

"Georgie, I am so sorry. I could not sleep. I came to search for a book."

"As have I." She hesitated for a moment and looked down at the floor. "Lizzy, may I talk to you about something very personal?" Georgiana was still breathing hard. "I feel I would like to tell you, but I do not want to impose on you."

"Of course you may. You may tell me anything."

Georgiana walked Elizabeth to a sofa where they sat down. During this walk, Georgiana had started to tear up. Elizabeth noticed her glossy eyes, but decided to remain silent and allow Georgiana to begin the conversation.

"Lizzy, I did something awful last summer. I hurt my brother very much." Georgiana started to cry. Speaking through her tears, she said, "I persuaded myself that I was in love with a man named George Wickham. He was a childhood friend of my brother. Mr. Wickham used to play with me and amuse me when I was a child. He was very nice and told me he loved me. I thought I loved him, and we wanted to be married. He was very secretive, though. He did not want my brother to know we were to be married; he wanted to elope. He told me my brother did not really like him anymore and may not give his consent, but if we eloped, then it did not matter. And I believed him."

Georgiana broke down into sobs. Her whole body was shaking. Elizabeth sat close to Georgiana and held her tightly, but she seemed to be beyond comfort. Her crying was filled with doubt, regret and guilt that had been mounting inside of her for months.

"He told me he loved me… And I believed him…" By now, she was nearly screaming. "I hurt my brother so much…"

Elizabeth rocked her as she would an upset infant, speaking soothing words to her and stroking her hair. The poor girl had no mother. Who could really comfort her at such a time? Elizabeth felt so inadequate. She understood the feeling of devastation. Suddenly, the door opened and Mr. Darcy loomed in the shadow of a candle he held. He began to walk towards the sofa until arrested in his progress by a glance and a nod from Elizabeth. Their eyes connected. Darcy had heard enough to know Georgiana was talking about Wickham. And now Elizabeth was telling him with her eyes that she would take care of Georgiana and that it was not his place — not now. It was his turn to trust. What should he do? His sister — his girl — was sobbing and wailing over Wickham, hanging onto Elizabeth. Could he leave the room and trust her? He laughed to himself. He knew he would trust Elizabeth with his life, so why not with his sister. He gave her a slight affirming nod and quietly left the room.

Georgiana finally quieted, but she still held tightly to Elizabeth, who returned her embrace.

"My brother called on me unexpectedly before we were to leave for Scotland. I knew Wickham was upset. I knew he did not want me to see my brother, but I loved him; how could I not? My brother asked what I was doing with Wickham. I had to tell him everything. I ruined everything with Wickham." She pulled back from Elizabeth and sat next to her on the sofa. She leaned her head on Elizabeth's shoulder and held her hand in both of hers.

"My brother said that if I were to leave with Wickham, that I would be unhappy, that he would not treat me well. He told me that Wickham was only interested in my dowry. Did you know that it is thirty thousand pounds? I hate it. I cannot marry where I want. I only found out then from my brother that if I were to marry without his consent, he would not have to give my husband my dowry until I turn thirty years old. What is worse is that my brother is not my sole guardian. I have a cousin who must also give his consent. Neither of them would approve of Wickham. I went to Wickham at his lodgings, alone, and told him of my brother's refusal. I knew he had expected it, but why should that have mattered? We had decided we would marry anyway. He seemed nervous when I told him about my cousin, Colonel Fitzwilliam. When I told Wickham about my dowry, he was shocked. He did not say a word to me for a full five minutes. He looked at me very strangely. I was so afraid, as if I had done something wrong."

Georgiana started to cry again. Her heart seemed broken. What a tender heart she had.

"I told him, 'I will not go back to my brother's home or to Mrs. Younge's. Let us be off to Scotland tonight, this very moment.'"

Georgiana continued, "He just looked at me, and then he started to laugh. He laughed so hard he had tears in his eyes. Lizzy, he was laughing at me. I started to cry."

"He said, 'Little girl, do you really think I care for you for any reason other than your dowry? And since it appears that I cannot have your money, what use do I have of you?'"

"I told him that we loved each other; that was why. He started laughing again. 'Love you? Love the sister of my greatest enemy? Who do you think you are?' And with those words, he bowed to me and walked out of the room. I have not seen him since."

"Oh, Georgie, I am so sorry. I do not know what to say. You are a very kind, gentle young lady. Your heart will heal. It was horrible for him to use you so, but it is just lucky, I suppose, that you found out before you were married to him. How awful it would have been to be bound to him when all he thought of was your money. If he hates your brother, how could he ever truly love you? All he did was deceive you. You are not to blame." Elizabeth was thoughtful for a moment, struggling for words. "I am sure you must feel great pressure from having such a dowry."

"I know my father meant well leaving me so much money so that I could marry well, but to marry equally as to fortune often rules out the ability to marry equally as to love. I know I disappointed my brother very much and I hate the thought of that. What about you, Lizzy? Shall you marry?"

"I can almost laugh. I have no dowry at all. I used to have but fifty pounds a year after my parents passed away, but I have been cut off even from that. I will only marry for the deepest love, and any man who would take me for nothing would be crazy, and I could never love a crazy man. When I leave your family once my mourning is over, I shall become a governess to a gentleman's family and spend my days shifting for myself in the world."

"Must you leave? You need not. I should like to have a companion with me. Mrs. Annesley is very kind, but I cannot speak to her as I do to you. If you must go somewhere and teach, please stay with me and teach me. Please do not leave me. I know that my brother would not like you to leave."

"You are very kind, Georgie, but I do not want to be a burden on anyone. I do not want to be dependent on anyone."

"You cannot possibly be a burden on us. You must consider it, I beg you."

"I will, Georgie. Now, I think you should return to bed. Do you think you can sleep? I will come and sit with you tonight."

"No, Lizzy, I will be fine. Thank you." Georgiana returned to her room with a lighter heart than she had carried with her for many months. Elizabeth quickly followed her, not wanting to see Mr. Darcy, and went to her room with a heart a little heavier than usual, feeling sorry for Georgiana and wondering how such evil could possibly exist in the world.

LIFE FOR ELIZABETH IN FEBRUARY and March passed mainly in the music room. While she had no heart for singing, she would play. Indeed, it was the only distraction a cold winter day afforded if one was tired of needlework or reading. Elizabeth had never practiced as she ought to have. As a result, she did not know many pieces by heart, and having left all of her sheet music at Longbourn, she had the discouraging task of starting afresh learning songs from Georgiana's extensive library of music. At least she was not lacking in choices. Mozart was all the rage. No wonder Mozart was the favorite; his songs seemed to make the most sense. He died at such a young age. What else could he have accomplished? What else could Jane have accomplished? Georgiana seemed to favor *The Marriage of Figaro*. To Elizabeth, *Don Giovanni* seemed more to suit her mood.

The easiest occupation for Elizabeth seemed to be listening to Georgiana play. She was less shy with Elizabeth, and she would sing for her; she could play for hours without needing a piece of music. Her style was eloquent and her movements at the instrument graceful. Watching her was as pleasurable as listening to her, and it was not long before Elizabeth had company. At first, the gentleman would stand outside the door so he would not be seen; if he were present, Georgiana would become embarrassed and leave the instrument, so he would listen from a distance. Every day he would come and stand after breakfast while she played, and Elizabeth would watch him as he leaned against the wall. After a week of this, it appeared on a particular day that Georgiana was especially involved in her music and oblivious to intrusion, so he quietly walked to the nearest chair and sat down, not moving, breathing, or even looking at her, fearful of bringing notice to himself. Georgiana continued her song and remained at the instrument a while longer.

Before she could stand up, Elizabeth spoke to her, afraid his sudden appearance may frighten her. "Georgie, Mr. Bingley enjoyed your performance very much." Elizabeth glanced at Bingley, willing him to silence.

"Mr. Bingley?"

"Yes, he joined us while you were playing."

"Oh! Mr. Bingley." Georgiana colored. "I do not usually play for other people."

"Yes, but you know me tolerably well, and I am not a total stranger to you; you should not be uncomfortable playing for me."

"Well..." She paused, feeling uncomfortable. What could she say? "I... I suppose not, Mr. Bingley. I hope I did not play too poorly, sir."

"No, indeed, you played beautifully. Thank you for allowing me to stay. Please do continue."

"No, I thank you, but I believe I have played enough for today." She gave Elizabeth a small, crooked smile and walked out of the room.

"Very good, Mr. Bingley," said Elizabeth in a conspiratorial tone. "Our shy girl may yet come out of her shell."

From then on Bingley was welcome when Georgiana chose to play, and as she did not play any less than before, Bingley spent more and more time in the music room than he was wont to do in the past.

IN THE MIDDLE OF THE month, Darcy approached Elizabeth.

"Miss Bennet, I know that sufficient time has passed now in your mourning that it would be appropriate for you to go into company again. It is my desire to introduce you at a dinner party to some of my acquaintances in the neighborhood of Pemberley and Lambton. How do you feel about such a plan?"

"Well, I..."

"Would you feel comfortable attending such an affair? The invitation list would include perhaps 24 people, nothing too large but not too intimate. All depends on your feelings on the matter. We will do nothing with which you are uncomfortable."

"Mr. Darcy, you are very kind, but you should not allow me to determine whether you have a party at your home."

"We had hoped to introduce you into society hereabouts, so indeed it does concern you. Please be honest with me. What are your feelings on the subject?"

"I had not thought to do anything while in mourning, but it is now acceptable, I suppose, for me to go into company. I must admit I am nervous about meeting your friends. I am just a country girl with no connections, being allowed to remain at your home by your own graciousness. I do not know whether I feel equal to the task."

"Miss Bennet, in this case you have excellent connections: you have Georgiana and me. We shall see to it that you are well met and introduced as our friend and guest. And please let me reassure you that it is a pleasure to have you in our home. Georgiana and I both value your friendship very much and are pleased that you are here. You are very welcome here, and I do not know how to thank you enough for all of the attention you have given to Georgian — in helping her overcome her shyness, in loving her, in being her friend, and in giving back to her the life that seemed to be lost when our father died. I do not know what we would have done without you." He turned his head away, blushing in a most becoming way at the expression of her importance to him. But it was true, and he wanted her — needed her — to feel welcome and comfortable at Pemberley.

"Well, Mr. Darcy, I appreciate your kind words very much. You must know I would be destitute without your assistance."

"Please say nothing of that, Miss Bennet. Regardless of your circumstances, we would be honored to have you with us. Indeed, Georgiana and I would have come to Longbourn, stolen you away, and brought you with us had you remained there under the happiest of conditions," he said smiling.

Elizabeth could not help but laugh at this picture of Mr. and Miss Darcy rushing into Longbourn with swords and pistols to take her away to Pemberley. All she would have needed was Jane to make it perfect.

"Mr. Darcy, I would love to come to your party."

After dinner, Darcy was able to tell Georgiana the news that Miss Bennet was willing to attend the dinner party. Georgiana asked whether she could make all the arrangements herself for the first time. Darcy agreed as long as she checked with him along the way. He wanted everything to be perfect for Miss Bennet. They decided that they would hold the party on March 26.

Georgiana immediately enlisted Elizabeth's help, much to the latter's satisfaction. Elizabeth still suffered through bouts of melancholy over Jane's death, and being confined indoors due to wet, cold and snowy weather did nothing to improve her spirits. Helping Georgiana with the dinner party would be a welcome relief, however trifling it seemed.

The invitation list would include Lord and Lady Beecham of Hillcock Manor and their son, a principal landholder in the neighborhood, second to Pemberley; Dr. and Mrs. Southwood, the rector of the Lambton church;

Mr. and Mrs. John Bemmerton of Filmore; Mr. David Tuesby, second son of the Earl of Ingleford and many more names Elizabeth could not remember as she lay in bed that night willing herself to sleep. Oh yes, and of course, Mr. Bingley. Dinner would be at seven o'clock, and everyone was invited to come any time after six. Because of the weather, Mrs. Reynolds was asked to prepare rooms for each of the guests in case traveling became too difficult. This fact was included on the invitation. Every hospitality was extended to these guests to encourage them to come.

"Lizzy, I have drawn up a map of the table for the two courses, assuming we can convince Cook to provide twenty-five dishes. I have tried to limit the number of 'removes' so that the servants will not always be running in and out."

"If you must know, Georgie, I do not always like soup and am glad when they bring the fish."

"Lizzy, we have to have soup at a dinner party! How could we not?"

"Well, I shall not have any."

"Do as you will," Georgiana laughed. "I do not know why they call all of these other dishes corner dishes when there are only four corners on a table."

"That is one of the advantages of being a cook. You get to know all of the culinary secrets. Maybe we can peek into the kitchen one day, look over her shoulder and find out what really goes on in there," Elizabeth teased.

Georgiana was laughing. "You are going to get me in trouble, Lizzy. My brother said I could manage the details of this party, but you keep making me laugh. I am going to forget something."

"I am sorry. I cannot help it. But I do agree with you: there are only four corners on a table." The girls burst into laughter again. Just then, Mr. Darcy walked into the drawing room where they had been *working*—so to speak. The ladies would afterwards say they tried their best to be serious, but they could not. They looked at him and then at each other, and more peals of laughter rang through the house. Darcy just smiled at them and went to the library. He left the door ajar, though. He loved the music of Elizabeth's laughter, which was such a rare treat.

Georgiana and Elizabeth finally resumed their work. The first course would contain meat and game, sauces, vegetables and perhaps a sweet pudding. Following the first course, the table would be completely re-laid by the servants with the guests present. The second course was lighter than the first and would include several main dishes of meat and fish, but with a greater variety of puddings, creams and tarts.

The ladies decided on the following dishes:[1]

Salmon. Trout. Soles
Fricando of Veal
Rais'd Giblet Pie
Vegetable Pudding
Chickens. Ham
Muffin Pudding
Curry of Rabbits, Preserve of Olives
Soup. Haunch of Venison
Open Tart Syllabub. Rais'd Jelly
Three Sweetbreads, larded
Macaroni. Buttered Lobster
Peas. Potatoes
Baskets of Pastry. Custards
Goose

THE DAY OF THE DINNER party arrived, and everything was in preparation. Georgiana had seen to it all with Mr. Darcy's approval, and Elizabeth had been Georgiana's faithful assistant. Cook reported that all was proceeding on schedule and that no catastrophes were expected. It was a beautiful day outside, though the ground was wet, and while Elizabeth could not walk about, at least she could sit for a few minutes and feel the sun. She had enjoyed the hustle and bustle of the past two weeks getting ready for the dinner party that night. Elizabeth was going to miss it, for once it was over, there would be nothing to interrupt thoughts of Jane and her family.

The mood of the house was one of anticipation, like the sun dawning on a spring day. Mrs. Reynolds moved through each room like a general commanding an army as new smells curled through the house from the kitchen. Pemberley had not seen preparations like these in a long time. The Darcys had not entertained on such a scale since the late Mr. Darcy had passed away.

Elizabeth and Georgiana went up to dress at four o'clock, and Elizabeth was down again before five. She knew that Georgiana would be longer as

---

[1] *Menu from a dinner provided for Prince William of Gloucester by the Dean of Canterbury in 1798, and attended by Cassandra Austen.*

she always was on dressy occasions. Since no guests were expected until six o'clock, Elizabeth went into the relative privacy of the drawing room and sat down to her work. It was nice to be still and quiet; getting everything ready had taken up a good part of the day. This party was the grandest affair with which Elizabeth had ever been involved, let alone attended. Her mother's parties had never been this large since there was not enough room at Longbourn to hold so many people. A larger number than those invited that night could be entertained easily at Pemberley. Even now, servants were passing back and forth past the door with too much frequency for her taste. She had not seen Mr. Darcy or Mr. Bingley all day.

Her reverie was suddenly interrupted by a servant.

"Excuse me, ma'am. May I present Mr. David Tuesby." The servant turned and left.

Mr. Tuesby was tall, though not quite as tall as Mr. Darcy. He had light-colored hair and deep blue eyes. He was well built and very handsome. Though a gentleman, his hands looked strong and appeared used to work. He was immaculately dressed — not a fold or a crease out of place. He held his chin high. Depending on how he spoke, Elizabeth thought, she would judge him proud. It was too early for the dinner guests to arrive. Where was Mr. Darcy? Why was Mr. Tuesby there with her?

"I am Mr. David Tuesby, ma'am," said he, with a formal bow, "your humble servant at your service, of course. And you are...?"

"Miss Elizabeth Bennet, sir," said she with a deep curtsey.

"I am here by way of invitation for the dinner, Miss Bennet. Because of the distance I must travel and the uncertainty of the roads today, I am unfortunately — no, let me say that again — I am *fortunately*," he said looking at Elizabeth, "arrived very early, and so I am to have the pleasure of your company."

"I do not know where Mr. Darcy is, sir; he should be here to greet you."

"Darcy? No matter about him. Tell me all about you."

"There is not much to say," she said meekly. She did not like Mr. Tuesby but would be civil to him. Mr. Darcy would be there shortly, and then she could leave the room.

"Well then, I shall say it. You are young, unmarried, beautiful, wear lavender fragrances, have the darkest of dark, piercing eyes, are not from Derbyshire, have not long been in this house, and Darcy should go to the devil for hiding you from me."

Elizabeth was quite shocked and embarrassed. She sat back down to her work and said nothing. Perhaps he had had too much drink — but so early in the day. Oh, where was Mr. Darcy?

Mr. David Tuesby took to pacing the drawing room like a predator toying with its prey. Every time he approached Elizabeth, he stared at her with unblinking eyes that made her skin itch. She felt naked before him. She sank back into her chair as far as she could, her eyes pleading with the door for anyone to enter the room.

"Miss Bennet, I see that you are in mourning. A father or a mother?"

"My sister."

"I am sorry. Death seems to take satisfaction in whomever it finds. Was she young?"

"Yes. In the bloom of life."

"No doubt Death disappointed some young man, then. Well, everybody must learn to face it. My mother, my brother and both sisters are dead. Everyone in my family is so dead, I consider myself lucky to be alive." He laughed at what he thought was a joke.

Elizabeth was becoming ill. He would not take his eyes off her, and she was afraid of him. *How is it possible to be alone in a house so full of people? Where is Georgiana?* she thought.

"So, how do you like being here with Darcy?"

His tone of voice seemed to imply that she had an intimate, inappropriate relationship with Mr. Darcy, and that revolted her. How dare he be so personal with her!

"I am the guest of Miss Darcy."

"What is the difference? But do not worry; Darcy is a gentleman just the same. Darcy and I were in school together, and he got me out of a couple of scrapes if you know what I mean, but not Darcy — always the gentleman. The ladies loved him, too. He could have had... Well, anyway."

Tuesby sat next to Elizabeth on the sofa she occupied. She cringed and leaned against the arm.

"I have always considered Mr. Darcy to be the perfect gentleman, Mr. Tuesby."

Still no one came to the room. The clock said 5:35; it was yet some time before the others would arrive. Where was Mr. Darcy? Mr. Tuesby smelled of port wine. Maybe she could get away.

"You must excuse me, Mr. Tuesby." Elizabeth set her work aside and made to stand.

"No, Miss Bennet... Elizabeth, please do not go." Tuesby quickly grabbed her arm and forced her back onto the sofa.

"Mr. Tuesby! You are hurting me! Please, sir! Release me; I must go!" She struggled against him, but he held on to her more tightly.

"Elizabeth, please settle down and talk to me. I feel like I have known you my whole life. I know there is a connection between us if you would listen to your heart. Look at me, Elizabeth; look at me!"

Elizabeth would not answer but closed her eyes and turned her head away. He was hurting her arm, and she was scared. Her eyes stung with tears.

"Elizabeth, if you will just let me—"

Elizabeth started crying. "No, no, no..."

With his other hand, he grasped the back of her neck, pulled her head towards him, and kissed her harshly, bruising her lips.

"Do not fight me Eliz—"

"NO!" Elizabeth screamed.

"You do not understand; I need you."

"Do not touch me; do not touch me!" She could taste the stale wine on his lips. She wanted to vomit.

He began to squeeze her neck. It hurt so badly that she saw white light around the edge of her vision. He kissed her again, and the last thing she remembered before she fell helpless across his lap was somewhere, in the back of her mind, a bolt of lightning and a crash of thunder that sounded like someone yelling, "TUESBY!"

ALMOST EVERYONE HEARD IT. It sounded like someone had died.

'NO!'

Elizabeth! Darcy recalled he had not seen her all day; everyone had been so busy with the party. He ran to the drawing room. There, on the far sofa, was Mr. David Tuesby and Elizabeth. He had one hand on her arm, which he appeared to be holding, and another on her neck, which he was also grasping, and he was kissing her, against which she was struggling—for just a moment—then she collapsed on his lap.

"TUESBY!"

Tuesby was startled by Darcy but kept his hold on Elizabeth. "What do you want?" he asked bitterly.

Darcy was moving towards them when Tuesby suddenly stood and threw Elizabeth to the floor as if she were a doll. She fell without a sound.

Bingley and a servant had just reached the room. Darcy picked up Elizabeth and walked carefully towards the door. As he passed Bingley, he said, "Keep him in here; do not let him leave."

Bingley did not quite know what was going on, but there was no mistaking the look in Darcy's eyes or the tone of his voice.

As Darcy headed towards the stairway with Elizabeth, Georgiana was on her way down.

"Fitzwilliam! What happened to Elizabeth?"

"Come with me to her bedchamber." Georgiana followed him, opened the door, and led him in with a candle; he laid Elizabeth down on her bed.

"Call for her maid and Mrs. Reynolds. Have Mr. Edwards, the apothecary, sent for immediately."

Georgiana went in search of a footman to send on the errand, dispatched him, and came back to Darcy.

"What happened, Brother?"

"I heard a scream while in the library just a moment ago. It was Elizabeth. I went into the drawing room, and that monster, David Tuesby, had his hands on her, and he was forcing her to kiss him. As I shouted at him, Elizabeth collapsed in his arms. When I approached him, he threw her to the floor as he stood to face me. I went to her and carried her here."

"Oh, Lizzy! Brother, has she said anything? Has she opened her eyes?"

"No, she has not moved. He had a strong hold on her arm and her neck. You must attend to her. I have to remove Tuesby from the house and see to our guests who will be here at any moment. I will send up Mr. Edwards when he arrives."

"Please send up some warm water so I may wash her."

"Yes, of course. Please send me word after Mr. Edwards leaves."

"Tuesby, you appear to me, by both sight and smell, to be drunk. It is beyond my belief that you would come into my home and assault my guest in such a manner. Of what are you thinking?"

"I feel as if I have known Elizabeth all my life"

"You may refer to her as Miss Bennet, Tuesby."

"Darcy, I feel I have known Miss Bennet all my life. I feel we are destined for each other. She would not listen to me. She would not look at me."

Darcy's heart nearly stopped. What had he done wrong that she was left alone with this man? How is it that she could not be safe in his house? Pemberley was supposed to be a sanctuary for her from her family and her grief—a place for her to recover from Jane's death—not a place to be further hurt and insulted. Who knew what other damage might come from that evening?

"If you felt so strongly about her, why did you hurt her?"

"Hurt her?"

"Yes, you were gripping her neck so hard she collapsed on your lap after you forced yourself on her. And then you threw her to the floor. Are these the actions of a man who feels deeply for a woman?"

"I would never hurt her. I love her."

"You hurt her. And if you have hurt her severely, you will be hearing from me again. I have called for your carriage. Leave my house."

Darcy's other guests were polite enough that, if they had heard what happened, they said nothing of it. Mrs. Reynolds was so efficient that three places were removed from the table without much notice so it would not appear that Miss Bennet, Miss Darcy or Mr. Tuesby were missing. Because no one was expecting a Miss Bennet, Darcy had only to make excuses for his sister; she had suddenly fallen ill just that afternoon, and she was confined to her room. Mr. Edwards had been called for, and he probably would arrive during dinner, but they should not be alarmed.

Normally, Georgiana would have been shocked into immobility and unable to do anything, but here was Elizabeth, physically and emotionally hurt. She had not moved from the position in which Georgiana and the maid had left her after changing her into loose-fitting nightclothes. She had made no sound. Georgiana could not tell whether she was sleeping or unconscious. She knew she was breathing lightly but steadily, and her heart was beating slowly and firmly. She had the beginnings of a bruise on the arm Tuesby had been holding. Her lips were swollen and looked sore. There were red marks on her neck where he had squeezed it. Georgiana took a soft towel and washed her mouth with warm water until she could no longer smell the wine from Mr. Tuesby.

To Georgiana this was awful. If this had happened to Elizabeth after being in Tuesby's company just a few minutes, what risk had she been exposed to with Wickham? What would he have done to her, especially after securing her dowry? Her brother had probably saved her life. How was she ever to trust anyone? How would Elizabeth ever trust anyone? Life was so uncertain, and people like Mr. Tuesby made it almost unbearable at times. *Oh, where was Mr. Edwards?* Elizabeth's maid, who was about Georgiana's age, looked frightened. Georgiana went to sit next to her, took her hand, and they waited together until there was a knock at the door. Georgiana went and opened it.

"Good evening, Miss Darcy. It is a pleasure to see you again. I am sorry to be here under such circumstances. I saw Mr. Darcy in the hall, and he explained to me a little of what happened to Miss Bennet. Please tell me all that you know."

"Thank you for coming to quickly, Mr. Edwards. My brother carried her here. Her maid and I changed her into nightclothes. Her arm, where he was holding her, appears to have a bruise on it, her lips are swollen, and there are red marks on the back of her neck. She does not appear injured otherwise. He did throw her onto the floor, my brother said, so I do not know if she is hurt and it is not visible."

"Has she moved or spoken?"

"No, sir."

"I will examine her."

While Mr. Edwards was examining her neck, Elizabeth woke with a groan. Georgiana jumped and ran to the bedside and gently rubbed her cheek.

"Oh. Lizzy, please wake up; please talk to me."

"Georgie," Elizabeth whispered, "is he gone?"

"Yes, Fitzwilliam has sent him away. You shall never see him again."

Elizabeth sighed in relief. Never had she been afraid of anyone before, but she was afraid of Mr. Tuesby.

"Did Mr. Darcy..." Elizabeth was too embarrassed to say anything.

"What Lizzy?"

"I must talk to your brother."

"He is at the party."

"The party? Oh, I forgot. You must go down. They are expecting you; please go." Elizabeth sounded upset.

"No, Lizzy. My brother made my excuses. He asked me to stay with you."

Elizabeth felt a tear roll down her cheek. "Your brother is so kind. I do not deserve it."

"Of course you do."

"No I do not. I feel so dirty. What did I do wrong? Why did he hurt me?"

Mr. Edwards interrupted. "Miss Darcy, I will return again tomorrow. She seems to be doing much better, and I am in the way now. Good evening."

"Thank you, Mr. Edwards." He saw himself out and shut the door.

"Lizzy, you did nothing wrong. None of this is your fault. He was drunk. He was trying to control you and hurt you. Why? I do not know, other than to say that you were at hand, and had I been in the drawing room, it would have been me and not you. It is my fault, you know. I should have come downstairs when you were ready. I never should have left you alone. How was I to know?" Georgiana started to cry. "I must send a note to my brother."

Brother,

Mr. Edwards has come and gone. He did not complete his examination of Elizabeth because she woke during it. She is ill—her mind more so than her body, I think. She blames herself. She asked if Mr. Tuesby was gone from the house. I assured her he was and promised that she should not see him again. I hope that is true.

She has a bruise on her arm where he was holding her, her lips are swollen, and she has red marks on her neck. She has made no physical complaint, but she is much disturbed and upset by the whole affair. I intend to spend the night with her.

She has asked to see you, Brother, though she will not say why. If possible, I would appreciate it if you could leave your guests for a moment and come to her.

I feel responsible for this business, Brother. I should have gone down with her when she was ready. I never should have left her alone. And also I have to thank you again for rescuing me from Wickham. If this happened to Elizabeth on such a short acquaintance, I am certain Wickham would have killed me once he had my dowry. Oh, Fitzwilliam!

GD

Chapter 6

The table was being re-laid for the second course when the footman brought Mr. Darcy the missive from Georgiana. Darcy excused himself and went to his library to read the note.

To say that Darcy was shocked did do give justice to what he felt. Elizabeth was not complaining of any physical injury, which was hopeful, but perhaps meant nothing in the face of the mental upset she was enduring. It was unbelievable that she blamed herself for doing anything wrong. She was the victim of a drunken womanizer, and she was not herself. This Elizabeth was a frightened little girl — not the woman he brought to Pemberley. He had failed to protect her, and she blamed herself when she should be blaming him. His heart ached. Georgiana, in her empathy for Elizabeth, felt her old wounds opening once again. How much anguish had Tuesby caused? How was it ever to be repaired? How were peace of mind and security ever to be restored to Pemberley? How were these two women ever to feel safe there again?

Was the only answer to call out Tuesby to a duel and hope for the best? Darcy had no doubt he easily could defeat Tuesby — at the least, humiliate him and at worst, kill him. If they were caught, it was ten years in the Tower. If he killed Tuesby and it were found out, he would be hanged.

Elizabeth! She wanted to see him. He would go to her immediately.

Darcy knocked gently on the door of her bedchamber. Georgiana opened it slightly.

"Please wait a moment." She shut the door, and shortly, she came back to let him in.

Darcy rushed to Elizabeth's side and took her hand. She jumped back from his touch and pulled her hand away. He was hurt but instantly understood.

"Miss Bennet, you asked to see me."

Elizabeth said nothing but looked at him. He had wanted to touch her, and he appeared hurt. But there was something else. She could not decide.

"Mr. Darcy, thank you for all that you have done for me. Thank you for bringing me to my room—for sending away Mr. Tuesby. I know that you are going to blame yourself or expect me to blame you. Do not." She felt like she was a child in trouble with her governess. "Who could imagine that someone would try to hurt me in your home? I do not blame you. I only thank you and feel a great deal of gratitude for all the kindnesses you extend to me." If only he would not look at her. She turned her head away.

"Miss Bennet, you should not have been left alone. I should have protected you."

"Mr. Darcy, being in your home is protection enough, and you know very well that I seek out opportunities to be alone. Do not take responsibility for this upon yourself." She paused. "Sir, I do have one favor to ask of you."

"Yes, Miss Bennet, anything."

"Sir, I do not want you, in the name of honor, my reputation, or any other reason, to fight with Mr. Tuesby. I could not endure the thought of it," she pleaded.

"Miss Bennet, he has insulted you, me, Pemberley, and all that I believe in and care for." He blushed.

"Please, Mr. Darcy! I will recover and be fine. I will leave Pemberley so that any damage to my reputation will not dishonor it." She was saddened at the thought, and growing frustrated with Mr. Darcy. Why could he not just agree with her? Did he not understand?

"If this is important to you and your happiness, then I will agree. But in exchange you must promise me something."

"Very well, Mr. Darcy."

"You must promise that you will not leave Pemberley."

"Are you certain?"

"Nothing would distress me more than your leaving. Georgiana and I cannot do without you regardless of the circumstances."

"I feel the same, sir," she whispered. "I will not leave," she said more loudly.

From that time forth, Elizabeth recovered her strength. She had no physical injury that a few days rest could not heal.

Mr. Darcy did not leave things the way they were, however. He wrote to the Earl of Inglesford explaining, in part, what happened with his second son. The good earl wrote back, saying his son was embarking later that month on a two-year grand tour of the Continent, he and apologized for any harm that came to Miss Bennet and the insult to Pemberley House. He also thanked Mr. Darcy for not calling out his unruly son. Miss Bennet received the news gladly and, later that month, resumed her walks around the park.

IT WAS THE BEGINNING OF April, and Darcy felt he must go to London to take care of pressing business that he had been putting off since Elizabeth had come to Pemberley. His solicitor had finally insisted that Mr. Darcy must come to town. There were matters of the estate to take care of, such as new tenant leases, and grain and supply negotiations for the upcoming winter; also, Darcy was always eager to add to the Pemberley properties by purchasing any new land that came available for sale in the neighborhood. Mr. Darcy further wanted to give directions to his London housekeeper, Mrs. Thomas, to redecorate one of the family apartments. Mr. Bingley chose this time to see his own solicitor about terminating the lease at Netherfield and to begin inquiries into any eligible purchases in a location near Derbyshire.

The gentlemen left for town in mid-April. Even though the ladies had been given a week's notice of their departure, it was still a sad hour. Elizabeth had grown used to the gentlemen's company and felt herself quite dependent on Mr. Darcy for all her needs and comforts. It was not that she was not self-sufficient, but since Jane's death, she liked knowing she could depend on someone else to help her. Since the episode with Mr. Tuesby, she was occasionally afraid of being alone, even though she knew he was out of England.

It was a teary farewell for Georgiana, who felt deeply any separation from her brother, no matter how short a time it would be. Elizabeth said her farewell in the hall to allow Georgiana time alone with her brother outside. Georgiana hugged him closely and wept into his shoulder, begging his speedy return. She felt insecure away from him, particularly for the first few days as she was reminded all over again of those feelings that accompanied the death of their father. Darcy was well aware of what she was feeling, and it pained him to have to tear himself from her grasp, but he must be off, he told her, if he was to return by the end of the following week.

"Of course, Fitzwilliam," she meekly replied. "I am sorry."

"I understand how you are feeling. Miss Bennet is here. Take comfort in her."

Georgiana brightened at the thought. She had forgotten about Elizabeth.

"Yes. Thank you, Brother. Have a safe journey, and please write often." With that, she kissed him on the cheek. He stepped into the carriage where Bingley was already waiting, and they were off to London.

"Well, Bingley, this is my first time away from Elizabeth since she came to Netherfield. I do not think I shall like it. I wish I did not have to go. It takes every ounce of my strength not to turn this coach around right now, and we are not even out of the park yet."

"You must care for her a great deal, Darcy."

"I do. I love her very much. Bingley, how are you doing? How are you dealing with your loss?"

"I suppose I am recovering. I am glad you brought us to Pemberley. It was the right thing to get us away from Netherfield. I am feeling better, and I believe that Miss Bennet is, also. I still miss Jane very much."

"I know you do, but you will love again. You must."

"That is what Miss Elizabeth said. She said it for herself, and she said that is what Jane would want for me. It is just hard to imagine myself with anybody else. But it is also hard to be alone now."

"You are a very sensitive man, my friend. You are a person who needs to love and needs to be loved. You should not apologize nor feel bad about it." Darcy hesitated for a moment to gauge his friend's mood. He had something to say that he wanted Bingley to hear, but he did not want to offend him. "Bingley, there is someone very similar in disposition to Jane—sweet tempered, kind, gentle hearted—and who I believe does love you and could love you much more."

"Whom do you mean?"

"My sister, Georgiana."

"Darcy—Georgiana? But I think of her as my friend and your sister." Bingley glanced out the window. He said impatiently, "Jane has not been buried a year."—and more angrily—"Of what are you thinking?"

"Bingley, I am not saying you have to do anything. I am only suggesting a possibility. Who better to love than your friend? A part of you will always love Jane, and Georgiana will not expect you to forget Jane. Indeed, your challenge may be in convincing her that accepting your affection may not be disrespectful to Jane and her dear friend Elizabeth. Talk with Georgiana. She will accept whatever attention you give her at whatever pace you choose to proceed."

"Do you truly believe this is the right thing for me?"

"You will have to decide that. I can only say that she has the ability to soothe much of the ache you feel in your heart and soul. And I know that you, of all people, deserve to have that pain taken away."

"I have your consent, then?"

"You have my consent to court her, Bingley. Should you offer her your hand and she accept it, you will have to ask again," Darcy replied with a smile.

Bingley spent much of his time thinking about their conversation. It was true; he had to confess that he was a better man for having been loved by Jane. Miss Elizabeth had told him that Jane would want him to love someone else and be happy. He did not love Georgiana—he had never thought of her in that way—but he had to agree with Darcy. If ever there was a young woman of similar nature to Jane, it was Georgiana. Would this not be a betrayal to Jane? If Jane were alive, he would never consider it. However, they had had no home together, no children together—nothing. There was nothing on which to hold. He could either join Jane in the grave or appear to be living and try to move slightly forward with his life. Georgiana would not expect him to forget Jane. She would not be affronted by her memory. Any other woman would. Darcy was connected to Jane in life and death, and he hoped to marry Miss Elizabeth in the fall. He could soon come to love Georgiana and could surround himself with those same friends who had shared his greatest pain. There would be no need for new attachments or new relations. All the love he needed in the world was already his. Darcy was right. He had Darcy's consent, to be sure, but perhaps more important would be one other person's. He would do nothing to hurt Miss Elizabeth.

Bingley and Darcy returned to Pemberley within the appointed ten days' time. Their business had gone well. Most important to Bingley, Netherfield was now gone. He had gladly paid off the rest of the lease just to be rid of the place. His servants would be moving his belongings back into his townhouse in London. Some other time he would look for an estate in the country, perhaps some place in Derbyshire. Darcy would know what to do.

Georgiana was overjoyed to see her brother safely returned. He had written to her from London, giving her the expected day and time of their arrival, but so many things could go wrong, and Georgiana had been nervous all day. Finally, they heard the sound of an approaching carriage, and there they were. Georgiana ran out the door to greet him as a servant pulled down the carriage step. Elizabeth was also pleased to see them. She had felt no less nervous but had done a better job of hiding it. When she asked herself the reason, either she could not or she would not know why, but she felt a great sense of relief and pleasure knowing that Mr. Darcy had returned to Pemberley.

THE NEXT DAY WAS WARM and beautiful, as all spring days should be, and Elizabeth could not resist the urge to walk out alone in the morning to enjoy the air, smells and sounds, so while she thought everyone was at their usual morning employment, she escaped for an hour of refreshing solitude. Elizabeth had barely left the house when she heard the sound of footsteps behind her. For just a moment, she thought it might be Mr. Darcy. As she quickly berated herself for having such silly thoughts, Mr. Bingley came up beside her.

"Good morning, Miss Bennet."

"Good morning to you, Mr. Bingley. I thought you were busy in the library."

"I must confess I was keeping an eye on you, hoping you would be tempted out on such a day and that I might have the opportunity to speak with you alone."

"Is there anything I can do for you, Mr. Bingley?"

"I do not know how to begin. I am afraid of offending—of being disrespectful."

"Mr. Bingley, I doubt very much that you ever could offend me, much less be disrespectful. Is it of Jane that you wish to speak?"

"Yes, in a way it is. You once told me that she would want me to love again, to be happy, and to remember her." He stopped walking, looked down, and then faced her. "How can I do those things together?"

Elizabeth paused. She had to craft her answer carefully. What she said could affect Mr. Bingley for quite some time, and she would not be held responsible for his happiness or lack thereof. "I know that Jane would want you to be happy. I know that she would want you to remember her. I know that she would not want you to stop living because of her."

"Ah...Jane," Bingley whispered. Elizabeth noticed tears in his eyes. He continued, "I do not know if I can or ought to do this."

"Do what, Mr. Bingley?"

"Ever love someone else."

"You can, Mr. Bingley, and you must—for Jane's sake, for your comfort, and for my own satisfaction."

"Satisfaction, Miss Bennet?"

"Yes. In knowing that, in loving Jane so well and being loved by her, you have found that you cannot do without those feelings in your life. It would give me great satisfaction to know you are happy with another. I know you would not forget Jane. There would always be a small place in your heart for her."

"It is of this I would like to speak, Miss Bennet. Mr. Darcy has made an observation to me, and he has told me that I am a person who must love and who must be loved, or I cannot be happy. He has told me there is one, he feels, who could love me and that I could love in return, and that this person would not be threatened by memories of Jane or ask me to give them up."

"And do you agree with him, Mr. Bingley?"

"I do. He is right. And what Jane, you, and he want for me could all come to pass for me in a relationship with this woman. I do not love her now, but I respect her very much; she is a good friend, and I could easily love her if I could reconcile myself." Elizabeth hoped he was not referring to herself. She knew she could never love him though she could not say why. "I have known her a long time and have no doubts as to the goodness of her character."

"Mr. Bingley, if you are seeking my permission to court a young woman, you certainly do not need it. I shall not interfere in your affairs."

"But I *am* seeking your consent, Miss Elizabeth. I could do nothing that would offend either your or Jane's memory."

"I assure you, sir, you would be doing neither."

"Thank you for your assurances. I have not wanted to do the wrong thing. I have been afraid to do anything—even to speak to you."

"Oh, Mr. Bingley, you should know by now that you do not need to be afraid of me. Pray tell me if it is possible—who is this young woman?"

"Georgiana Darcy." By now, Elizabeth was not surprised to hear the name.

NOT ALL SPRING DAYS ARE pleasant, and on one such day towards the end of April, it rained. Elizabeth chose to spend the morning in her room by the fire reading all the letters she had received since the time of Jane's illness. There were not many, and the memories they brought back were horrible. How could her mother, her own mother, accuse her of hurting Jane? Things would have been so much simpler if she had just died with Jane. Indeed, part of her had.

She felt ill. She wanted to cry, but tears would not come. Her shoulders ached and her stomach hurt. She knew she should put away the letters and lie down or go out for some air, but she would not take the trouble to move away from her memories or from the fireplace. Would this never end?

There was a knock at the door from her dressing room, a sure sign it was her maid.

"Come in."

"Ma'am, are you ready to dress for dinner?"

Dinner—Elizabeth suddenly felt overwhelmed by the thought of having to dress, of having to do anything at all. "No, I shall not be going down for dinner today. If you would please tell Miss Darcy I am not feeling well and will not be joining them."

"I will have Cook prepare a tray for you to take in your room, ma'am."

"No, thank you, I do not care to eat. Ask that I not be disturbed."

"Yes, ma'am."

DARCY WAS THE FIRST TO arrive in the drawing room. He always enjoyed dinner with his friends. He felt good knowing he was able to provide for them, and their conversation was so engaging that he wished no meal would ever end. Georgiana and Bingley soon joined him but not Miss Bennet, which was curious, for she was never late. A footman came to Mr. Darcy with a note from Elizabeth's maid, informing him that Miss Bennet would not be down for dinner, was not feeling well, and wished not to be disturbed. Elizabeth's maid wanted him to know that Miss Bennet refused a tray from the kitchen. Darcy's brow furrowed in frustration.

"Brother, what is the matter?"

"It is Miss Bennet. She will not be coming down to dinner nor will she take anything in her room. She has asked that she not be disturbed."

"That is not like her at all," said Georgiana. "Something must be very wrong. Start dinner without me; I will go to her."

"But she asked not to be disturbed," said Darcy, who did not know what to do.

"Well, I *am* going to disturb her. I will break the door down if I must, but I am not going to leave her alone with whatever she is thinking or feeling. It must be awful, or she would come down to be with us." With that, she gave them a doubtful smile and went upstairs towards Elizabeth's room.

When Georgiana arrived outside the door, she stopped to listen quietly. Hearing nothing, she knocked gently on the door. She received no response.

She knocked again, a little more firmly. "Lizzy, it is Georgie"

Once again, Georgiana received no response. "Lizzy, please let me in. I am so afraid. Please!"

She waited again. She was sure Elizabeth would answer, but she did not. Georgiana was becoming quite alarmed.

"Lizzy, I am not going to leave you in there alone. I am going to come in now even if you will not let me in." Georgiana carefully turned the doorknob and walked quietly into the room. Elizabeth was not in bed. She walked softly to the other end of the room towards the fireplace. As she grew close, she saw Elizabeth on the sofa with her knees brought up against her chest. Her whole body was shaking as if she were chilled from a high fever. Elizabeth was staring blankly into the fire and seemed unaware of Georgiana's presence in the room.

Georgiana continued to walk towards her, calling her name, "Lizzy? It is I, Georgie. Will you not say anything to me?"

Elizabeth did not answer. Georgiana went to her and sat down on the couch next to her.

"Lizzy." Georgiana reached out her hand and touched Elizabeth's shoulder. Elizabeth recoiled from the touch, quite startled, and stared at Georgiana. Gradually, a look of recognition greeted Georgiana. She shuddered to think what could have happened had she left Elizabeth to herself all night.

"Come here, love." She turned Elizabeth on the sofa and cradled her against her chest like an infant, supporting her head in the crook of her elbow. Elizabeth had stopped shaking.

Suddenly, Elizabeth cried, "Do you think I killed Jane?" With those words, she broke out in tears, crying almost hysterically. Georgiana held Elizabeth close, stroking her hair and shoulder.

"Lizzy, you would not have hurt your sister. Mr. Bingley has told me of all you did for her, day after day, night after night. There was nothing more you could have done. You did everything right. Jane was just too ill. It is so sad, Lizzy; I know how you feel. I remember the pain I felt and still feel from the death of my father. I never knew my mother."

"But my mother said—"

"Do not listen to her. I know what she said, and she was wrong. She was not with you at Netherfield. She does not know all you did on Jane's behalf: how you helped the physician and nursed her. She is looking for an excuse for her own failure as a mother. I am sorry to pain you further. Those were cruel words, but she was trying to hurt you, and you did not deserve it. Please do not listen to her. Believe the ones who truly love you, the ones who were there. Mr. Bingley and Fitzwilliam do not believe you did anything except to try to save her. Oh, Lizzy."

Elizabeth continued to cry for most of the night while Georgiana held her, comforted her and cried with her. Elizabeth's pain was so profound that it swallowed up everything around her.

THE GENTLEMEN DINED WITHOUT THE ladies. They were concerned, nervous, and uncertain, but they felt they must trust Georgiana and hope that Elizabeth would be well by morning. They amused themselves with a game or two of billiards after dinner but had no heart for it and decided to retire early.

Mr. Darcy could not sleep; he was too worried about Elizabeth. What had gone wrong? Had he done something to disturb her? He felt all the frustration of a lover helpless in the face of struggles in the life of his beloved. He wanted to send a maid for word but knew Georgiana would tell him about Elizabeth as soon as she could, and any interruption would be unwelcome. He would respect their privacy. He was never as grateful as now for his decision to bring Georgiana from London to be with Elizabeth. She and Elizabeth had become dear friends, which pleased him immensely. And never before, it seemed, did Elizabeth need a friend as much as she did that night.

GEORGIANA KEPT ELIZABETH IN BED the next day. She ordered tea brought to her and fed Elizabeth herself. She stayed with her the whole day, dozing off when Elizabeth slept but keeping a constant vigil over her friend. Elizabeth had finally stopped crying late into the night, and Georgiana persuaded her to change into her nightclothes and go to bed. Georgiana felt helpless. What could she do for her that would protect Elizabeth from such a night ever again?

Mrs. Reynolds came to Elizabeth's room to inquire about Miss Bennet's health on behalf of Mr. Darcy, who was quite anxious and concerned. Georgiana did not have a fair report to give her, relating briefly the details of the night and her plans for attending to Elizabeth throughout the day. Mrs. Reynolds offered to send up Elizabeth's maid to sit with her so that Georgiana could retire to her own room for some needed rest, but she refused to leave.

"Thank you for your thoughtfulness, Mrs. Reynolds, but I cannot leave Miss Bennet. Please reassure my brother that I am well."

Elizabeth did not wake often during the day, and when she did, she did not speak. She would follow Georgiana's instructions to eat and drink, but would not or could not respond to her questions. That night, Elizabeth seemed to sleep much more peacefully, and Georgiana was encouraged as to her health. During the night, she slipped out to her own room to rest.

Elizabeth's mind was in a torment. No matter how hard she tried, she could not wake up. She had repeated dreams of placing Jane in her coffin. In one dream, Elizabeth found herself buried in Jane's coffin, only to discover she was alive and trapped. Her mind would scream, but her voice remained silent. In another dream, she imagined her whole family gathered around her as she stood next to Jane, accusing her of murdering Jane, pointing their fingers at her, screaming at her, taunting her, beating her with their fists, stripping her of her clothes, leaving her naked in the road, bruised and torn, laughing at her. There was nowhere for her to go, no one to comfort her, no place to hide. She was shamed and embarrassed. In another dream, she was a little girl with a skinned knee, running into the house crying. She went to her mother for comfort but she just laughed at her, told her she was too busy for her and that she should go away. She went to her father in his library, and he told her to get out so that her blood would not stain the leather furniture. She finally ran to Jane, and Jane asked her, 'Why did you kill me?'

"I EXAMINED HER THOROUGHLY, MR. DARCY," said the apothecary, "and I can find nothing wrong with her physically. She would not answer any of my questions. It appeared that she did not even hear me, but if I gave her a command, such as 'lift your arm', she would follow it precisely. Has she suffered any head injuries or any other type of nervous trauma?"

"Her sister died in November, Mr. Edwards. They were very close—the best of friends—and she has been estranged from her family since then. I suppose the strain and pressure of this became too much for her; I did not realize the extent."

"Well, sir, I will come every day to examine her. I do not know what to tell you regarding her condition."

"Thank you for coming, Mr. Edwards."

Every day Georgiana would help Elizabeth's maid dress her, and she would take her on walks out in the pleasure gardens. She would talk to Elizabeth about anything she could think of, telling her everything she could about her own life. Every now and then, she thought she saw a spark of recognition in Elizabeth's eyes, but just as quickly it would pass away. During the rest of the day, Elizabeth would sit in the drawing room and stare out the window.

Darcy was half agony, half hopelessness. His Elizabeth had somehow been taken from him, and he was powerless to do anything about it. He sat with her in the drawing room, holding her hand and talking to her about all the affairs of the estate—anything that came to mind. When they were alone, he opened his heart to her. He told her that he had fallen in love with her while she was at Netherfield and she had touched his heart and soul in a way no one had ever done before or would again. He told her about the beauty he saw in her eyes, in the silky softness of her skin, in the lightness of her touch. He told her about the energy he felt pour through him whenever he kissed her hand or she took his arm. He explained the passion she had ignited in him that would find an outlet only in her. He told her that he wanted her to be the mistress of Pemberley and bring her ringing laughter to the silent halls of his childhood home. He expressed his hopes of enjoying a family with her and seeing her beauty in the faces of their children who would be as dear to him as she was. He spoke of how he missed her voice, her conversation, her teasing and her playfulness. He told her how much he loved her and would always love her, and if this was all she could give him, then he would gladly take it. He said he would love and protect her for the rest of her life, and she would stay with him always and not be afraid.

Elizabeth heard everything. The dreams had finally ceased. Indeed, she had no dreams at all, which was a relief. She was no longer afraid of falling asleep and had started to feel rested again in the mornings. The days seemed so long, and the walks with Georgie nearly consumed her strength. It was all she could do not to collapse when they arrived back. She loved Georgie very much, and she did not know what she would have done without her constant care. Was this how Jane would have felt? Was it possible that she did not hurt Jane, but that Jane was comforted by her and her mother was wrong? Mr. Darcy told her he loved her. Elizabeth was surprised at the boldness of his confession though she did grant that he thought she did not hear him. But she did, and she was grateful to him for his affection. She knew two people loved her now—sincerely loved and appreciated her—and that nothing in this world would take that away from her. Mr. Darcy would not love her if she were a bad person, to be sure, and she had long ago decided to trust him. She knew she could trust him. If he loved her, then she could love herself—and she would love him. She did love him. She would accept him. She would become his wife, his companion, his friend, the mother of his children, the mistress of Pemberley. She would allow him to protect her and love her for the rest of her life.

"Mr. Edwards, is there any change in Miss Bennet?" asked Mr. Darcy. He was praying for a positive answer, but he did not need the apothecary to tell him her condition. He spent enough time with her to know. He would know when she began to improve. He would be the first to know.

"She is healthy and fit, Mr. Darcy. She is being well cared for, and I commend you and your sister for it, but as to her mind, I can find no change."

"Thank you, Mr. Edwards."

The following day, while Elizabeth was sitting in the drawing room, she felt a weight being lifted off her shoulders. She blinked her eyes in wonderment at where she was and began to turn her head to look around her. Darcy saw her action and immediately went over and sat next to her, watching her carefully. She turned her head and looked him straight in the eyes. He felt that she was piercing his soul, and he knew then that she had heard every endearing word he ever spoke to her. She slowly raised her hand to his face and, cupping his cheek, said, "Thank you for finding me, sir."

He took her hand in both of his, slowly kissed her fingers and held them to his heart. "Thank you for being there, Elizabeth."

Elizabeth quickly regained her physical strength and slowly regained her mental stamina. She would startle easily at sudden noises, preferred quiet conversation to laughter, and spent much of her time in the drawing room, looking out the window—now with a feeling of resolve. Georgiana or Mr. Darcy would often sit with her. They rarely spoke as this appeared to them to be a time of healing and rest for Elizabeth. And indeed it was. Jane was gone, and her family was gone, but Elizabeth was still loved and cherished and did not have to feel alone. Not only would she live, she could be happy.

ONE HAPPY DAY IN THE first week of May, Georgiana took Elizabeth for a long walk in the park. She had much to tell her but did not know where to begin.

"Lizzy, how are you feeling?" Georgiana was still worried about Elizabeth. She knew that Elizabeth could put on a strong face while truly hurting.

"I am fine although I am still a little weak, and my mind does wander. But I am able to rest now, and you take such good care of me that I want for nothing. I could not ask for a better friend than you, Georgie. You have indeed helped me to realize that I could not have hurt Jane at all, that my mother is wrong. You have been such a comfort to me, and I know that I would have been the same for Jane. I understand now that she was just too ill; nothing could be done.

"I am so glad to hear that from you, Lizzy, and I know it to be true. You could never hurt anybody. I know that Jane must have been so glad to have you there. Indeed, Mr. Bingley has told me on many occasions about your love and devotion to her. He loved her very much, you must know."

"Yes, he did, Georgie. His loss was very severe, and I feel so sorry for him. They were a perfect couple. But Georgie, he must love again. Jane would want that for him." Elizabeth stopped and turned to face Georgiana.

"Georgie, do you love Mr. Bingley?"

"Oh, Lizzy, do not be angry with me, please!" Georgiana sounded almost frantic.

Elizabeth took her hand. "I am not angry, Georgie. If you love Mr. Bingley and he returns your affection, I am happy for you both."

"I do not want to offend you or be disrespectful to Jane's memory. I love you as if you were my sister and would not do anything to hurt you. I would give up anything to keep your love."

"Georgiana, please listen to me. Mr. Bingley cannot spend the rest of his life pining after Jane, but she will always have a place in his heart. Will that be offensive to you?"

"Oh, no, I would not want him to give up his memories of her. I want to share his life, not take it from him."

"You have many of the same qualities he admired in Jane. You are kind and gentle. You have a tender heart, and I know you would love him very much. You would allow him to heal, and together you would build your own life. He would have his best friend for a brother. Who could ask for better connections?"

"Thank you, Lizzy. Thank you so much. But Lizzy, you must not leave me. If Mr. Bingley makes me an offer, you must come and live with us. I cannot bear the thought of your leaving."

"I told you before that I would consider it, Georgie. I know that it would be hard for me to be away from you. It is many months before that might happen, so let us remain happy."

The next day, Bingley, Georgiana and Elizabeth were out walking together. Elizabeth had arranged herself to be on the far side of Georgiana so that Georgiana was firmly attached to Bingley's arm and chatting primarily with him. Elizabeth did not mind. It was obvious that these two needed a little help, and perhaps a few minutes alone in the park would be welcome to them.

"Mr. Bingley," Elizabeth announced, "I need to run back to the house for a moment, but I shall not go if you two do not continue without me."

"Miss Bennet, we can accompany you. You should not have to be alone."

"Well, sir, I know my way around here very well, and I think I can manage easily. I shall catch up to you in a few minutes."

"Are you sure, Lizzy?"

"Yes, Georgie. You will not even know that I have been gone." And with that, Elizabeth turned towards the house and, in a very unladylike gesture, gathered her skirts and ran off. Bingley and Georgiana, no longer surprised by anything she might do, just laughed and returned to the path.

Chapter 7

"Miss Darcy, I would like to take this moment while we are alone to let you know that I have received your brother's permission to court you." Bingley held his breath.

"Thank you for asking, Mr. Bingley. I would welcome any attention that you could spare for me."

"You are teasing me, Miss Darcy."

"Indeed, I am not, sir. I am very serious. I am grateful for the time you spend with me, and if my brother has given you his consent to court me and this is your wish, well then, sir, I welcome it very much."

"Thank you, Miss Darcy. I am glad to know that I am welcome. I did not know how you would feel as you know how I felt about Jane, and her death being so recent."

"I am sensitive to that matter, sir, and I grieve with you. There will always be a place in your heart for her, a place I will share as long as I have the rest." She smiled at him. This was quite forward of her to say and perhaps a little provocative as well, especially for two people just courting.

"I appreciate your understanding. Your brother said that this would be your opinion and encouraged me to talk to you. I am glad I did."

"Mr. Bingley, I have something to say to you that might make you change your mind about wishing to know me better in such an intimate way."

"I cannot imagine any such circumstance, Miss Darcy. Please, do not be afraid on my account."

"Well, I am afraid. Very much so. Do you know Mr. George Wickham?"

"I may have heard his name."

"Last summer, I was attended to Ramsgate by my companion, Mrs. Younge, who apparently had a connection with Mr. Wickham. Mr. Wickham was a childhood friend of my brother, and I also knew him. He spent hours providing amusement for me when I was a child, and I liked him very well. When I encountered him at Ramsgate, it was not difficult for him to persuade me to believe that I was in love with him."

Bingley began to feel uncomfortable. "Miss Darcy, you do not have to relay this account to me."

"Indeed I do, sir. You must know who I am before you decide about any future with me. I cannot form an attachment with you only to have you hate me later when the truth comes out." Tears were forming in Georgiana's eyes, her distress evident.

"Mr. Wickham told me that he was not on good terms with Fitzwilliam and my brother never would consent to a marriage between us. We decided, then, that we must go to Scotland and be married, that we must elope." A tear rolled down her cheek. "My brother unexpectedly came to Ramsgate to see me just two days before we were to be off for Scotland. Mr. Wickham told me to say nothing to my brother about our planned elopement, but I could not conceal anything from him. Mr. Bingley, my brother was so disappointed in me. He told me that Mr. Wickham never could make me happy, that all he wanted was my dowry, that he would make my life miserable and break my heart, and that he did not love me at all despite what he may be telling me. He explained that if I were to marry against his wishes, he could withhold my dowry until I reached age thirty. He said I must give Mr. Wickham that information. He also said that my cousin Colonel Fitzwilliam was joined in my guardianship and I should tell him that as well.

"I left my brother's lodgings in a fit of anger and went to where Mr. Wickham was staying. I told him that we must away that very night for Scotland. When I told him what my brother had said about my dowry, Mr. Wickham got a strange look on his face. He questioned me, asking whether it was true that I would not receive any money until I was thirty. I said it was so. I told Mr. Wickham that it did not matter, that we were in love and should be off right away, and that all would work out to our benefit and blessing. Then the most horrible thing happened. Mr. Wickham began to laugh. He laughed so hard he almost cried, and he was laughing at me. I asked him why, and he said that he could never be in love with me, his enemy's sister, and that all he wanted was my money and revenge on my brother. He said he never cared for me at all and that, if he had to wait until I was thirty to get at my dowry, I was of no use to him at all. Then he picked up a bag, looked at me one last time, started laughing again, and walked out the door. I had been completely abandoned—completely humiliated."

"Miss Darcy, I am so sorry. What did you do?"

"I did not know what to do. I knew that eventually I would have to face my brother. I decided he was the only person with whom I would be safe, so I went back to his lodgings and told him all that had happened. I expected him to be so angry with me, but he was not. He was kind and gentle, loving and forgiving. I will never forget how well he treated me. I felt safe and protected. The next morning we left directly for Pemberley.

"Mr. Bingley, I want you to know this, to know the woman with whom you may be getting yourself involved—unsteady, ridiculous, and unworthy of true affection."

"Not so, Miss Darcy. You were deceived by a cruel fortune hunter who took advantage of your loving heart and innocent trust, characteristics that make you the special young lady you are. You need not be ashamed of what happened. Your secret is safe with me—safe in that I think more highly of you than I did. You found you had made an error, and you corrected it as soon as possible by going to your brother directly. You showed great strength and resolve. Any man who does not prize that in a woman is a fool."

"Are you sure, Mr. Bingley? I do not want to lose your good opinion." Georgiana shed a few more tears.

Bingley stepped closer to her, took her hand, gently raised it to his lips, and gave it a soft, lingering kiss that shocked them both with its warmth and passion. "I am very sure, Miss Darcy—very sure indeed. You need not worry on my account."

Georgiana gasped for breath and turned away from him as she colored. Bingley noticed her discomposure with satisfaction and then diverted the topic of conversation.

"I wonder where Miss Bennet is," Bingley mused.

"I know where she is not and will not likely be for the rest of the afternoon."

"And pray, where is that?"

"With us." Georgiana giggled.

"Well, then, shall we continue our walk around this area of the park?"

"Certainly, sir, I would be happy to do so."

AT DINNER, DARCY ANNOUNCED THAT he had received an invitation to a ball at Hillcock Manor to be given by his friend Lord Beecham in a week's time. The invitation included himself and three guests. The news, however, did not receive an enthusiastic reception. All were aware that Elizabeth's mourning would not allow her to accept the invitation, and leaving her alone seemed unconscionable.

Elizabeth spoke first in a cheerful, encouraging voice. "Mr. Darcy, you are well aware that it is impossible for me to accept this invitation. But I would be very pleased if you, Georgiana and Mr. Bingley were to go and tell me all about it when you return. It sounds like it will be a happy affair, and by no means should you suspend your pleasure on my account."

"But, Lizzy, how could we possibly think of leaving you here alone?"

"Very easily, Georgie. You know I spend much of my time alone in quiet reflection, and I will have Mrs. Reynolds to keep me company. I will ask Mr. Darcy to choose a book from his library for me, and I shall retire early. I shall be very happy, indeed, knowing you are at a ball and having a wonderful time." Elizabeth glanced from Georgiana to Mr. Bingley, causing them to smile and blush. "Indeed, it would hurt me greatly were you to refuse the invitation because of me. Surely you do not intend to remain housebound for the next six months of my mourning! Please go to the ball and be happy. You have given me a great deal of care and comfort. You deserve a night of pleasure."

"Are you sure, Lizzy? I would gladly remain with you," replied Georgiana, sincerely.

"I am very sure, Georgie."

Thursday arrived, and Elizabeth assisted Georgiana's maid to help her dress and arrange her hair. When they had finished, Georgiana looked in the mirror and told them that she had never looked as well as she did then.

"Thank you, Lizzy. You cannot imagine how important tonight is for me."

"Yes, I can, but do not worry. You look beautiful. I have never seen you in greater beauty. Mr. Bingley will surely be in love with you after tonight. You must tell me how it all goes."

Elizabeth saw them safely into the carriage and felt gloomy when they left. She would prefer not to be alone, but she was in mourning, and it would not be proper to go. For Jane's sake she would not go. To entertain herself, Elizabeth decided to walk the halls of Pemberley, beginning with the large picture gallery on the third floor. She looked at all the former residents of Pemberley, trying to find similarities in features between them and Mr. Darcy. From time to time, she thought she saw that same shape of mouth or look in the eye, but she decided that he was mostly unique. She made her way down the gallery to his likeness. There he was, looking down at her. She had seen the gallery before on a quick tour when she first came to Pemberley, but this was her first chance to study it. She was now glad to be alone.

Elizabeth thought back to the time that he had found her after the scene at the officers' ball in Meryton. She had felt so warm and protected when he held her, and she knew then that he would be the standard by which she would judge other men. She remembered the way he looked at her when she was at Netherfield attending Jane. At first, she did not know what to think, but she soon knew that his look was one of affection. He seemed to be very concerned about her; he told her to trust him, which she did, and he had been faithful to her on every occasion since. It could only be a proof of his love, which he had confessed to her during her illness—a confession he did not know she heard.

She never would forget his words to her. He had told her that he had been in love with her since she had come to Netherfield, about the beauty of her eyes, the softness of her skin, the lightness of her touch. He told her how he felt when he kissed her hand or when she took his arm, or the passion that he felt for her. He wanted her to be the mistress of Pemberley, to make a home and enjoy a family with her. She remembered how warm she had felt when he told her how much he loved her, and would love her, and how he would protect her for the rest of her life; she would stay with him always and should not be afraid. How could she not be moved by such a declaration of love as this? As she stared up at his likeness, his eyes looking down at her, she remembered every word he said to her.

"Yes, Mr. Darcy," she said aloud, "I love you, too. I feel the same passion when you kiss my hand or I take your arm. I would like nothing more than to be mistress of Pemberley and be protected and loved by you. Thank you for loving me. Please tell me again, sir, now that I am able to answer you."

Dearly Beloved

Early Friday morning, Georgiana came to Elizabeth's room to talk about the ball.

"Oh, Lizzy, it was wonderful. My brother insisted on the first two dances, but then Mr. Bingley asked me for the next set. Dancing with him was heavenly. Being held in his arms, I thought I should faint from pleasure had I not wanted to assure myself that I was not dreaming. I then danced with Lord Beecham's son and then his nephew. They were very gentlemanlike, and both seemed as though they would enjoy my thirty thousand pounds very much and me just a little." Georgiana had to stop here, and both girls laughed.

"And then I danced the next two with Charles, uh, Mr. Bingley…"

"Georgie…Charles?"

"When alone, we agreed to address each other by our Christian names," Georgiana said shyly.

"So, how was this second set with Charles?" Elizabeth teased.

"Just like the first. I wish it could have lasted all night. Mr. Bingley asked my brother if he would consent to his asking me to dance a third time. Brother asked Charles whether we had reached an agreement between us, and Charles said we had not. Then my brother said that, perhaps for propriety's sake, we should not dance a third set."

"Your brother is very wise, Georgie; I hope you are not angry with him."

"No I am not. I know he only wants my happiness, and I would be mortified to overstep the bounds of decorum, even for Charles. So we just talked together the rest of the evening. We tried to include my brother, but he would just smile at me and then walk off to talk to someone else. I do not know why."

Elizabeth smiled at this picture of Mr. Darcy as matchmaker. "Shall we go down for breakfast? We do not want to keep the gentlemen waiting, do we?" She winked at Georgiana, who blushed in a becoming manner.

When they arrived downstairs, they found that Mr. Darcy had left early on estate business, but Mr. Bingley was waiting for them. He greeted the ladies cheerfully, and his spirits seemed as high as Georgiana's.

"How did you enjoy the ball, Mr. Bingley?" asked Elizabeth, unquestionably knowing the answer.

"I liked it very much," he replied with a sidelong glance at Georgiana that did not go unnoticed by Elizabeth.

"Well, I am very glad. And how do you think Mr. Darcy liked it?"

"He seemed happy enough, which is saying quite a lot for Darcy at a ball. He only danced with Georgiana and Miss Beecham and spent most of his time with other gentlemen who chose not to dance but preferred to discuss politics and sport."

"I do hope he did not pass his time unpleasantly." Elizabeth was relieved that his list of dancing partners was short.

"The only comment of regret I heard him utter throughout the evening was that he wished you could have been there, a feeling we all shared, I am sure." Elizabeth turned away as she colored, not wanting to give rise to any supposition on Bingley or Georgiana's part regarding her feelings for Mr. Darcy.

While they were eating, a footman came in with the post, giving a letter to Elizabeth. She was shocked to find it was from her sister Mary. Trembling in apprehension, she folded the missive into her skirts and ran out the door. She crossed the pleasure gardens and into the park, where she was sure of seclusion. The fact that Mary would write to her was such a marvelous thought that she could hardly bear it. If anyone, she had expected to hear from her father. To be sure, she had been disappointed by his silence. Lingering in the shade of a tree, she broke the seal.

Longbourn, Wednesday, May 7

Dearest Lizzy,

I do hope that you will forgive me for not writing to you. Mama forbids it, you know, but I feel I must take the chance on this occasion to write of dreadful news concerning Lydia. To own the truth, she and Mr. Wickham, an officer in the militia regiment quartered here, have eloped, and it is said they are off to Gretna Green. They left Monday night, and they were not missed until yesterday morning. Kitty was privy to all the details and triumphantly told Mama and Papa about the whole business before a search for Lydia started. Apparently, he and Lydia agreed to meet on Monday night by appointment. There has been a long-standing flirtation between Lydia and Mr. Wickham, but of course Mama found nothing wrong in the business, not willing to turn any suitor away. Papa never was at any of the assemblies or even out of his library at home when Wickham was here even to notice what was going on, so she was allowed to behave just as she felt, much to my disgust, of course. You must know that Lydia and Kitty have been very disrespectful of Jane's memory. They are supposed to be in mourning, yet so often it seems, they are found meeting with officers, and Papa searches them out and brings them home again. I cannot imagine what he says to the men—apparently, not enough, for Kitty and Lydia do it repeatedly. To Lydia, it is all a great joke, of course, and you know that Kitty will follow wherever Lydia leads.

Mr. Wickham says his father was the steward of Mr. Darcy's estate, and the late Mr. Darcy had promised him a living in the church, but your Mr. Darcy refused to give it to him. I used to believe that story until now. Just this morning, Aunt Philips returned from town, reporting rumors of Mr. Wickham's leaving debts with nearly every tradesman and gamester. She also reported that some of the tradesman's daughters were not treated well by him. I think it odd that none of this knowledge comes out until now, but even if only some of it is true, it certainly lays a black shadow across Mr. Wickham. Poor Lydia. She does not know any of this about him.

Lydia has been very jealous of you since you went off with Mr. Darcy and Mr. Bingley. She says it would be so much fun to be away from home. I try to tell her that you have been sent away by Mama because of a fierce argument over Jane's death and that none of it is by your choice, but she never would listen to me. She is the most selfish person I know.

I must get this to Meryton and post it before Mama or the servants know I have written, or I shall regret it dearly. Give my compliments to your friends. I hope they are taking good care of you.

Mary

Elizabeth felt as though she had been hit on the head, so severe was the blow from this news. Wickham! Georgiana had told her about the depravity of the man. Now he had persuaded Lydia to elope with him. Having pursued Georgiana for her thirty thousand pounds, what did he expect to gain from Lydia? She had fifty pounds a year on the death of their parents. Their father's estate was entailed away to Mr. Collins. What could he do for Lydia? Nothing! Wickham marry Lydia? Impossible. He had only wanted Georgiana for her money, and when he found he could not have that, he laughed at her and left her alone at Ramsgate. What could persuade him to take Lydia from Meryton?

He was not going to marry Lydia. They were not going to Gretna Green. Was Lydia so lost as to forget everything and live with him without being married? Was she too stupid to know that he would never marry her and would eventually leave her somewhere, poor and alone—or worse? Why had she forsaken her mourning and forgotten Jane? Did she not love Jane? Oh Lydia! All the hurt and pain of the last days before Jane's death came back to Elizabeth—all the feelings of guilt and thoughts filled with doubt and self-recrimination. *Did I actually hurt Jane? Was Mama right?* Elizabeth slid down the tree to the ground—like a fallen leaf to the grass—and wept as the memories washed over her.

DARCY HAD BEEN OUT ON a morning ride inspecting the park and two tenant fields that were adjacent to it. There was no necessity for the inspection other than a need to ride out. Sometimes Pemberley, as large as it was, seemed so small with Elizabeth in it. He loved her dearly and longed to profess his feelings for her, but he knew it was not yet time, and patience is not a virtue to a man in love. He was on his way home, lost in thought, when he heard soft, steady crying.

There was hardly a breeze that morning. The air was clear and pure, warm and fresh. It was the air of love, disturbed only by the sound of crying. Darcy's blood chilled. With the discernment of a lover, he knew immediately who was crying. He dismounted and followed the sound around a small stand of shrubbery to a large tree. In a heap of skirts and shawl at the base of it was Elizabeth. He ran to her, knelt beside her, took her up in his arms and held her against his chest. She continued to cry softly. Her arms were pulled up hard against her body; her skin felt cold, and she had not opened her eyes. Darcy looked around him, trying to understand what could be the matter, and noticed a letter with a broken seal. It had her name on it, and it was addressed from Longbourn. Her mother! It had to be her mother again!

Elizabeth's eyes flickered open, and she found herself swallowed up in Darcy's gaze. It was filled with a look of agony. Never had she seen him thus. What could be wrong? As she began to recollect herself, she realized he was holding her as he knelt on the ground. The letter! The letter from Mary! Wickham! Oh, should she tell Mr. Darcy? He had told her to trust him.

Darcy was grateful to see her eyes open. It seemed as if she was a moment in recognizing him, and he felt profoundly concerned. Then she did the most wonderful thing: She wrapped her arm around his waist, helping to support her weight and pulling her body close to him. She had yet to explain herself or to say a word, and Darcy dared not speak. Her look swore him to silence; an explanation would come when she was ready.

And it did come. Elizabeth decided she had to trust him. She wanted to trust him. Had she not trusted him since the day she met him? Did she not love him? She reached across her legs and picked up the letter.

"I must thank you once again, sir, for finding me."

"I am grateful, madam, that I was at hand."

"I must reveal to you another terrible secret, a dreadful happening that has just occurred in my family. And it does concern your family in a way. It might make you hate me." She paused. How to continue? The truth would soon be known. She must trust him.

"Mr. Darcy, my youngest sister, Lydia, has eloped, has thrown herself in the power of Mr. Wickham." She sat up and away from him, coloring from the embarrassment of this current piece of family weakness.

"Are you certain, absolutely certain?"

"Oh, yes. They left Meryton earlier this week with the reported intention of going to Gretna Green to be married. Mr. Darcy, Georgiana has told me all about her dealings with Mr. Wickham. I doubt very much that he intends to marry my sister for the fifty pounds a year she can provide." Elizabeth rose to her feet and walked a few paces away from him, suddenly discomforted by his presence. "I thought you should know."

She walked back towards him and handed him the letter, stepped away from him, and began a slow walk across the park back to the house.

Darcy read the letter in growing fury. Wickham! How did he manage to touch everything and everyone he loved?

AFTER DINNER, WHEN THE LADIES had separated to the music room, Darcy asked if he could speak with Bingley in the privacy of the library.

"Bingley, I have to go to London in a few days. I would ask that you take care of Elizabeth...the ladies...for me in my absence."

"What happened? We were not to go to town until after Miss Bennet's deep mourning."

"Something has come up—something concerning her family that only I can take care of."

"What is it, Darcy? Can I be of service to you?"

"It concerns Miss Lydia Bennet and my old friend George Wickham."

"Did you say 'Wickham'?" Bingley shot back.

"Yes, do you know him?"

"Georgiana, I mean, Miss Darcy, has told me of her past relationship with Wickham. What does Miss Lydia have to do with that scoundrel?"

"He has prevailed on her to elope with him on pretense of marrying her in Gretna Green. Elizabeth does not believe it will happen, and neither do I. Her father can give Miss Lydia nothing. I believe he is using Miss Lydia to disturb my life once again by trying to get at me through Elizabeth. Wickham knows that Elizabeth is here because Miss Lydia does. If he can ruin Miss Lydia's reputation and cause a scandal in the family, he must presume that I will no longer allow Elizabeth to remain here. He must assume some form of attachment between her and me, but I cannot allow it to happen. No scandal would change my feelings or intentions towards Elizabeth, but I cannot allow any more pain to enter her life. It is too much, just too much."

"What do you intend for us to do, then?"

"'Us,' Bingley?"

"Yes. I am now as much involved with Wickham as you are, and you will need someone with you when you meet him."

"I do not intend to call him out, Bingley."

"I know, but I do not intend to allow you to do anything else that might be stupid and prevent you from being Miss Bennet's husband sometime in the future."

Bingley and Darcy stared at each other for a moment and then joined the ladies in the music room. Elizabeth entertained them with two new songs she had been learning. When she finished, Darcy spoke.

"Miss Bennet, will you trust me?" He caught her eye, and Elizabeth met his gaze, returning his piercing stare. "Yes, Mr. Darcy, I will. I have complete faith in you."

"Then you must please allow me to say what may for a moment pain you."

"As you wish, sir." Bingley and Georgiana looked at each other with no little alarm.

"Georgiana, Miss Bennet's sister, Miss Lydia Bennet, has eloped with Mr. Wickham."

Elizabeth began to color.

Georgiana's hands flew to her mouth, and she gasped. "No, it cannot be true! That could not ever happen, could it?"

"It could, because he was never publicly set down when he humiliated you—which was not your fault, allow me to add. Also, he knows that Miss Bennet is here and, I believe, presumes some type of attachment between the two of us."

With this statement, Darcy and Elizabeth renewed their intense gaze, which was noticed by their companions. Elizabeth started to blush. Darcy recollected himself and continued.

"It is my opinion that he is using Miss Lydia to try and force one of two things:

"One, some sort of scandal in the Bennet family that would supposedly force me to send Miss Bennet away from my household." Their eye contact resumed for a brief moment.

"Or two, to force me to prevent that from happening by tracking him down in London, which should not be too difficult, and bribing him. This would be in the form of payments of debts to tradesmen, debts of honor, and the like. What he is also hoping to secure, I imagine, is a sizeable settlement on Miss Lydia that will induce him to marry her, thereby removing the scandal from the Bennet family, leaving Miss Bennet and myself unmolested." Their eyes were drawn together once again. "It is my intention to do just that."

"But, sir," Elizabeth cried, "we are talking about my family. We have only caused you grief. You are already burdened by my presence. Surely, you take too much upon yourself. If Lydia had observed mourning as she ought, this would not have happened. If you must, find out where they are in hiding and let my father know; he can decide what to do. It need not concern you. You must not put yourself to any trouble on my behalf. I am not worth your trouble and have already been too much of an inconvenience." Elizabeth was out of breath at the end of this speech. She felt she had lost all control over her own life.

Darcy cleared his throat. "Miss Bennet, Elizabeth, please understand that you will never be a burden to me, ever."

Silence fell over the four friends. The implications of his statement were clear.

Bingley interrupted the quiet. "Miss Bennet, Wickham is partially my responsibility now, or may soon be," he glanced briefly at Georgiana, "and

I cannot escape the obligation I have, along with Darcy, to rid him of any access to those we love. Please allow us to do this."

"What will you do to see that it never happens again?"

Darcy answered her question. "That I cannot tell you, and perhaps it is not possible to say that it can be done. But he will be publicly bound to your sister, employment arranged, debts paid, and a place in society given them. Choosing to leave it would be their decision, of course, but not a very intelligent one. It will be uncomfortable, and it means your sister marrying while in mourning, but at this point, that cannot be helped. The only question left is: Do you wish to come to London with us? You can remain with your aunt in Gracechurch Street, or Georgiana and Mrs. Annesley can accompany us while you stay with them at the townhouse."

"Fitzwilliam," asked Georgiana, "I may have no say in this discussion, but if I do, I would prefer Elizabeth go to the townhouse with Mrs. Annesley and me. I desperately want to see that monster made to marry Miss Lydia. I do not want to remain at Pemberley. I have a right to some form of closure in my life, do I not?" Georgiana was proud of the longest speech she had ever uttered to her brother requesting something she was sure she would not get.

"Miss Bennet, do you want to go?"

"Yes, Mr. Darcy. As much as Lydia is to blame in all of this, she will have no one there for her; she should have someone with her on the occasion of her wedding. Thank you for making it possible for me to be there."

"Miss Bennet, since you know Georgiana so well, what do you think of her request?

"I would agree with her under one condition, Mr. Darcy. Can you keep her safe?"

"I can keep you both physically safe from Wickham, but you will have to see to her heart."

Mr. Darcy told the party that his solicitor had an associate who was skilled at locating 'missing things,' as he put it. In the morning, Mr. Darcy would send an express to his solicitor seeking help in locating Mrs. Younge, Georgiana's former companion, who was a very close acquaintance of Mr. Wickham and was sure to know where he was staying in London.

"Good morning, Georgiana."

"Good morning, Elizabeth, can I do anything for you?"

"Well, yes. I was wondering whether you would take me into Lambton so that I might purchase things for the second mourning. I should not need them so soon, but it seems that I cannot wait any longer." Elizabeth's face was tight, and tears were welling up in her eyes. She was unable to fathom how, her family once again was destroying everything that was precious to her.

Georgiana seemed to understand her feelings. She said nothing but walked over to Elizabeth, took her in her arms, laid her head on her shoulder and gently rubbed her back until she felt Elizabeth gently sobbing. "I love you, Elizabeth."

THE PARTY DISCUSSED THEIR PLANS and decided to leave for London on Thursday morning after an early breakfast, spending two nights on the road and arriving at the townhouse by Saturday around dinnertime. The second night they would spend in Meryton. Elizabeth had not been back since they left Netherfield, and she had a desire to see the completed memorial stone in the Bennet chapel wall. She was hoping that, by arriving there in the late afternoon, she could avoid the notice of her family, who she was sure would not take kindly to her appearance, but it could not be helped. Jane was her first priority. Poor Jane.

THE WHOLE PARTY WENT INTO Lambton on Wednesday to make purchases for the trip. While everyone was shopping, Mr. Darcy met his steward at the Lambton Inn to discuss the acquisition of a new parcel of land that had just become available. Mr. Bingley wanted some new gloves, and the two young ladies went to the modiste to pick up Elizabeth's gowns, to the milliners and then to the shoe sellers. Elizabeth thought to herself that she had never had so many new things as she had in the past six months. She tried to pick out fabric for the gowns that might eventually be of use for general wear around the house when not in mourning. Not much could be done about the new bonnets and certainly not the gloves, but the shawls would probably pass well enough.

THE PARTY, INCLUDING MRS. ANNESLEY, arrived in Meryton Friday afternoon. Three of the party descended the carriage. The step was put back up and the door quietly shut.

"Rossiter."

"Yes, Mr. Darcy."

"We passed through Longbourn village on our way here; did you happen to see it?"

"Yes sir. It is a fine village, sir."

"Please take Miss Bennet and Miss Darcy to the church. Wait for them one-half hour then return them here. Do not under any circumstances leave them alone, even if that means being late. If you are, I will assume you are detained at the church, and I will come in search of you myself. I am entrusting you with these two young women, Rossiter. Miss Bennet refuses to allow anyone but Miss Darcy to accompany her, so you are my only hope of an escort for her."

"I will not let you down, sir."

"Thank you."

Elizabeth overheard most of Mr. Darcy's instructions to Rossiter. *I know he loves me*, she thought. She wanted to call out to him, change her mind, and have him come along, but she knew she must do this alone. Georgiana, being a woman, would understand what she was feeling.

They rode to the church in silence, and when they arrived, Rossiter stopped the coach, jumped down and handed them out. Elizabeth stood still for a moment, hoping to recognize the familiar sounds of people, birds and animals from the estate. Somehow, nothing seemed to be the same, though. How could it be? Jane was dead and gone. Elizabeth did not hear any people, for which Rossiter was grateful. He would be very glad to have these two delivered safely back to Mr. Darcy. He was not certain he liked the implications he heard in Mr. Darcy's tone of voice when given his charge concerning the two young ladies.

Elizabeth could see the corner of her old home, but she was no longer welcome there, and she still did not know why. She walked towards the little chapel. Carved in stone across the top was the word "Bennet" in block letters. Was it a name to be proud of? If she ever married, it would no longer be her name. What kind of pride is there in that? Her father had no sons. *Would that mean this little chapel is boarded up after Papa dies? Jane does not belong in here. She is supposed to be a Bingley. Poor Jane. How she loved him. How she loved almost everything. Why did it have to be her? It should have been me. I am the one with the bad disposition who disappoints one's parents, who had no marriage prospects, whom no one likes. Everybody liked Jane. Bingley has five thousand a year.*

Elizabeth had not even gone inside, and tears were wetting her cheeks. She had seen so much suffering, and a grave site was not a place to see less of it.

Georgiana looked on helplessly. She had insisted that Elizabeth allow her to come with her. Now she felt like an intruder, but she would not leave Elizabeth alone. Elizabeth was dealing afresh with Jane's death and with her abandonment by her family. Georgiana was too young to remember her mother dying, but she did remember her father's death and still had tears for that. She also understood abandonment quite well, thanks to George Wickham, so she could at least empathize and could certainly sympathize with Elizabeth's feelings. And so Georgiana just stood there, sometimes watching Elizabeth and sometimes looking around. When Elizabeth moved, she would move with her, making sure Elizabeth had plenty of freedom of motion and a feeling of privacy while still maintaining a sense of connection to Georgiana. When Elizabeth wanted Georgiana, she would be there, and until then, Georgiana would shore up her emotional reserves for what she knew was sure to follow.

As women did not attend funerals, Elizabeth was unsure where Jane's memorial stone would be located. However, she used to play in the chapel as a girl, much to the chagrin of both her father and the rector of Longbourn, so she knew things had changed. She could see where the floor had been broken up to make a place to bury Jane's coffin, and from that point, she looked upwards. There it was:

Jane Bennet
Daughter of Thomas Bennet, Esq.
Born 12 Dec 1789
Died 26 Nov 1811

"JANE! Jane!" Elizabeth sobbed, "Oh, Jane."

Georgiana was startled by the scream. She quickly moved towards Elizabeth but stopped when she saw Elizabeth immediately quiet.

Elizabeth leaned against the wall of the chapel, and with her fingers re-engraved the inscription on the stone, tracing each letter and number. Tragedies happen to other families, not hers, she thought. She laid her face against the cold stone, mingling her tears with the engraver's dust.

BACK AT LONGBOURN, MARY HAD thought she heard a carriage drive by, but then the sound had stopped, so she decided she had been mistaken. She was sitting in the entryway of the house out of the way of the commotion. No one seemed to notice when she sat there with her book. Who would think of sitting in such a place?

"Jane!"

Mary had not heard that name in quite a while. She wore mourning clothes, as did Kitty and her mother—even her father had black crepe around his hat—but mourning thoughts were another thing. They never spoke of Jane anymore because that meant they would have to speak of Lizzy, and no one was allowed to breathe her name in front of Mama. It was not fair.

Of all her sisters, she wished most that she could be like Elizabeth: so full of life, energy, and excitement. She seemed to be eager for everything. On the other hand, Mary was eager for nothing and preferred nothing exciting or out of the ordinary, and certainly anything that even encouraged activity beyond reading was distasteful to her. To talk of Jane and Lizzy would be a great relief to her. To know they had a proper place in their parents' memories was important in establishing what that place should be in their children's memories. Now there was nothing but confusion in Mary's mind. Was she still allowed to love them? Had her parents ever loved their children? Was she loved? What was her place in the family now that she was the eldest daughter at home?

Mary had heard Jane's name. It could only be Lizzy.

Mary closed her book, left her seat, and went outside and across the paddock towards the gate. She looked around and saw a carriage. *So I did hear a carriage. Someone is at the church.* Mary went in that direction and noticed a man standing near the wall.

"Good day, sir. May I be of assistance to you?"

Rossiter was not pleased. Perhaps this was the intrusion of which Mr. Darcy feared.

"Good afternoon, Miss. I have brought two young ladies to the church."

Elizabeth jumped up when she heard voices outside. *Mary!* She ran out of the little chapel to find her standing with Rossiter.

"Lizzy! I knew it would be you! When did you arrive here? Are you come home now?"

"Oh Mary! It is so good to see you!" Then she said sadly, "No, I am not come home. I am traveling to London and staying this night at the Inn at Meryton with my friends; I have come just now to see Jane's memorial stone. I shall leave you now so you are not punished for being seen with me."

"Please do not go yet. No one saw me leave the house, and I was alone there. Nobody will miss me for a little while at least. See! We are out of sight of the house."

"Very well, Mary." Elizabeth should have felt glad, but Mary's comments about being seen with her had begun to anger Elizabeth.

"Elizabeth, I am to marry Mr. Collins after the mourning time."

"Mary, I am so happy for you. Do you truly love him?"

"He is awkward, but I believe very strongly that he will be a fine companion for me. I feel not love, I suppose, but a great deal of respect for him and his talents. I know that most people do not like him, but that is of no concern to me. He says that he loves me. Time has proven his affection sincere, and so we will be married from Longbourn in December. "He comes about once a month to stay with us for a week, so we see him rather frequently. Mama likes him because he is to marry me. Papa, I think, does not like him too well, but that allows me to keep him to myself. We spend time reading together, walking and talking. I am looking forward to being in our own family party at Hunsford, and I am pleased that the future of my family is now secure. While this was not my primary motive, it certainly was a reason for allowing myself to be his choice of wife. If you and my sisters are not married by the time Longbourn falls to Mr. Collins, you will all be welcome to stay here. You need not be afraid. You do not know what comfort it gives to me to know that I can provide this for my family.

"I am not romantic, you know, not like you, Lizzy. I have never really sought marriage or men. I have attended balls and parties because my mother expected it of me, but I can hardly remember ever dancing. I now have a man who says he loves me, whose love has been sincere over the course of six months now. You cannot imagine what this has done for me. I hope you will be happy for me, Lizzy."

"Mary, if Mr. Collins has been able to win your affection, and you have his, then I am so happy for you! I am very glad that his affection has been put to the test of time and that he has proven sincere, and that likewise you still desire to be his wife after all this time. It gives me nothing but pleasure to know that you will be well settled. You certainly deserve it. Why did you say nothing of this in your letter?"

"I did not want to mix my happiness with Lydia's disgrace, that is all. I must go in now, Lizzy. Thank you for your kind words."

The sisters gave each other an affectionate hug, and Mary returned to the house to a mother calling for her. Elizabeth and Georgiana, assisted by Rossiter, stepped into the carriage for the short ride back into Meryton. They arrived in good time. Mr. Darcy was just thinking of walking after them when they arrived.

Chapter 8

The ladies stepped out of the carriage.

"Miss Bennet."

"Yes, Mr. Darcy?"

Georgiana walked passed them into the inn.

"May I ask how you are? I hope old wounds have not been reopened."

"You may always inquire into my wellbeing, sir. I shed a few tears, and I am afraid I alarmed dear Georgiana. I was quite overwhelmed for a few moments. Seeing Jane's memorial stone in the chapel came as quite a shock even though I knew what to expect and had seen her after she died."

Elizabeth noticed a familiar look on his face. Where had she seen it before? Oh yes, when she opened her eyes after crying in his arms in the park at Pemberley when he came upon her after she read Mary's letter — a look of agony.

"I am so sorry, Miss Bennet. I wish you had allowed me to accompany you."

"And what could you have done for me, Mr. Darcy, that Georgiana could not?"

"I...I do not know. I suppose...I suppose I just could have been there...with you." His voice and expression had softened perceptibly.

She was not sure how to respond. "I also had quite a surprise; I saw my sister Mary."

"That must have been agreeable for you."

"I still have not decided. I do not know. She came out to see me, somehow knowing someone was in the church or thereabouts. I wanted to leave right away, and I must say that Rossiter looked nervous. Nothing has changed at Longbourn. I am still an outcast, but Mary is to wed Mr. Collins. She seems pleased with the match. I am sure my mother is overjoyed." She said this sarcastically and Mr. Darcy could not but agree with her. He wondered how Mrs. Bennet would react when she found out that Elizabeth was to become his wife. He laughed to himself. He wondered how *he* would feel. Sometimes he forgot that it was not a foregone conclusion.

"I hope that Miss Mary will be happy. When are they to marry?"

"In December after Jane's year," she said. "Mr. Darcy, I want to thank you very much for bringing me here. I know very well that you did not have to and that it was at some inconvenience to yourself. You cannot know what a comfort it was for me to see Jane's memorial stone, as simple as it is. I am sure it is nothing to you, as you were able to attend the funeral, but it means so much to me."

"You are very welcome, Miss Bennet. I will do everything in my power to make your life happy." He smiled at her, becoming lost in her eyes.

She paused for a moment to return his smile and then walked to the stairs and up to her room to dress for dinner. Darcy felt he had never loved her as much as he did at that moment.

ELIZABETH DID NOT SLEEP WELL that night. Her mind was filled with thoughts of Jane, her mother, Mary and Mr. Collins, and all that had happened since Jane's death. It was all too horrible. Her thoughts were in a complete turmoil when she awoke on Saturday morning. She looked forward to arriving in Town. It would be the third strange place she had slept in as many days, but at least she would be settled there for quite some time, as Mr. Darcy said they would stay through July. She was looking forward to spending time with her Aunt Gardiner.

The only excitement the ride to London afforded was the ride back through Longbourn village. Once again, she could not see anybody, and she was sad to leave it behind her. Pemberley was very grand, and Mr. Darcy, Georgiana and Mr. Bingley very kind, but they were not her family. Then, she supposed, neither were the occupants of Longbourn House.

The party arrived early Saturday afternoon. Elizabeth never had seen such houses as she now beheld before her, and Mr. Darcy's home was the grandest of them all. Mrs. Thomas, the housekeeper, met them at the door. She was a woman in her forties who had newly come into the position, having assumed the post from her mother. Since her youth, Mrs. Thomas had been a servant in the home, and for the past few years, she had been training closely with her mother. Mrs. Thomas was a very capable woman, and Elizabeth would find that she was, like all the servants, very zealous of the Darcys' happiness, courteous to all they brought into the home, efficient in their work and happy and well treated in their positions. The Darcys were loyal to those in their employ, and they had very little turnover in their staff.

Darcy introduced Elizabeth. Mrs. Thomas knew everyone else very well. "Mrs. Thomas, this is Miss Elizabeth Bennet, who will be our guest during our stay here. Miss Bennet, Mrs. Thomas, our housekeeper."

"It is nice to make your acquaintance, Miss Bennet. Please call on me for anything that might make your stay with us more comfortable. You must be tired from your journey. I will show you to your rooms if you will follow me."

Elizabeth was shown into an apartment containing three rooms: a sitting room, a dressing room and a bedchamber. There was a fireplace in each room. The furniture was not modern and seemed to be of a fashion more appropriate twenty years earlier, but it was tastefully done and was very beautiful. The room had been decorated in the light colors of spring. In front of the fireplace were a settee and a sofa with a small table between them. There was a vase of fresh flowers on the table. The bedclothes were white and rose with lace trim, and the curtains were of the same pattern as the bedclothes. They were open and admitted the afternoon sunlight. The room faced north, opposite the street, so it was quiet. Over the large mantelpiece was the likeness of a woman and a small boy. Elizabeth wondered if these were Darcys of some past generation. This room was obviously decorated to suit a woman's taste, and it recently had been refinished. Once again, she was overwhelmed with the depth of Mr. Darcy's love and thoughtfulness. Elizabeth would be comfortable spending the next few months using it.

Her sitting room had cherry furniture in a feminine style, including armchairs, a sofa, and a writing table. Her dressing room had a large copper bath, room for more clothes than she had ever owned, a mirror, drawers for her personal items and a beautiful comb and brush with the Darcy crest on them. She wondered what they could be doing there. She would ask her maid about it later. That was a thought: 'her maid.' Ever since she had been with the Darcy household, she had been given a personal maid. She was not quite sure what to do with such a luxury, having had to share such services with her sisters. Mr. Darcy took exceptionally good care of her.

THE SEARCH FOR WICKHAM BEGAN in earnest with Darcy's visit to his solicitor to see whether he knew the whereabouts of Mrs. Younge. His solicitor's research had been successful; he had the information Darcy needed. Darcy went to the address he had been given and knocked on the door with his walking stick.

Mrs. Younge's housemaid opened the door. "May I help you?"

"Yes, I have come to see Mrs. Younge on a matter of urgent business." Mrs. Younge was in a sitting parlor very near the door and heard Mr. Darcy's voice. She felt her blood run cold. In her mind, she was begging her housemaid to send him away, but she knew it was too much to ask.

"Please come in, sir. I will let Mrs. Younge know that you are here."

Mrs. Younge wondered whether she had finally been found out after two years for having stolen the Wedgwood figurines from the townhouse. She had made a pretty penny by selling them. She knew he could put her in prison for it.

"Mrs. Younge, a gentleman is here to see you."

"Thank you. Please show him in."

This was a great deal easier than Darcy had anticipated, which only caused him to worry more. He had to get Wickham's address out of her. He followed the maid into the sitting parlor, and Mrs. Younge rose to her feet.

"Mr. Darcy, what brings you to London?" She tried not to let the fear show in her voice. He had been furious with her at Ramsgate, accusing her of being delinquent in her duty and of not overseeing and protecting Georgiana as she knew she ought. He also implied that, instead of looking out for Georgiana's best interests, she had been seeking her own lustful gratification and certainly not following the specific directions he had given her regarding the care and management of his sister. Mrs. Younge felt she had been attending to his sister with great care. She was only trying to bring two very deserving young people together, who, she thought, could love each other very much. She had known Mr. Wickham from her previous position in Mr. Weyton's home in London, and he had always shown himself to be a respectable young man. She did not know what Mr. Darcy had against him; whatever it was, it was vile and hateful. She abhorred Darcy. And in her weakness for revenge at being taken away from Georgiana, whom she loved, and her position, which paid a great sum, she took the figurines and sold them. They had been family heirlooms, though little noticed. Unfortunately for her, they were in a place in the house to which only she had general access, and circumstantially, she would appear the likely felon. Appearances were not always deceiving.

"Does the name Wedgwood conjure any images in your mind, say images of prison?"

"I know not of what you are speaking," she replied softly.

"Oh, I think you do. I am willing to overlook the matter, perhaps, if you were to provide me with a little information."

There is very little he does not already know. Why is he here? "What sort of information?"

Darcy could see her relaxing her shoulders, though her countenance remained unmoved.

"I am looking for a friend of mine."

What friends could he possibly have? And why would his so-called friend be hiding from him?

"And your friend is...?"

"...Mr. George Wickham."

"He is not your friend. You have certainly proven that, I would say. Who do you think you are, calling him friend? You have no business with him. You have nothing to do with the young woman. I shall certainly not tell you where he is. Ever."

"So you have seen him recently. Where is he?"

"I will not tell you!" she said looking all about her, anywhere, except into his eyes.

"You mean to say that you will not tell me whether living in this lovely house is preferable to prison?" Darcy paused to let his words become clear to her and to decide what he would say to her next. "I know you have much to think about. I will come back tomorrow, and you can tell me what you have decided. Do not play games with me, Mrs. Younge. I will know where Mr. Wickham is, and you most assuredly will tell me."

As Darcy headed for the door, he turned to her and asked, "How much is Mr. Wickham paying you to keep his little secret?" With that, he exited the house into the dirty alleyway.

Mrs. Gardiner opened the door and invited her niece and her young friend to step in. It had been ages since she had seen Elizabeth, and so much had happened. There was no one connected with the family who was not touched by Jane's death and Elizabeth's removal to Derbyshire.

"Lizzy, please come in. Oh, it is so good to see you." The two ladies hugged and kissed each other. It had been too long for Elizabeth. Her aunt always made her feel better about herself.

"Aunt, how are you? How are my uncle and my cousins?"

"Everyone is well, Lizzy. Please introduce me to your friend."

"Mrs. Gardiner, this is Miss Georgiana Darcy."

"You are very welcome, Miss Darcy. Thank you so much for the kindness you and your brother are showing to Elizabeth."

"Thank you, Mrs. Gardiner. I can assure you, it is no kindness at all, but a pleasure. We do not know what we would do without her. She is my very best friend. And I know that my brother is quite taken with her."

Georgiana gave a start, and put a hand over her mouth, realizing what she just let slip. "I... I mean... he is fond of her. Oops." Georgiana blushed furiously. Elizabeth lost her composure in a brief fit of coughing. Mrs. Gardiner smiled at the girls, recollecting a similar time when she was young.

After the necessary but uncomfortable pause and a little uncertainty on her part, Elizabeth began, "Aunt, for particular reasons, Miss Darcy is well aware of Lydia's elopement with Mr. Wickham. Indeed, I have accompanied her to assist her brother and his friend Mr. Bingley, of whom I believe you have heard, in search of Lydia. Mr. Darcy believes he has sources of information that will very soon lead him to their whereabouts."

"Does your father know this, Lizzy?" asked her surprised aunt.

"No, he does not. Mr. Darcy does not want him to know unless we meet with success. Mr. Darcy has no patience with my family regarding their treatment of me, and he does not feel himself obliged to disclose his activities unless he is able to find Lydia. If he does, he will ask my uncle for his assistance."

Mrs. Gardiner was concerned. This was quite unusual. "What kind of assistance?"

"It is Mr. Darcy's intention to persuade Mr. Wickham to marry Lydia as a means to bring about an honorable end to the elopement. To make that come about, quite a bit of money will have to be laid down. My father cannot afford even half the sum that will be required. Mr. Darcy will need my uncle to convince my father that he has put up the sum himself so that my father will accept the assistance. Mr. Darcy, in fact, will bear the burden of the whole himself."

"Does Mr. Darcy give the reasons for this extraordinary involvement?"

Rather shyly, Elizabeth replied, "He desires that no further pain or disappointment come upon my family." She looked down at her feet when she felt herself blush.

Mrs. Gardiner saw the confusion on Elizabeth's face and began to have some ideas of her own. "Or to you," she added.

"Or to me," whispered Elizabeth, understanding once again the depths of Mr. Darcy's affection for her.

DARCY AWOKE WITH A START. As usual, he had been dreaming about Elizabeth. He looked at the calendar as he did every morning. It was Tuesday, 19 May 1812. In one week, Elizabeth would throw off her black mourning clothes and change into the more subtle hues of gray, lilac and dove—colors of the second mourning. She would consider herself freer to move about and go into company, and then so would he. She did not appear to grow weary of the obligation to her sister, and he would never tire of her. The following week, to let her know that he remembered Jane, and that he remembered Elizabeth and cared for her, he would give her a gift.

He left his townhouse after a late breakfast and returned to Mrs. Younge's home. He had no fears that she would not be there. There was no place for her to go. He could take everything she had if he wanted to, so she had no choice but to defend it in some manner. Besides, he had offered Mrs. Younge something to ponder. He had brought up the subject of money, and her circumstances were not so comfortable that his assistance would not be useful, and certainly, Wickham could do nothing for her. His darker side would have preferred to intimidate her with prison, but it would be far simpler and quicker to bribe her, and his real concern here was Elizabeth. She was more important than any revenge of his and more valuable than any amount of money.

So it was with pleasure, Darcy thought, that Mrs. Younge herself opened the door after his loud knock. Once again, she seemed fearful and uncertain. This insecurity he would do nothing to abate.

"Come in, sir."

"Thank you, Mrs. Younge."

Mrs. Younge seated herself as a signal to Mr. Darcy to sit down. She did not speak. She would not be prevailed upon to begin the conversation.

"Will you tell me where Mr. Wickham is?"

"Why should I?"

"You mentioned that he is in the company of a young lady. That young woman's family has not seen her for several weeks. She disappeared with Mr. Wickham, unwed, in the night with no forwarding address; she has eloped with him. Her note to her favorite sister indicated they were to go to Gretna Green to be married. As you well know, they are here. She has not written to her family to announce any marriage. It is imperative that you allow me to see Mr. Wickham that I may endeavor to correct this situation."

"Why you, Mr. Darcy?"

"The family is in mourning for the loss of another of this young woman's sisters to serious illness six months ago. They have not the means or ability to locate Mr. Wickham and bring about an honorable end to this elopement. I have taken upon myself their troubles as a friend of the family. You must see the injustice of this circumstance. You must help me remedy this situation and allow me to be of use to the young woman and her family."

"I do not trust you," she said hesitantly. She was actually beginning to believe him, but she could not so easily let go of the means of getting money from him.

"How can I persuade you?"

"How do I know you will not hurt him?"

"I suppose there is no way for you to know that unless you want to accompany me on my visits to him and see the girl for yourself." Darcy tried to imagine himself allowing this to happen, and he could not.

"No, I do not want that." She was letting him get away. She had to be more direct. "You must know that the cost of maintaining such an establishment as this is quite a burden, particularly when improvements need to be made."

"Oh, and are you planning any improvements?" The conversation was finally going in a direction about which he could do something.

"Yes, a room or two could use some new furniture, some pictures for the walls. Little things make a room so much more pleasant." She felt dirty, but she was sure she would get something.

"Well, Mrs. Younge, perhaps when I come back this afternoon, you could have Mr. Wickham's directions for me, and I could be prepared to make a contribution to assist in your improvements. Do we have a bargain?"

"Yes, Mr. Darcy, we do."

DINNER THAT EVENING WAS AT the Gardiners' home in Gracechurch Street. As Darcy, Bingley, Elizabeth and Georgiana rode through the London streets, Darcy explained his business of the day.

"Well, I do have some good news. While I was out this afternoon, I called on Mrs. Younge for a third time, having seen her last night and again this morning. She has provided me with Wickham's directions here in London. His lodgings are located on the other side of Town from here." He had been addressing himself to Elizabeth. "After breakfast tomorrow, when it is not too early, Bingley and I will ride over in the carriage and call on Wickham and try to see your sister. We have not discussed this, Miss Bennet, but what would you like me to do? I had always imagined that he should marry her. Is that your wish?"

"I… I had not…" What could she say? She had assumed that Mr. Darcy knew what had to be done. "I cannot imagine my sister having a great deal of happiness in her life attached to that man, but the consequences for Kitty and Mary will be ruinous if he is not made to marry her."

"And what of yourself, Miss Bennet?" asked Darcy.

"I do not care to think of myself, sir."

"I am sorry, Miss Bennet, I did not mean to distress you. I—"

She reached out and brushed his arm with her fingertips. "No, you did not! I mean, I am not distressed about that. I believe they should marry, sir. There is nothing else to be done."

"With your permission, I will consult with your uncle tonight after dinner."

"Yes, please, Mr. Darcy. Georgiana and I saw my aunt yesterday and anticipated your desire to speak with him." Her lip quivered. "Mr. Darcy, you cannot imagine the shame and embarrassment I suffer knowing what mortification you bear on behalf of my family. It is beyond imagining. I cannot thank you enough and cannot express to you my heartfelt gratitude in such a way as to communicate what I feel when I consider all that you have done and yet will do before this miserable business is concluded. My family can never repay this debt to you.

"Miss Bennet, I pray you, please be the only member of your family who knows of my assistance and be assured that my thoughts are only for your happiness. That is the only satisfaction I require for my troubles, if they can be called such." He hoped he had not said too much. He did not want her gratitude but her love. However, he did not want to trifle with her. It was a risk he was forced to take. She deserved to be here on the spot in the hunt for her sister rather than remaining at Pemberley, wondering what was happening and not understanding his absence. Maybe he should have left her until he was certain of the outcome, but he was selfish, too. He could not be away from her. There was no doubt he could make Wickham's life with Miss Lydia much more agreeable than life without her. All he could hope for was that Mrs. Younge had not lied to him and that there was a small shred of decency left in Wickham.

Mrs. Gardiner's hospitality was comfortable and pleasant for the small party. She had kept her children up to meet their cousin and her three friends. They had acted shy and darling as small children of tender ages ought to do. They were particularly pleased with Mr. Darcy, who found room on the small sofa for all five of them: himself and the four little Gardiners. Somewhere from under the laughter could be heard Darcy's low growls and grunts that seemed to stir up even more screams of delight. Georgiana, standing next to Bingley, was happy to see her brother let his guard down with these little children. She rarely saw him behave so freely. Mr. and Mrs. Gardiner were quite pleased with their children, as all proud parents should be.

Elizabeth was filled with many emotions, most of which were shocking to her. She had never considered herself a lover of children beyond the affections she felt for her young cousins. But seeing Mr. Darcy, a man she had openly avowed to herself that she loved, playing with these small children, created in her heart such feelings of longing for a child—his child—that for a moment she was forced to look away to prevent a tear that threatened to fall. She had to admit to herself that she felt jealousy. She wanted Mr. Darcy to put off propriety and decorum, to hold her in his arms, and to say things to her that would make her laugh with delight. If she could for just a few minutes, she wanted to have the pain and anger of the past six months lifted from her heart, and if she could have that, she wanted to spend those few minutes with Mr. Darcy. She never loved him more than she did at that moment.

The lightness of the occasion passed with the children. With dinner came the politics of dinner small talk—what to say and not to say while everyone became acquainted. The Gardiners wanted to talk to Elizabeth about Bingley, and she to them about Jane. Darcy wanted to discuss Lydia; Bingley would have been grateful to hear the Gardiners' feelings for Jane, but he would not approach that for the world with Georgiana there. And she was pleased to be anywhere with her friends and hoped that the Gardiners would like her; she remembered her embarrassment from the previous day when she said a little more than she should about her brother's feelings for Elizabeth. She noticed Mr. Bingley's discomfort and wondered at it, but then she recalled that Elizabeth told her she and Jane used to come to visit the Gardiners frequently, and perhaps he was uncomfortable because of that.

The ladies separated to the drawing room after dinner. Mr. Gardiner served the gentlemen port and decided to begin the necessary discussion. "Mr. Darcy, I understand that you have come to town with the intent of searching for my missing niece. Is that correct, sir?"

"Yes, sir, it is."

"And what does Elizabeth say to this?" Mr. Gardiner wanted to get an idea regarding this young man's feelings for his niece. She had been a long time under Darcy's protection and, as things stood, would continue to be for some time to come. It would be unfortunate if she were some place where she was not respected and appreciated. Mrs. Gardiner was confident that some kind of attachment was forming between the two of them.

"Miss Bennet has suggested to me that, if I can find Wickham and Miss Lydia, I report this information to her father and then do no more."

"Do no more? Do you not feel that any efforts on your behalf are officious, to say the least?"

"I am not concerned about Mr. Bennet's opinions of me. His treatment of Miss Bennet leaves me with no patience for him or his family. I proceed solely in the interest of Miss Bennet's well-being and happiness." Darcy's tone of voice reflected his impatience. "I am sorry, Mr. Gardiner."

"No, do not be. I cannot account for Mr. Bennet's tolerance for this treatment of Elizabeth. And frankly, I have very little patience with it, either. As they are all my family, I must have a little more understanding to avoid a complete rift with what remains of them."

"I understand, sir. I would act similarly if in your place."

"Mr. Darcy, what do you intend to do?"

"I have been able to locate Mr. Wickham's directions. In the morning, Bingley and I will go see them. I share Miss Bennet's opinion that the only honorable conclusion to this supposed elopement is their marriage. It will take more influence and money than Mr. Bennet has at hand. I willingly supply both. but I need you to assume the responsibility for the outcome. I do not want my part in it known to the family. I do not believe that Mr. Bennet would accept or want my help, yet he must accept it because I cannot bear that this pain be upon Eliz— Miss Bennet any longer than necessary."

"I see. Very well. I do not know how Mr. Bennet would look upon your interference in his affairs. On the other hand, how relevant is that when there is nothing he can do about it anyway? After all, you are only looking after the welfare of two of his daughters—one, we need not add, for whom he seems to have done very little." Mr. Gardiner would allow himself to like Mr. Darcy. He was obviously in love with Elizabeth, which meant she would be well taken care of. Mr. Darcy did not seem to hold too high an opinion of Mr. Bennet. Well, why should he? But should he still not ask his consent to marry Elizabeth? Then again, why should he ask Mr. Bennet anything? Elizabeth nearly fled to Mr. Darcy's home with nowhere else to go. Is not that consent enough? Mr. Darcy would be very welcome to the family. Whether Mr. Darcy would welcome anyone beyond Elizabeth remained to be seen.

THE NEXT DAY, DARCY AND Bingley left their carriage in front of the lodgings to which Mrs. Younge had directed them. They went inside, asked the landlord for Wickham's room, and they were directed upstairs. Darcy knocked on the door, which Wickham answered.

"Darcy, welcome to London." He did not seem surprised by his visitors.

"Wickham, this is my friend, Mr. Bingley. We have come to see Miss Lydia Bennet."

"Lydia?" *Not 'Mrs. Wickham.' That confirms they are not married,* Darcy thought. Wickham said, "You have just missed Lydia; she has gone to buy a few things."

Bingley asked, "You sent a lady out unescorted in this part of town?"

"Oh, she is not a lady, Mr. Bingley," replied Wickham with a laugh. "How is your little sister, Darcy? I daresay she liked me very well. We would have made a happy couple, but she was just too nice, though I suppose I did not quite get the chance to find out how nice. Too bad about the dowry. Did she get over the heartbreak? By the way, thank you for coming. I was counting on it."

"Be careful, Wickham," Darcy growled.

Bingley could not believe what he had just heard. Never in his life— How did Darcy just stand there and take such abuse from this man?

"So, Darcy, these Bennet girls can be quite a handful. You have one for yourself now, I hear. Too bad one of them is dead. But that leaves two others. Maybe you would like one, Bingley?"

Most individuals, man or woman, and even Bingley, can absorb a considerable amount of pressure when it is gradually exerted on them. However, when it comes upon them all at once, in many cases, just like a dry twig, they will snap.

Several things were happening all at the same time to Mr. Bingley. He was unable to breathe, and he was unable to see colors. He had a piercing ache in his head. He lost control over his body. From some point above the floor, he watched himself quickly cross the room in long strides towards Wickham, his fists clenched dry of blood. He saw his arm pull back and suddenly Wickham doubled over with an expression of discomfort, stumbling backwards. Before Wickham had a chance to stand up again, he saw himself reach out, grab Wickham's head, and thrust it downwards on his knee. Then he stepped back. For just an instant, Wickham hung there in the air. Then, there was the sound of a body hitting the floor.

Bingley quickly inhaled and staggered back, falling into a chair. Tears were pouring down his face. Every memory of Jane was passing through his mind at that moment, her memory having been irreverently invoked by the mouth of the greatest evil Bingley had ever known. His whole body was shaking.

Darcy was shocked. He had witnessed such things in his days at school, but to see such violence come from Bingley was unthinkable. Not that he disagreed with it—just that it came from Bingley. He went to check on Wickham. He would wake up stiff but alive and, undoubtedly, would be more cooperative the next day.

Darcy took Bingley the long way home, allowing him time to compose himself before they arrived. When they entered the townhouse, Bingley went straight to his room. Darcy could not blame him. Either Wickham's remarks about Georgiana, Jane, or both, obviously upset him. He walked into the drawing room, where Georgiana was sitting alone with her work.

THE LONG RIDE HOME TO allow Bingley time to recover himself had mostly failed. He was unequal to anybody's attention. If he were to speak, he felt as if his voice would falter, so he said nothing. If Darcy did not ask him questions that could be answered with just a nod of the head, he did not answer him at all. How was he to face Georgiana? He had stood by and listened to Wickham speak ill of her. Yes, it had angered him, but he had borne it with patience. But when he mentioned, even in reference, Jane Bennet, he came completely undone and committed what were for him unspeakable acts. Never in his life had he behaved in such a manner. Was this one result of loving a woman? Perhaps it was better to be alone.

He opened his door and hailed a servant to bring him some brandy and water. He had not decided which it would be—dining on ashes with Jane or dining on hope with Georgiana. Brandy for Jane, water for Georgiana. He should have stayed at Pemberley. He was starting to feel better there, resolved to the past, reconciled to the present, and hopeful for a happy future with Georgiana and Darcy. Now Wickham had ruined his peace of mind. He felt guilt over his behavior toward Wickham, but he would have to face him the next day. He would never let Darcy near him alone, not after what he himself had done with so little provocation. And guilt over Jane. Yes, he had loved her and he did love her. And guilt over Georgiana. He was beginning to love her. Had Jane not died, there never would have been a Georgiana. But Jane did die, and he needed to love. Darcy was right. He would always love Jane, but he would love Georgiana, too. He had seen Jane placed in her coffin, had seen the lid bolted down, had seen her lowered into her grave and had seen the floor of the chapel rebuilt over her head. All hope was gone. There was not a possibility of mistake.

"WELCOME HOME, BROTHER, WHERE IS Mr. Bingley?" Darcy smiled. *She is always thinking about him now. She reminds me of Bingley when— Well, enough of that for today.*

"He went to his room as he was not feeling well. He is perhaps a little overheated." Darcy would never tell her what happened. He would not mention any details of Bingley's involvement with Wickham. Everything in her life was being stained by that man.

"But it is not hot today."

"I am sure he will be fine. I will ask him later whether he intends to come down to dinner."

At that moment, Elizabeth came in from the library with a book. "Hello, Mr. Darcy."

"Hello, Miss Bennet. We had a brief conversation with Mr. Wickham this afternoon. I am afraid it was not too productive. He asked us to stop by again tomorrow. Unfortunately, Miss Lydia was away or we would have spoken with her, as well. I know you are worried about her. Please believe that we would have seen her if it was at all possible."

Elizabeth looked at him with an arched brow. What was he hiding? He sounded like a convicted man. She had not said a word about her sister, and here he was apologizing about not seeing her? She could not very well ask him right in front of his sister, and so she would approach him later. She had to know.

THE SERVANT RETURNED WITH BINGLEY'S brandy and water. He took a small glass of brandy. *In memory of Jane.* It would be his last sad memory. From now on, he would only remember her in death as she had lived in life: as a happy woman. He took a small glass of water. *To the future.* He drank this water slowly, allowing it to purify his body as it coursed down his throat. *To the future,* he repeated. He stood up, washed his face, straightened his cravat and coat, and went downstairs to Georgiana.

ELIZABETH INSISTED THAT SHE JOIN Darcy and Bingley on the next visit to Wickham, where she hoped to meet with her sister. Before they entered the carriage, Darcy addressed her.

"Miss Bennet, you should know that Mr. Wickham had a little accident yesterday. Unfortunately, he made some disparaging remarks about Jane, my sister and you. Something happened to Bingley — set off his anger. Before I knew what was happening, he had laid Wickham out on the floor. Bingley cannot explain his own behavior to himself or to me. If Wickham should make some reference to it today, I do not want you to be surprised."

"Very well, Mr. Darcy. Thank you for telling me. Is Mr. Bingley recovered from this?"

"Yes, Miss Bennet. He is doing much better than I imagined. I had anticipated he would not join us for dinner last night, but he came downstairs almost happy."

Bingley joined them in the carriage, and they were off across town to Wickham's lodgings. Elizabeth was surprised at the condition of the neighborhood. It did not appear to be a very safe place at all, and she wondered that Wickham would bring Lydia there until she remembered that Wickham did not care at all for Lydia. It brought a tear to her eye. Darcy saw her distress and could only imagine what she was thinking. It was only going to get worse for her.

When they arrived, Darcy asked Elizabeth to remain in the carriage until they ascertained that Lydia was home and they had separated her from Wickham. Darcy did not want Elizabeth spending any more time in Wickham's company than absolutely necessary. Elizabeth agreed with a silent nod.

Chapter 9

Wickham opened the door but immediately stepped back on seeing who it was.

"Are you not going to invite us in, Wickham?" asked Darcy.

"I suppose," he replied, clearly not wanting either of them inside.

Bingley looked around the apartment, seeing more than he had the previous day. It was one room with a single bed in it, and Lydia was sitting on it, smiling at him coyly, blushing as if she were a new bride. The room was cluttered, their belongings scattered about. There was a chair by the window on the far side of the room, a desk and chair on the left side. The desk was littered with empty wine bottles. The room was not well lit, and what light it had came from cheap candles that were smoking. It was an eerie, uncomfortable place, and it was difficult to believe that Lydia would exchange the relative comfort of Longbourn for it.

"Wickham, Miss Elizabeth Bennet would like some private time with her sister. Would you please join Bingley and me downstairs so that we can continue our conversation there?"

The gentlemen began to move through the door.

"Where are you going, Wickham?" asked Lydia.

"Downstairs to talk to Darcy and Bingley. Please remain here. I believe your sister Miss Elizabeth is coming up to visit you."

"Oh, that will be wonderful. How I have longed to see her."

Darcy followed Wickham downstairs where he had procured a private room. Bingley went out to the carriage, escorted Elizabeth up to Wickham's room, and remained outside the door.

"Lydia, what have you done? Do you not realize the pain you are causing our family? They do not know where you are, whether you are well, or whether you are coming home!"

"Oh, there is nothing to that. You can tell them everything."

"You know very well that I cannot. Come home, Lydia. Mr. Darcy will take you to Longbourn this very day. We will tell Papa that this whole affair was Mr. Wickham's doing and that you should be forgiven and allowed back into the family."

"There is nothing to forgive, Lizzy, for I have done nothing wrong. I love Wickham; we are going to be married at some point, and until then, it does not signify that we live together a little ahead of time. It is not as if anybody cares about those sorts of things these days."

"People care about those sorts of things very much, Lydia. You are bringing quite a scandal upon our whole family. You are ruining the marriage prospects for the rest of us, and making life very troublesome for Papa."

"Mr. Darcy will marry you no matter what I do, I own,"—Elizabeth could not but help blush at this—"and Kitty is too jealous of me. Nobody ever thinks about me and what I want."

"And just what do you want, Lydia?"

"To marry Wickham, brush out his red coat every morning, polish his buttons and be happy."

"Do you think someone who takes you from your family without marrying you first will love and take care of you and truly make you happy?"

"He did not take me away. I left."

"Why?"

"Because he was leaving and I did not want to stay at home. Papa and Mama do nothing but argue since you went away. I cannot bear the noise. No one cares about what I have to say anymore. Everyone is cross and angry. Even Hill does not attend to me. She just squints at me, tells me to behave, and runs off to Mama."

"About what do they argue?" Elizabeth was beginning to feel afraid.

"About you. Papa says Mama is being unreasonable in sending you away, that it is not your fault that Jane died. Mama says that it is either you or he must go and then what a scandal that will cause and could he possibly do such a thing to his daughters."

Elizabeth turned in surprise. "What? She wants him to leave the house?"

"No. Only if he insists that you be allowed to return home. She says she will have none of it."

Elizabeth sat on the bed and leaned against the bedpost. "Oh, Papa," she said quietly.

"What, Lizzy?"

"Um, oh nothing, Lydia." Elizabeth reflected on her last moments with her father, beating on his chest, screaming at him, then the darkness. "Lydia, how soon would you be willing to marry Mr. Wickham if it could be arranged?"

"Tomorrow, of course."

"Please come and stay at Aunt Gardiner's until the arrangements can be made. This cannot be a comfortable place for you. Please?"

"Very well, Lizzy."

"Then pack your things. Mr. Bingley will assist you in taking them downstairs. I will await you in the carriage." With that, she stepped into the hallway.

"Miss Bennet, you do not look well. Let me call for Darcy, and we will take you home."

"I will be well enough. We are taking my sister to my Aunt Gardiner's until a wedding between her and Mr. Wickham can be arranged. If you would be so kind as to assist her with her things, I will await her in the carriage."

"Of course, Miss Bennet. I will escort you down to the carriage."

After Bingley had shut the door, she moved to the far side of the coach and leaned her head against the glass.

"Oh Papa," she cried. "Oh Papa." And all efforts to contain her tears failed.

IN RESPONSE TO DARCY'S FIRST question, Wickham said, "I have no intentions towards her. She is an amusement for me. You know very well I must marry for money, and she has none."

"So what did you intend to do with her?"

"Just leave her when I grew weary of her, which will be soon, as she is growing tiresome. How about your Miss Bennet, Darcy; is she growing tiresome?"

"If you do not want a repeat of yesterday, you had better confine your remarks to Miss Lydia Bennet."

Wickham opened his mouth to make another comment. "Miss Elizabeth is—"

Suddenly, Wickham found himself on the floor, rubbing his eye.

Bingley cheered. "Bravo, Darcy!"

"Wickham, I told you that this conversation does not extend beyond Miss Lydia. I will no longer tolerate your abusive language towards my sister or any of the other Miss Bennets. Sit back up in the chair!"

Wickham pulled himself back into the chair, a humbler man than he was before. "What do you want, Darcy?"

"I want you to marry Miss Lydia and put an end to this pretended elopement in an honorable fashion. I want you, for once in your life, to exercise a shred of decency and do the right thing. What is it going to take?"

"Well, Darcy, it will take something you have that I do not."

"Which is?"

"Money."

"How much?"

"My debts sum up to a pretty penny, over £1000 in Meryton, an additional £200 here in London. I certainly will not marry Lydia on her dowry of £50 per annum after her parents die. No, I figure that to marry her I will require at least £7500."

"Wickham, be reasonable!" Bingley shouted.

"I am being reasonable. I do not have the luxury of magnificent wealth and a grand estate like my friend here, something that I deserved to have at least a portion of and hope yet to get. If he really loves his Miss Bennet and wants to avoid a scandal in her life, he will provide for me."

"Darcy, may I speak to you outside for a moment," asked Bingley.

"Certainly. Excuse us, Wickham." They departed the room into the hall, shutting the door behind them.

"Miss Elizabeth has finished her interview with Miss Lydia. She seemed rather upset, and she has retired to the coach. She did persuade Miss Lydia to remove to her Aunt Gardiner's home until a wedding arrangement can be negotiated with Wickham. Miss Lydia is gathering her things, and I will help her to the carriage when she is ready. I think we should take the ladies home, Darcy."

"Very well, Bingley. Let me have a little more conversation with Wickham while you assist Miss Lydia to the carriage."

Bingley went upstairs to help Lydia finish her preparations and then board the carriage. Elizabeth heard them coming. She did not want Lydia to see her crying, so she pulled herself together the best she could.

"Wickham, I am prepared to spend a certain amount to cover your debts so that you can come out of hiding and marry Miss Lydia. I agree that more money should be settled on her. I am not prepared to turn you into an idle, independent gentleman. You must have a profession. What shall it be? A clergyman? I hardly think you fit for looking after the spiritual needs of other people, let alone yourself. The law? You long ago decided that was not an option for you. The navy? You are too old to enter that respectable field. I see that the only real place for a man like you is in the army. You can no longer stay with Colonel Forster, so it remains to be seen where you will go. I will contact my cousin Colonel Fitzwilliam about using his influence to obtain a commission for you in a regiment with which he is connected in the north. The regiment is part of the regulars, so you will take your chances at being sent abroad should there ever be war on the Continent or in America. The regulars have more respect and honor than a commission in the militia, which may hold some attraction for you. What do you say, Wickham?"

"How much money will be settled on Lydia?"

"We will have to decide that another day. I will return tomorrow. Lydia has agreed to remove to her Aunt Gardiner's until the wedding. Tomorrow, I will provide you with the directions and ensure that you have access to their home when you wish to see her. It will take a week or so to get word on your commission in the north. Until that is finalized, your wedding cannot proceed, of course."

"Why are you doing all of this, Darcy?"

"Because I am a friend of the Bennet family, and I am trying to be of use to them, that is all. This will all work out for your benefit. Having your debts paid off, marrying Miss Lydia with some money settled on her, a new commission in the north, all of this is to your advantage, so do not run off and cause me to look for you again."

"I will be here, Darcy. I will see you tomorrow."

Darcy went to the carriage, wondering whether Wickham really would care that he would not be with Miss Lydia that night. Darcy thought that, in his own situation, he would find it unendurable to be separated from Elizabeth. He was determined that she would not leave his household until they were married, at which time she would never leave it, a thought that gave him a great deal of comfort.

Lydia talked the entire way to the Gardiners. She spoke of what a great deal of fun she had running off with Wickham and how excited she was about the wedding. Elizabeth, on the other hand, said not a word but looked blankly out the window. Darcy was becoming concerned. What had happened in Lydia's room to cause this turmoil in her mind? Surely, she was prepared in some degree to see Lydia's situation. She could not be that surprised. What had happened?

Bingley did not say much, either. He was disgusted with both Lydia and Wickham, and he would say nothing to her. Darcy tried to play the polite host and humor Lydia as best he could. Fortunately, she did not need attentive listeners. She was content just prattling away about her adventures.

The Gardiners were pleased to see Lydia and welcomed her into their home. Elizabeth helped her settle upstairs while Mr. Darcy explained the situation to Mr. and Mrs. Gardiner. They were horrified to learn of the conditions in which she and Wickham had been living. Darcy assured them that he would find better lodgings for Wickham once the financial arrangements had been worked out.

On her way down the stairs from Lydia's room, Elizabeth overheard the following conversation:

"Mr. Darcy, thank you very much for all that you are doing for Lydia. You are really taking too much upon yourself," said Mr. Gardiner.

"No, sir, I am doing whatever is required to ensure Miss Elizabeth's happiness and peace of mind."

"You must care for her a great deal, then.

"Yes sir, I do—a very great deal."

"She is lucky to have gained your friendship."

"Thank you, but I am fortunate to have gained hers."

Elizabeth was blushing when she decided to finish her trip down the stairs, fearful of being caught eavesdropping. Lydia was settled in; they could leave now.

Elizabeth walked over to Mr. Darcy, placed a hand on his shoulder, leaned against him and whispered into his ear, "Mr. Darcy, I am not feeling well. Could we please return home?" She gently pushed off him to stand straight again. Mrs. Gardiner noticed the little intimacy with a smile.

"Mrs. Gardiner, I need to return to my townhouse to finish some business I have been neglecting and to send off an express to the north to inquire about a commission for Wickham. If you will please excuse us, we must be off now."

"Yes, of course. Please come again soon when you can all stay for dinner."

"We would enjoy that very much."

Elizabeth kissed her aunt and uncle goodbye, and they were off.

THAT EVENING, DARCY PENNED A note to his cousin in the North.

London, Friday, May 22nd 1812

My dear cousin,

This note concerns George Wickham. He has once again invaded my life. Do not fear; he has done nothing to Georgiana. My present involvement regards his elopement with a young lady by the name of Lydia Bennet. Her sister Elizabeth, who is currently staying with Georgiana, is in mourning for their late sister. Lydia does not share her sister's sense and ran off with Wickham several weeks ago. I have found them in London, unmarried, with no intention to marry. To save Miss Elizabeth from further pain of scandal, it is my desire to bring about a marriage as soon as possible, but I need your help. I want to acquire a commission for Mr. Wickham in a regiment in the North, away from his acquaintances here. I will pay the cost, whatever it is. Time is critical. They cannot be married until I have obtained this commission for him.

You may ask why I am doing this for him after his behavior to my family and me. In response to that, I can only say that I am not doing it for him but for Elizabeth.

I will look forward to hearing from you at the earliest possible moment.

Fitzwilliam Darcy

He posted it express and could do nothing then but wait.

On Saturday, Darcy and Bingley went back to talk to Wickham. He greeted them a little more solemnly.

"Hello, Darcy, Bingley."

"Good morning, Wickham," said Bingley. Darcy said nothing. He was already doing enough; he did not need to exchange pleasantries as well.

"Wickham, I have sent a note off to my cousin in the North to obtain his assistance in procuring a commission for you in a regiment there. I expect to hear back from him soon.

"Well thank you, Darcy, I am much obliged. So, I assume you are going to pay off my debts in Meryton and London, which are about £1200, then purchase the commission for me, which is £200. We will need money for traveling, setting up a dwelling place, new clothes for Lydia and the like, which I would imagine would be another £100. That is £1500. We can ask her father for her cost of bed and board at Longbourn, which is, perhaps, £100 per annum? You can settle another £6000 on her, which at the 4 percents, would be £240 per annum, plus the money from her father would give us £340 per annum to live on, plus my income from the military, which, you know, is not much. That totals £7500, just as I told you yesterday."

"Darcy, that is an incredible sum," said Bingley. "How can you possibly afford that?"

"Oh, the master of Pemberley can afford much more than that, Bingley; I am being generous. I am only trying to claim what should have been mine all along."

"Why yours?"

"Because I should have had the living. My father did more for Mr. Darcy than what he honored me with in his will. I attended him almost constantly when I was at Pemberley. I deserve more. Now, with Miss Elizabeth tied around his little finger, he has no choice but to comply, or the scandal becomes public, the Bennets become further pained, Lydia is abandoned on the streets, and I walk away laughing."

"You are a monster, Wickham," said Bingley.

"I know, but I hope to be a comfortable monster and not have to live day to day wondering where my next meal will come from. And I figure the Darcys have so much money, they can easily provide that for me."

"What assurances do we have that you will not mistreat Miss Lydia?"

"You have none. I do not love her. She is pretty enough, but she talks too much, just like her mother. Perhaps being taken to the North, humbled by marriage, she will learn to hold her tongue," boasted Wickham. "Unfortunately, you are giving her the money, not me, so I will have to keep her with me."

Poor Lydia. Poor Elizabeth, thought Darcy. There was no chance of happiness for Lydia, but Elizabeth knew that.

"Wickham, this is the last time I allow you to interfere with my family and those I love."

"Ah, so you are in love with Miss Elizabeth, are you? All the better for me. Tell me, how shall you prevent my further interference?"

"I shall challenge you to a duel and kill you, regardless of the consequences to myself."

Wickham's blood went cold and drained from his face into his stomach, which immediately started to ache. He had never imaged Darcy would be that angry. He assumed he could blackmail Darcy against his emotions at almost any time. Perhaps it would be best to stay away.

"Wickham, both you and I are aware that I am more skilled at any weapon you could choose—and it would be my pleasure."

In his mind, Wickham had to agree.

"Wickham, I will not settle £6000 on Lydia, but I will settle £4000 on her, providing you with £160 from her settlement, £100 from her father. That is a total of £260, which is the best you are going to do from me—a total of £5500."

"Very well, Darcy."

"Pack your things. I am moving you to better lodgings closer to my townhouse. I would imagine that the wedding could occur in about two weeks' time. I will apply for a license for you. The Gardiners have agreed that you may call on Lydia, but she is not to leave their home. Make sure you are kind and gentle with her and do nothing to offend either her or the Gardiners or you will have no further privilege. Do you have paper and ink?"

"Yes."

"Then before we leave, address a letter to Colonel Forster resigning your commission in his regiment."

The letter was written, and Darcy posted it after Wickham was moved to his new accommodations.

ELIZABETH WENT EARLY TO GEORGIANA'S room and knocked on the door.

"Come in, Lizzy."

"How did you know it was me?" asked Elizabeth.

"Because nobody else comes to visit me in my room at such hours except my maid, and she knocks at my dressing room door."

"Am I disturbing you?"

"Oh, no. I am always very happy to see you, Lizzy."

"Georgie, it is May 26th, the end of my deep mourning. Jane died six months ago today. I have very different feelings."

"Oh, Lizzy!"

"I am fine, Georgie," said Elizabeth thoughtfully. "I am so glad to have known Jane. She was my model as to what was right and good in a person. I am happy to have been the one to care for her in the last days of her life. I was completely consumed in loving and nursing her. That was one advantage of being at Netherfield—I never would have been allowed to do that at Longbourn."

"Why not?" asked a surprised Georgiana.

"My mother would have required most of my time since Mama would have been ill due to Jane's condition and unable to exert herself. I would have been called on to care for my mother, and Jane most likely would have been left to the care of the housemaids."

"That is awful, Lizzy. Is your mother really like that?"

"Oh, yes. Whenever anything happens that is not to Mama's liking, she fancies herself ill or nervous and complains until one will do almost anything to silence her. My father pays her no attention but hides in his library, and she is left to the care of her daughters. I have tried to be patient, and for Jane's sake, I bore it the best I could, but I would have resented Mama's behavior a great deal if I had known that Jane was gravely ill and that I was attending to Mama and not to Jane. Now, after Mama's treatment of me, I wonder why I tolerated her at all."

"Because you are a loyal, loving daughter just as much as Jane ever was. Do not let resentment and anger eat away at the love in your heart."

Elizabeth laughed. "You sound just like Jane."

"Well, Lizzy, then you can trust me in this."

After dressing, the ladies went down to breakfast, where a buffet had been set out on the sideboard. The gentlemen soon joined them. Darcy looked at Elizabeth, trying to gauge her feelings, wondering whether she would accept the gift he planned to give her. He was fully aware of the day's significance to her. He knew he was putting himself forward, but he felt deeply on this occasion and wanted to express his feelings. Elizabeth had stepped away to a window for a moment, so Darcy took the opportunity to approach her:

"Miss Bennet, if it is not inconvenient or undesirable to you, would you please visit me in my library during the course of the morning? I have something I would like to give you."

"Mr. Darcy, it is certainly not inconvenient or undesirable to visit you on any occasion." Elizabeth favored him with a shy smile and then brushed past him to her place at table to finish her breakfast. That was indeed a surprise.

Elizabeth and Georgiana went into the drawing room after breakfast to attend to their embroidery. Elizabeth was feeling a little nervous. When should she go to him? Should she appear eager, calm or in love? How could it not be love?

Well, it must be time. Elizabeth excused herself from Georgiana, set down her work, and with the appearance of decided calm, walked towards the library. It was a good decision to be calm but a hard thing to do. Elizabeth had rarely been in the library—his room—but Darcy had asked to see her. He had something to give her. She knocked on the door gently and with some hesitation.

"Come in, Miss Bennet."

Elizabeth entered the room, shut the door and leaned against it. "You are the second person today who seemed to be able to look through the door and know it was me just by my knock."

"Who was the first?"

"Your sister. I went to her early this morning, and when I knocked at her door, she said the same thing, 'Come in, Miss Bennet.' She said I would be the only one to come to her at that time of day and that her maid would—" Elizabeth colored and looked down at her feet, twisting her hands.

"Miss Bennet, please continue."

"I am sorry, sir; I was rambling."

"Not at all. I enjoy hearing whatever it is you have to say. Indeed, few things give me greater pleasure." Now it was his turn to blush.

"Thank you, Mr. Darcy."

"Miss Bennet, I want you to know that I am aware today is the end of your deep mourning for your sister. This has been a difficult six months for you, and the treatment you have received from your family has been unconscionable. I am genuinely distressed whenever I think on it. My heart is deeply hurt when I see you in such sorrow. I do not know what I can do to relieve your suffering, and I feel helpless that I cannot. Your happiness and peace of mind have been my primary interest almost since I met you.

To be of service to you has been my greatest pleasure. Anything I can do for you, I will do."

Elizabeth was stunned. Such an open avowal of what he felt for her — she had not expected it so soon. Her heart was rejoicing. "Mr. Darcy, thank you, I—"

"Miss Bennet, please, you need not say anything. Perhaps I have been too forward. Indeed, I could say more." Darcy took a deep breath, exhaling slowly. "I have a gift for you."

To Elizabeth's ears, he might have said 'I love you...'

Darcy went to his desk and brought out a small box, prettily wrapped. He carried it across the room and put it in Elizabeth's hands.

She took it and examined it on all sides, savoring the feeling of having something that belonged to him in her hands. She could still feel the warmth of his hands on the sides of the box where he had held it. She imagined what it would be like if he were to hold her. She walked towards his desk, sat down on a chair in front of it, and saw him join her on a chair next to her. She caressed the ribbon and looked at him. He returned her gaze with a look that seemed to burn through her, and she felt her skin tingling. She looked down at her gift and then back to him again, glancing upwards through her lashes, gently biting her lower lip. She could feel her heart pulsing throughout her body; her breath seemed to be caught in her throat. She gave a loud sigh, laughed softly and then turned her attention back to her gift. She set the ribbon aside and took off the lid.

If Darcy had meant to surprise Elizabeth, then she could not have been more so. Inside was a small mourning brooch, about an inch long and a half-inch wide. In the center was a rectangle of glass, behind which was a lock of hair. Surrounding this glass, all around it, like a fortress, were faceted stones of jet, like shining black sentinels in the candlelight. On the back of the gold setting, the following words were engraved: *In Memory of Jane Bennet 26 Nov 1811*. It was the most beautiful thing Elizabeth ever had seen — and she had received it from Mr. Darcy.

"Mr. Darcy, I do not know what to say. This is a beautiful piece of jewelry. How did you get Jane's hair?"

"I was able to acquire some from the jeweler with your father's permission, though he seemed impatient with my request and just wanted me to be gone from his presence, so I do not know whether he knew to what he agreed. Do you like it, Miss Bennet? Will you accept it?"

"I love it very much, as I love—" Elizabeth cleared her throat. "And yes, I will accept it with pleasure. When I look at it, I will remember what you told me, sir, and I will remember you as well as Jane. Thank you very much for thinking of me."

"You are very welcome. I am glad you like it." He reached over and took her hand. It was so warm. To be held by those hands! She was incredible. Did she know what a treasure she was to him? How could he tell her? He raised her hand to his lips. She was wearing lavender today as she did nearly every day. Her skin was soft against his lips—so soft, so gentle, so delicate. The passion she stirred in him. How he wanted to reach out, hold her and protect her from all the pain in her life. She belonged with him—at Pemberley, at the townhouse, or wherever he was. His mind began to wander around the grounds at Pemberley, by the lake. There they were, the two of them, with a picnic basket on a blanket, the cool breeze moving the air, a bird calling from a tree, a mother duck with a small family of ducklings...

"Mr. Darcy..."

He felt Elizabeth gently pulling her hand from his grasp.

"I am sorry, I—" He was quite embarrassed. How long had he been daydreaming, holding her hand to his lips?

"Please, do not be sorry, Mr. Darcy. I do not know where you were just now, but thank you."

"You are too kind, Miss Bennet."

She laughed. "It is you who are kind, Mr. Darcy."

Elizabeth felt weak all over. Why did she pull her hand away? She could have stayed with him forever. How could she tell him? Setting down the box, she took up the brooch and pinned it to her gown. She looked him squarely in the eyes, took one of his hands in both of hers, raised it to her mouth, brushed it lightly with her lips and then stood quickly and hurried from the room. She stopped in the hall outside the drawing room and realized she was hot, flushed and confused; she could not let Georgiana see her like that. Elizabeth went to her room for a half hour to calm herself. Her only hope of composure was not to think of him, not to think of the time with him in his library, and not to think of the brooch proudly displayed on her shoulder. All this, Elizabeth knew, would be impossible.

Lewis Whelchel

On Saturday, Darcy received the following letter from his cousin Colonel Fitzwilliam:

Newcastle, Tuesday, 26 May 1812

Mr. Fitzwilliam Darcy,

  I am not certain who you are, but you seem to have the same name as a cousin. I know this cousin has a profound hatred of George Wickham, so I know you could not be the same one who is requesting my help in purchasing a commission for him; you must be someone else who is using his name. That being the case, I intend to travel to London on my next leave from the regiment and drink you under the table until I gain a true confession.

  A woman, Darcy? Who is Elizabeth Bennet that she can tame the lion? You, Darcy, fallen in love? I congratulate you, and I will love her for it, though I would much rather face Wickham with pistols than provide him with a commission.

  To your satisfaction, General Rothwell is seeking an officer of few talents and no ambition. I have told him that I know of a man from the militia in Hertfordshire who would suit his purposes. Without exerting myself too much, I have convinced the dear general to take on Wickham and have pledged the £200 for the price of the commission. He is to report for duty in Newcastle on Monday, June 22. I have told the general of the upcoming nuptials, and the general wishes me to offer his compliments to the new Mrs. Wickham and to assure her that she will find the officer's lodgings very comfortable for ladies such as herself. He hopes that she and her husband will dine with Mrs. Rothwell, others of the officers and their wives, and himself, of course, on the Thursday night after their arrival.

  The general is a very complicated man. He will give Wickham something to think about for a long time.

  There, I have done my duty to you, the general, Wickham, Miss Lydia Bennet, and, I dearly hope, to Miss Elizabeth Bennet as well.

  I wish you the best with Miss Elizabeth. She must be a very special woman if she causes you to expend such effort on behalf of George Wickham.

Yours, &c.
Richard Fitzwilliam

Folding up the letter, Darcy went in search of Elizabeth.

"Miss Bennet, I have been looking for you. I have good news from my cousin Colonel Fitzwilliam."

"Well, I hope I was not too hard to find, sir," Elizabeth teased. "Pray, what sort of good news is it?"

"Wickham shall have a commission in General Rothwell's regiment in the north at Newcastle. He is to report there on June 22."

Elizabeth colored and looked down. "Sir, I do not know how to thank you again for your kindness to my family. I know that they will never be grateful. Lydia is particularly undeserving and does not realize the great advantage you are providing for her. And I cannot be grateful enough. I am sorry, Mr. Darcy."

"Miss Bennet, this is wonderful news. Monday a week, June 8, should be the day of the wedding, allowing them a full two weeks to get to Newcastle. Perhaps they will be invited to Longbourn." Darcy stopped talking and looked at her until she met his gaze. "Miss Bennet, you must believe me, you must trust me, that everything I do, I do for your happiness. To see you smile is all the thanks I desire." Elizabeth could not help but smile at that. "There, I am well paid. Thank you." He turned and went to his library, wondering how the smallest gesture of affection and kindness from her could cause such happiness in his heart.

ELIZABETH WAS ALL GRATITUDE. SHE was mindful of the tragedy facing her family should Lydia's situation become generally known. All chances of a favorable marriage for any of them would be lost forever. Perhaps even Mr. Collins would break his engagement with Mary. At best, they all would be dependent on Mr. Collins for the rest of their lives. Elizabeth thought back to Georgiana's offer to remain with her after her mourning. It was so tempting. How she loved Georgiana. But what of Mr. Darcy? Would he ever condescend to become Wickham's brother? How could she bear staying in the same house with Mr. Darcy under any other circumstances? Her eyes started to burn. *Oh please, Lizzy, no more crying*, but it made no difference, and the tears came.

WICKHAM WROTE BACK TO DARCY that he would be prepared to marry Lydia on the 8th, at eleven in the morning at St. Clement's. Darcy wrote to

Mr. Gardiner, apprising him of Colonel Fitzwilliam's news and the wedding date, time and place. Although pleased, no one was happy about it except Lydia, and she did not seem to require anyone else's good humor. She was looking forward to being called 'Mrs. Wickham,' and signing her name 'Mrs. Wickham' and being able to chaperone Kitty at the balls in Newcastle when she would come to visit. She was sure she could get a husband for her. But not for Lizzy—she was too old and serious these days. She took this mourning business too much to heart. She looked ugly in those dark gowns; who would want to marry someone ugly except for Mr. Collins, who was to wed Mary. Lizzy's only chance was Mr. Darcy, and what was all the money in the world against a man in uniform?

For their part, Mr. and Mrs. Gardiner felt inadequate to their calling. In their home was a wayward niece. Yes, Lydia was not their favorite, but still she was family and needed their help, which they were happy to be able to provide. They wanted so much for her to realize, just for a minute, all the pain and anguish she had brought upon her parents and the potential loss faced by her sisters because of her actions, but she would hear none of it. They would talk to Lydia, and she would completely shut them out. She would later tell Elizabeth that she had not heard one word in ten. Only for Elizabeth's sake could the Gardiners retain any patience with the unworthy girl who deserved none of the attention she was receiving from Mr. Darcy. One thing worried Mr. Gardiner: Was Mr. Darcy aware of how completely ungrateful Lydia was for all he was doing on her behalf? Would he change his mind upon noticing her ingratitude? Mrs. Gardiner then reminded him, "My love, this has nothing to do with Lydia or Wickham. He is doing this for Lizzy."

"If that is the case, Lydia and Wickham shall get from him more than they deserve." Her husband laughed.

"Please, dear, this is a serious matter. Lizzy has six months of mourning left before they could possibly think of marriage even should they defy the usual custom of not seeking an engagement during mourning. So how does he tell her he loves her? What can he do to attach her affection? How does he confess the full feelings of his heart at this delicate time in her life?"

"How does he, Mrs. Gardiner?"

"He does everything he can to make her life happy. He took her into his home when she was cast out of her own. He brought his sister back from

London, her usual residence, to be with her. He kept Bingley with him—one of her friends throughout Jane's illness and death. She lives in luxury in his household. She has huge apartments, a personal maid, and servants at her beck and call. Now, a problem arises in her family. It becomes his problem, and he throws his entire stock of resources at it. He was able to find Wickham within a week, work out a financial deal with him within another, two weeks later, he had a commission for him in the north, and a week after that they will be married. No one else could have done this, and none of this mattered personally to Mr. Darcy until it involved Lizzy. As soon as it did, he spent every available minute working towards a successful resolution. Do you not see, Mr. Gardiner; he is treating her as if she were his wife already? And what a wonderful husband he will be. Indeed, he is the second most wonderful one I know."

And with that, she went over and sat on his lap. He gave her a surprised look but recovered enough to ask who the most wonderful husband of her acquaintance was. She snuggled up next to him, wrapped her arms around his neck and began to kiss him. He responded to her kiss by holding her closer, rubbing his arms along her back, thinking it was wonderful that the children were in bed already, and hoping that he was the most wonderful husband of her acquaintance.

THE WEDDING WAS FIVE DAYS away. Mr. Bennet was so angry at Lydia that he would give her no money for wedding clothes. However, Mrs. Gardiner thought she should have a new dress for her wedding, so she, Lydia and Elizabeth went to a modiste recommended by Georgiana to pick out a new gown. It was to be simple, thus elegant, but useful for wear after the wedding at dressier occasions, such as the forthcoming dinner with General Rothwell. Lydia was quite nervous, and she was prattling on about every thought that crossed her mind. Elizabeth was glad she insisted that Georgiana stay at home since she could not have endured Georgiana hearing Lydia's nonsense. Lydia liked each fabric they looked at, thought they all were desirable—the more expensive the better—and wanted her gown to be heavily trimmed in lace. Elizabeth tried to reason with her, but she was unsuccessful until Mrs. Gardiner, frustrated with all the noise and time it was taking, decided to take matters into her own hands.

"Lydia, this is what I shall provide you." Mrs. Gardiner then proceeded to choose a simple white muslin material with a very modest cut on the bodice—something Lydia argued against but Mrs. Gardiner insisted upon—and lace trim around the neckline and sleeves. She also purchased a matching bonnet, shawl and gloves in the same pattern. The ladies went to a shoe seller and bought slippers that went perfectly with the ensemble. Elizabeth was pleased. Lydia's outfit spoke of simple elegance, and it would be something Elizabeth might have chosen for herself, but then Elizabeth and her aunt had a similar taste in clothes. Indeed, in the past, Elizabeth had her aunt buy gowns for her in London and send them to Longbourn for her without ever seeing them, knowing that she would like them very much.

On Saturday morning, they went back to pick up the gown. Lydia dressed quickly, and just the hem needed some work. In no time, they were on their way to lunch, listening to Lydia's exclamations over how beautiful her gown looked, and was she not very clever for having picked something out that was so pretty and slightly different from her usual style. Elizabeth's patience was gone by the time she arrived back at the Darcys' townhouse.

Chapter 10

Mr. Bennet had given his permission for the Wickhams to come to Longbourn after their wedding, so it had been decided that a carriage would be let for the day to convey Wickham to St. Clement's and then take him and his bride on to Hertfordshire. This carriage arrived at the church on the appointed day at 10:30, just before Darcy's carriage. Wickham, dressed in his best blue coat, greeted the other party.

"Good morning, Darcy. Good morning, Bingley. Hello, Miss Bennet."

"You seem to be in a happy mood today, Wickham," remarked Bingley.

"A man should always be happy on his wedding day, Bingley."

"And you are happy?"

"I am very happy."

Darcy cleared his throat. "Shall we go in?"

The party walked down the main aisle of the church towards the altar. Elizabeth took Darcy's left arm with her right hand.

"I suppose I should thank you for arranging for the special license, Darcy." Wickham sneered. "There has not been quite three weeks for publishing the banns." Darcy did not respond. "So, Miss Bennet, how shall you like attending your sister's wedding today?"

"I had always imagined that she would be married from Longbourn church and that her whole family would be there to see her. I cannot help wondering how she shall feel about getting married quite alone."

"Alone? Why, you are her favorite sister, I am sure."

"Hardly, but come, Mr. Wickham, let us not argue. We are about to become brother and sister, you know."

Elizabeth sat down by herself on the left side of the church. Wickham and Darcy sat on the right; Bingley sat a row behind them. Just before 11 o'clock, Lydia and Mr. and Mrs. Gardiner came into the church. At the same moment, as if he had been watching, the pastor came and stood at the altar. Lydia, on Mr. Gardiner's left arm, gracefully moved down the aisle in her new gown.

Wickham seemed visibly struck by Lydia's appearance. Elizabeth had never seen Lydia looking so well. If only it could have been under better circumstances. Elizabeth's only comfort today, she supposed, was that the wedding was happening at all. How Lydia would be able to endure the marriage to come, Elizabeth hardly knew. Wickham joined Lydia in front of the altar.

The pastor was disappointed. Only five people were attending this wedding. Five! He did not delude himself about his calling. It was a living. He could hire a curate and do nothing if he chose, but he loved the people in his congregation and wanted to do the right thing. He did not know Wickham. He had met Darcy briefly, and he was told that Wickham needed to be married right away. Darcy had produced a special license for this couple, something he rarely saw, so he did everything he could to help. He had a general rule in mind when he viewed attendance at wedding services: Too many people attending and the wedding was a sham. Not enough people attending and it was a hushed-up affair. In either case, there was little chance of a successful marriage. Was that always true? No. He had married plenty of people from out of the area who were visiting their loved ones, wanted to be married in Town, and had only a handful of acquaintances. However, he knew that Wickham was supposed to be an officer in a militia regiment. He should have plenty of friends. Where were they? He knew that Miss Bennet was staying with her aunt. *His* friends could make it even if *her* family and friends could not. Something was wrong with this marriage, and he foresaw only sadness and misery for this couple. Moreover, he would have to say it was Wickham's fault. Lydia looked up at Wickham with a child-like eagerness that was almost pathetic while he appeared to be bored. Normally, he had difficulty keeping a couple's attention off each other and on the service. Now he would have given half his pay for the day just for a few glances between the two—any mark of affection on the groom's side.

Reading from the Book of Common Prayer, he began: "Dearly beloved, we are gathered together here in the sight of God, and in the face of this congregation, to join together this Man and this Woman in holy Matrimony; which is an honorable estate, instituted of God in the time of man's innocency, signifying unto us the mystical union that is betwixt Christ and his Church; which holy estate Christ adorned and beautified with his presence, and first miracle that he wrought, in Cana of Galilee; and is commended of St. Paul to be honorable among all men: and therefore is not by any therefore to be enterprised, nor taken in hand, unadvisedly, lightly, or wantonly, to satisfy man's carnal lusts and appetites, like brute beasts that have no understanding; but reverently, discretely, advisedly, soberly, and in the fear of God; duly considering the causes for which Matrimony was ordained."

That was the problem, was it not? This marriage was doing nothing more than satisfying man's carnal lusts and appetites. That man's lusts right there—Wickham's—and her problem was being enterprised, taken in hand, unadvisedly, lightly and wantonly. Wickham knew exactly what he was doing, and Lydia had no idea.

While the officiant was wondering these things about Wickham and Lydia, Darcy's mind had traveled across the aisle to Elizabeth. He was contemplating what he had just heard as if he were standing up with her and attempting to determine his own sincerity. While he admitted to feeling some form of lust for her, he was not seeking to marry her in order to satisfy it. He truly loved her. He wanted to be with her. He was ready to enter into commitments with her that were reverent, discrete, advised, sober, and in the fear of God; duly considering the causes for which Matrimony was ordained.

The service continued: "First, it was ordained for the procreation of children, to be brought up in the fear and nurture of the Lord, and to the praise of his holy Name."

The pastor felt sorrow here for the unborn children of this couple. Wickham would not raise them in the fear and nurture of the Lord—if he would even raise them at all.

Darcy was confident regarding this first point. He had enjoyed the Gardiner children, and while he was not up to that on a routine basis, he knew that most couples started with one child, and he would grow to love them as he loved Elizabeth. Elizabeth was so full of love. Her children would be beautiful, just as she was. They would no doubt have her fine eyes.

The service proceeded: "Secondly, it was ordained for a remedy against sin, and to avoid fornication; that such persons as have not the gift of continency might marry and keep themselves undefiled members of Christ's body."

Lydia plastered an emotionless expression on her face and hoped the preacher would quickly move on. He, however, enjoyed a little pause at this part to see who became uncomfortable, to find out what had really been going on with his young couples. Wickham looked down and rocked back and forth on the balls of his feet for a moment. Lydia just stared. Yes, he thought, they were guilty. It was sad. If they had no self-control now, how easy would it be to surrender it at other important times in their lives?

Darcy looked at Elizabeth again and was not quite sure why life without her would be considered such a higher level of living in God's eyes than life with her. She was the best thing He had created. How could she be accounted for sin?

"Thirdly, it was ordained for the mutual society, help and comfort that the one ought to have the other, both in prosperity and adversity, into which holy estate these two persons present come now to be joined. Therefore if any man can show any just cause, why they may not be lawfully joined together, let him now speak, or else hereafter forever hold his peace."

Elizabeth looked over at Darcy, who caught her glance, smiled at him and quickly turned away.

The pastor thought there were many reasons they should not be joined together: none of them lawful reasons. Either way, all would hold their peace.

Darcy received her smile with gratitude. Little did she know he was pledging his life to her in the middle of Lydia and Wickham's wedding—or did she? If he represented the prosperity, she certainly had suffered the adversity. Yet he knew that he was no closer to happiness than she was. The only hope he saw for himself was in her mutual society, to receive her help and comfort. And oh, how he prayed that she thought the same thing of him.

To Lydia and Wickham, the pastor said: "I require and charge you both, as ye will answer at the dreadful day of judgment when the secrets of all hearts shall be disclosed, that if either of you know any impediment, why ye may not be lawfully joined together in Matrimony, ye do now confess it. For be ye well assured, that so many as are coupled together otherwise than God's Word doth allow are not joined together by God; neither is their Matrimony lawful."

He gave them the customary five heartbeats to respond, but they were silent.

"Fitzwilliam Darcy, wilt thou have this Woman to be thy wedded wife…" Darcy returned from his daydream.

"… to live together after God's ordinance in the holy estate of Matrimony? Wilt thou love her, comfort her, honor and keep her in sickness and in health; and, forsaking all other, keep thee only unto her, so long as ye both shall live?"

Wickham said, "I will."

Darcy looked at Elizabeth and whispered, "I will."

Elizabeth looked up suddenly. She thought she had heard an echo, another 'I will.' She looked over at Darcy, who was staring at her. She turned away and looked at her hands.

"Lydia Bennet, wilt thou have this Man to thy wedded husband, to live together after God's ordinance in the holy estate of Matrimony? Wilt thou obey him, and serve him, love, honor, and keep him in sickness and in health; and, forsaking all other, keep thee only unto him, so long as ye both shall live?"

This is what Elizabeth wanted to hear. This was the desire of her heart. She looked over at Darcy and whispered, "I will." She watched him for a moment, his head bowed, as if he was contemplating the words being spoken. What could he be thinking? Was he thinking of her? He looked so beautiful.

Lydia broke the moment. "I will," she said meekly. Lydia was afraid.

The pastor saw her fear. It was about time, though a little late, he thought.

Wickham began to speak the words that were taught to him by the priest. Darcy turned to Elizabeth and she to him. The distance across the aisle seemed to narrow. He wanted to reach out his hand to her.

"I, Fitzwilliam Darcy, take thee, Elizabeth Bennet, to my wedded wife, to have and to hold, from this day forward, for better for worse, for richer for poorer, in sickness and in health, to love, cherish, till death us do part, according to God's holy ordinance; and thereto I plight thee my troth."

Darcy and Elizabeth were swallowed up in each other's eyes.

"I, Elizabeth Bennet, take thee, Fitzwilliam Darcy, to my wedded husband, to have and to hold, from this day forward, for better for worse, for richer for poorer, in sickness and in health, to love, cherish, and to obey, till death us do part, according to God's holy ordinance; and thereto I give the my troth."

Elizabeth was holding her breath. Darcy could not move. Wickham's voice was heard through the church as he spoke to Lydia,

"With his Ring I thee Wed, with my body I thee worship, and with all my worldly goods I thee endow: In the Name of the Father, Son, and of the Holy Ghost. Amen. "

At the end of what always seems to be a long service with all the Psalms, scriptures and prayers, the unhappy couple who were married that day entered their carriage and were off to Longbourn. The happy couple who were not married that day but who exchanged their vows unspoken returned with Bingley to the Gardiners' home for dinner. It was a quiet afternoon and evening.

In what seemed like a repeat of the previous winter, a servant came to the door of Elizabeth's sitting room to announce that a gentleman was waiting on her in the drawing room. When asked who it was, he answered, "Mr. Thomas Bennet of Longbourn, ma'am."

She had not seen her father since that day he brought her the mourning jewelry, since that day she had beat her fists on his chest, asking why she had been cast off by him and her family. And now he was back. Since then, she had learned some things from Lydia. She had learned that her parents argued over her, that her father was threatened with having to leave the house if he allowed Elizabeth to come back, that her father was not the problem, that he was only looking after his other daughters, and in some way herself, and that the true responsibility for this rested with her mother. Elizabeth felt tears in her eyes. How she had missed him; how she had misjudged him. She slowly descended the staircase and went to the drawing room.

She paused at the entrance. His back was to her.

"Papa?"

He turned to face her. "Elizabeth, my child."

She ran to him, threw her arms around him and cried into his chest. He held on to her with tears of his own.

"I am so sorry, Lizzy, so sorry."

They stood that way for what seemed like forever until he released her and held her at arm's length. "You look well, Lizzy. Mr. and Miss Darcy must be taking good care of you."

"Oh yes, Father, they are. I could not have better friends. They love me" —she paused— "and I love them."

"Mr. Darcy is a very fortunate man, then. I hope he deserves you."

"He is the best man I know, Father—the kindest, the most generous, the gentlest, the tenderest man I know—and I love him dearly."

"Have you two come to an understanding?"

"No, we have not spoken of it, but I know he feels the same for me. I believe he is hesitant because of my mourning. I feel great hope in the face of my sorrow over Jane's death. He loves me, Papa."

"I am so happy for you. You deserve some joy in your life."

"How are my mother and Mary and Kitty?"

"As you know, Mary is to wed Mr. Collins in December. We see him about once a month for the better part of a week. I do not know what she sees in him, but she really likes him. When a father gives away a daughter in marriage, it is more important for his daughter to like the man than himself, so if I have secured her happiness, I am satisfied. It is a good match for her, though that would not matter if she did not like him. I give her every chance I can to change her mind, but she will not. They whisper, talk, read sermons together, and write summaries of what they have read. I have to say that he truly loves her. It has been months now that he has been coming, and he has been faithful to her. Their affection has stood the test of time. Of course, your mother could not be more pleased. Mary is by far her favorite daughter now.

"Kitty is settling down. She is no longer as wild and as unrestrained as she was when Mrs. Wickham was living at home. She is disappointed, though, that I have refused permission for her to travel to Newcastle to stay with the Wickhams for the summer. Unless they come to visit, Kitty will never see Lydia again as far as I am concerned. I have learned my lesson, and Kitty will feel the effects of it.

"There is nothing to say for your mother. She fancies herself ill at the slightest provocation. She still blames you for Jane's death, and she will not cease to mention her feelings to any and every person who will listen to her. I take as much refuge in my library as before to avoid her ignorance and insipidity."

"Papa, Lydia told me that I am a cause of disagreement between you and Mama. Please do not argue over me. I am resolved to my situation, and I do not find it at all bad. I know you must think of Mary and Kitty, and even me, and must avoid any type of open disagreement between you as Mama threatens. You are doing the right thing." Elizabeth wiped away another tear.

"Why did you not tell me? It would not have hurt me so much."

"What was I to say, Lizzy—that your mother hates you? Would that have hurt less? I did not think so. I took the blame on myself as much as I could. I had hoped to write to you after you were settled and your mother could not hurt you anymore. I am hoping that I am not pre-judging your situation now."

"About what?" Elizabeth asked.

"I was caught by your mother in what appeared to be a compromising situation with one of Mrs. Long's nieces. She threatened to expose me to the neighborhood as an adulterer if I did not cast you out of the house. Indeed, I was doing nothing with the young lady, but I could not allow you and your sisters to be tainted by scandal. I knew that Mr. Bingley or Mr. Darcy would accept you into their household. My only fear was what would happen after Jane's year was over. I did not want to hurt you, Lizzy, but I had no choice. You do not know how it pained me to see you cry that afternoon when I walked out of Netherfield. If I were violent, I could have killed your mother."

"Oh, Papa, do not say such things; do not distress yourself. You can see that I am well now."

"It never should have happened. It was my own stupidity."

Mr. Darcy invited Mr. Bennet to remove from his rooms at the Knight's Inn to the townhouse, where he stayed for a week. During that time, Mr. Bennet carefully observed Elizabeth and Mr. Darcy together. While they did not exhibit any obvious signs of attachment, there was enough eye contact and lingering touches to leave Mr. Bennet in no doubt of their mutual affection. On the last day of his visit, he was able to encounter Mr. Darcy alone in his library. He approached him thus,

"Mr. Darcy, may I have a few moments of your time?"

"You are very welcome, sir; please come in." Darcy had come to like Mr. Bennet despite his disgust over his treatment of Elizabeth. He had a dry sense of humor that seemed to spare nothing that was ridiculous, and he was quite frank and open with his opinions, a trait that was refreshing to Darcy who was used to the guarded conversation of the social circles of London that took great care not to offend anyone of significance.

"Port or brandy, Mr. Bennet?"

"Please make mine brandy, and perhaps you should join me."

"Oh? I will then. What is on your mind, sir?"

"I would like to talk about Elizabeth," Mr. Bennet said, watching Darcy carefully, "and you."

Darcy nearly choked on a swallow of brandy.

"Of Miss Bennet and me?"

"I am probably violating her confidence, but I feel I have no choice. She has spoken to me at length regarding the affection she feels for you. She also told me that she is aware of strong feelings of attachment that you have for her. Apparently, during an illness she suffered in the spring, you opened your heart to her at a time when you thought she could not hear you. Well, she did."

"Mr. Bennet, I do not know what to say."

"You do not have to say much to me, but you need to say some things to Elizabeth. Talk to her openly of how you feel. She believes that you have not spoken to her out of respect for her mourning. I appreciate that very much. She, however, grows tired of it, I believe. She loves you very much." Mr. Bennet stepped over to the drinks table by the wall to refill his glass. "It is not easy for me, as her father, to see someone else become the most important man in her life. She describes you as the best man she knows."

"I love your daughter very much, sir. I have loved her since the days at Netherfield when she was caring for Miss Bennet. I believe I have done everything in my power to assure her happiness—as much as it could be secured given the circumstances—since her time at Netherfield. It is my intention to go on in that manner for the rest of my life."

"Mr. Darcy, the reason for my visit to you this evening is to give my consent to your marriage. I know you have not asked for it, but I do not know whether it will be in my power to see you at any other time. You cannot come to Longbourn on her behalf. You certainly cannot bring her there. Take care of her, Mr. Darcy. Love her. Cherish her."

"I will, Mr. Bennet. I will do all of those things."

"Please excuse me now, Mr. Darcy." Mr. Bennet took a lonely walk up to his room. He knew he had just parted with Elizabeth forever. Certainly, he would see her again—but when? And when he did, she would not be his. He had just given her away to Mr. Darcy, a man he knew by reputation only, a reputation almost entirely based on the words of the very woman he was to marry—hardly impartial testimony. Well, he would certainly like

Elizabeth's husband better than Lydia's or Mary's.

Darcy watched the door close on Mr. Bennet. He sat back in his chair, almost unable to support his own weight. Elizabeth loved him so very dearly, enough to speak of him to her father! Then her father would speak of those things to him and give his consent to a marriage without being asked? He knew without a doubt that there was an attachment between them. He knew of his own regard for her, and he knew that she was beginning to show signs of affection towards him, but all this? Incredible! Wonderful! It was all he could do not to run up to her bedchamber immediately and throw himself at her feet. Of course, it was not the time. But what happiness would be theirs when they could share their feelings for one another. He never would have said such things to her in the spring if he had known she could hear and understand, but he was grateful now. It seemed to be the basis of the understanding that would soon be theirs. Looking ahead, he knew they could not be married until after her mourning period was over, but that did not matter. He had known that all along. She was to be his. How could any man be more fortunate than he?

Recovering, Darcy sat down with a clean sheet of paper to write to his solicitor, instructing him to draw up settlement papers for his upcoming betrothal and to send his mother's betrothal ring. After folding and addressing the missive, he retired to his room. He was satisfied that he could look back over the course of their relationship and feel that he had done everything he could to make her life easier, to work to her advantage, to serve her—that everything he had done, he had done for her. He loved her so much. If only he could have taken away the pain of the last months. She did not deserve to suffer so. Darcy could not think of another person more harmless than she, yet all these struggles had been heaped upon her. Well, he would spend the rest of his life trying to ease her burdens and restore her to happiness. It would be no struggle for him. It was exactly what he wanted to do. He was glad he had given her the brooch. It was a tangible sign of affection given to her before her father came, a testament of his affection for her before her father kindled the fires. There would be no question in her mind of his love for her. He was so full of excitement that he was unable to sleep for hours, and when he did, his mind was happily employed with dreams of the new Mrs. Darcy and all of the things that would make their lives together happy.

THE NEXT MORNING WAS A melancholy one for Elizabeth. She had finally come to an understanding with her father after all those months, yet he could not be persuaded to stay with them longer, so she must say good-bye to him. Darcy and Bingley left them alone beside the carriage.

"Oh Papa, I wish you could accept Mr. Darcy's offer and stay longer."

"As do I, my child, but I must return to your mother at Longbourn. I told her I would be gone a week on business in London, and if I delay my return, she will grow suspicious of my having seen you. She believes you to be at Pemberley now."

"Did you not also?"

"Yes, until Brother Gardiner wrote to tell me how Lydia had been found and married. I knew he could not have done that. I did not know who could have, so I immediately set off to their home to confront him. They could not long deny the truth to me, and I came here immediately. Mrs. Gardiner first told me of your attachment to Mr. Darcy and the kind manner in which he treated you, and that I should be careful in my treatment of him or I would hurt you, which is something I will never do again."

"Oh, Father, that must have distressed you greatly."

"Indeed, it did at first until I realized that a young lover must have his way, and I am resolved. I do not know when I can see you again." He smiled at her. "Love, you should know that I related our conversation regarding Mr. Darcy to the man himself over brandy last night.

"Papa! You did not!"

"Indeed, I did. He had a similar story to tell me about you. Lizzy, I have given him my consent to marry you. He did not ask for it, but I know that sometime in the future he would have, and I do not know whether, at that time, he would be able to see me."

"I see."

"Lizzy, he loves you and has promised me to love you and cherish you. He has not spoken to you yet out of respect for your mourning. I told him that he must not wait for that."

"Papa, how am I to go back in the house and face him now?" Elizabeth asked fretfully.

"Easily. He loves you, and you love him. Go to him and express your love for him."

"Oh, Papa!" She blushed and then said, "You have a safe journey. I do not know how much longer we shall remain in London, but I will leave you word in Meryton. Give everyone my love as you are able."

"Indeed I will, sweetheart." With that, he leaned down and kissed her forehead. He stepped quickly into the waiting carriage, the servant put up the steps, and he was off. She knew not when she would see him again. She left him with tears in her eyes.

Not knowing what she would find in the house or who awaited her there, Elizabeth slowly turned and walked across the threshold, tears glistening in her eyes. Mr. Darcy was standing nearby waiting for her. She could not meet his gaze but walked over to him. He could see that she was about to cry and assumed it was because she was missing her father.

Elizabeth looked up at him and spoke in a quiet voice. "Mr. Darcy, thank you for the kindness you have shown my father. I know you have had no respect for him, but you must understand that he had no choice, that it was my mother's doing, and that I love him very much."

"I have enjoyed his company. He has a singular sense of humor that pleases me, and if you love him still, I will also." He smiled at her and took her hand. "Your father has given you to me."

She stepped closer to him and put her other hand on his chest. "Has he?" Her lips curled into a slightly provocative smile.

"He gave me his consent to marry you."

She leaned into him. "He did?"

"Yes."

"Had you asked for his consent?"

"No, I had not. I imagined that this would come later."

"Later?"

"Well, it has been my intention to ask you to be my wife after your mourning is over."

"And now?"

"Your father said that I probably could not see him later, not on your behalf at least. He told me about your conversation with him concerning me. He was fearful of violating your confidence but felt I had to know your feelings."

"And?"

"And I told him how I felt about you."

"Which is?"

"I told him that I loved you. That I have loved you since the time you were at Netherfield caring for your sister. I told him that all I have done has been to insure your happiness, as much as possible, since I have known you."

"You told him that?"

"Yes."

"And what did my father say?"

"To love you and to cherish you. He also told me that it was difficult for him to see another man become more important in your life than he was. He said that you told him that I was the best man you have ever known."

"I did." She smiled at him. "And then?"

"I told him I would do all of those things for the rest of my life."

"What things?"

"To love and to cherish you."

She took her hand from his and began to trace the outline of his lips. Darcy was not expecting this, to be sure, though it was certainly not unwelcome. She moved her ministrations to his face with a curious expression on her own, a look mixed with love, happiness and sorrow. Darcy did not understand her, but someday he hoped he would. He put his arms around her waist and drew her near to him. She was so warm, so soft. She took both her hands, framed his face, bent it towards hers, and gently kissed his lips. She was the first to break the kiss. She had a happier smile now, one of relief and contentment.

"I love you, Elizabeth."

"I love you, Fitzwilliam."

"Elizabeth, my love, will you marry me? Will you marry me just as soon as we can?"

"Yes, and I also promise to love and cherish you forever."

"I am so fortunate to have you. I have always wanted you. I could not wish for anything else."

She looked at him with tears in her eyes and such a look of love and tenderness as he had never seen from anyone before, which made him love her more than he ever felt possible.

He reached up, touched her lips, and caressed her cheeks and the soft skin below her ear. Elizabeth rewarded him with a sigh and turned her face into his hand, kissed his palm, and leaned against his chest. He felt so strong; she felt so secure in his arms. She knew she had found her home. He held her close, their bodies forming a single person, to be joined in love for the rest of their lives.

When the ladies went up to dress for dinner, Elizabeth followed Georgiana into her room.

"Georgie, there is something I would like to tell you."

"What is it, Lizzy?"

"Your brother and I are engaged to be married," said Elizabeth shyly.

"Oh, Lizzy, that is wonderful news." Georgiana jumped up and gave her a hug and a kiss on the cheek. "We are truly to be sisters, and you are not to move away. Oh, I am so excited. When is the wedding to take place? How did he ask you?"

"We cannot be married until after my mourning is over. I shall ask Mr. Darcy if we can be married on November 28 at the Lambton church. As far as asking me — I confess I believe we asked each other today in the entryway after my father left."

"Oh, Lizzy, you are not serious."

"I am very serious. My father has been playing matchmaker with a little help from my Aunt Gardiner. I love your brother so very dearly, Georgie. I hope you are not angry with me. I know he shall be giving me much of his attention."

"Lizzy, I am happy for you. I could not have chosen a better wife for him. My brother needs someone he can overwhelm with love. He has a big heart if he will risk showing it and a great capacity for love. He has been starving for it. I cannot supply it but perhaps his wife can. Oh, Lizzy, I know you can. You deserve such happiness in your life."

"Charles, do you have a moment to spare for me in the library?"

"Darcy, you never call me 'Charles.' What have you done? Or what have *I* done for that matter?"

"You have done nothing yet. I am hoping that you will be groomsman at my wedding."

"You are to be married? You finally asked Miss Bennet? Darcy, that is wonderful!"

"I cannot tell you how much I love her, Bingley, and coming to an understanding with her makes me love her that much more. It is wonderful.

I have never been so happy."

Dinner that evening was a joyous affair for the friends and lovers.

THE NEXT DAY, ELIZABETH AND Mr. Darcy paid a call on the Gardiners so that they could share in their joy. Mrs. Gardiner was very pleased for her niece, who, for the first time in a long time, had a look of joy in her eyes.

Business seemed to be concluded in town. By the beginning of August, the party had arrived back in the cooler environs of Derbyshire and Elizabeth's future home at Pemberley. Indeed, Darcy's motive for their removal from town was to give the future mistress an opportunity to redecorate her apartments and other rooms as she felt appropriate. It had been a long time since Pemberley had felt a woman's touch, and it was long overdue.

Elizabeth was glad to be back at Pemberley. She did not realize how much she had missed it. Being afraid to become attached to any place as her home, she was suddenly aware of the freedom that was before her. She went out every day—sometimes alone, sometimes with Mr. Darcy, usually with Georgiana—to enjoy the walks, spending time viewing the house from different angles and at different times of day to enjoy the changing light.

"Georgie, I love this place. I am the most fortunate woman in the world to be able to call Pemberley my home. I have never seen a place more happily situated."

"Indeed, it is a beautiful place. I will miss it."

"Are you to be leaving it, Georgie?"

"I cannot stay here forever, you know. I do want a home of my own some day. And I do not expect that it could ever be as beautiful as Pemberley. I just hope I do not live far away."

"Georgie, has Mr. Bingley found a place yet?"

"I do not know about Mr. Bingley, Lizzy. He is kind and nice, but he seems afraid of me sometimes. I do not know whether he thinks I am too young or whether he just loved Jane too much ever to be happy with another woman. He does not seem happy, and it breaks my heart. I would do everything I could; I would spend every waking moment trying to make him happy."

"Georgie, you are too good, and if Mr. Bingley does not choose you, then some other young man will. You will always have a home with us. I could not be parted from you."

"Thank you, Lizzy. It is strange to think of your taking my place in that house, and I am glad to release my brother to your care. I do not think I did a very good job of it. He thinks I am too young to confide in."

"Most men will be more comfortable with their wives than they will with their sisters, particularly one who is so much younger as you are."

THE NEXT DAY ELIZABETH HAD a new experience. She toured the mistress's apartments at Pemberley with her intended. Darcy had arranged with Mrs. Reynolds to have the rooms aired out and cleaned. He had been in them only a few times since his father had died. Formerly, he had accompanied his father into them to 'visit' his mother after she had died. Those were difficult memories, but soon he would share them with Elizabeth. She would understand. She would understand everything. Elizabeth also understood the implications of the one door along the common wall of the room that adjoined her bedchamber to that of Mr. Darcy. She blushed to think about it but anticipated its use just the same.

The room was decorated in deep cherry colors and lighter wallpaper with cherry furniture. Darcy told her she could make any changes she wanted to the rooms, and indeed, there were things she thought she might like to change. However, she also knew that Darcy had many memories associated with these rooms, and until she knew what they were and what kind of pain they held for him, she was not going to change a thing.

Chapter 11

So it had come to this: mistress of the whole house. What a change it was, and what a place Darcy had taken her from the scared, lost young woman she had been so many months before during her escape from the officers' ball in Meryton. It seemed a lifetime ago. Jane would have loved this place.

But she must cease comparing everything to Jane. All of those memories led her back to Bingley, and he was to become someone else's; she could not begrudge him that or his new love. She would not give up his friendship, regardless of the person to whom he attached himself, and he must know that she approved his choice and did not hold Jane against him. Mr. Darcy needed to know there was no ghost in her past motivating her actions.

August passed peacefully and uneventfully, a wonderful happening for Elizabeth and Darcy, who took great pleasure in each other's company and seemed to enjoy Georgiana and Bingley even more. Mrs. Annesley wisely gave the lovers as much time together as they needed.

The friends gradually resumed the daily habits they had adopted at Pemberley before their untimely removal to Town. Georgiana spent much time in the music room, and thither went Mr. Bingley almost daily. He had to go through a period of readjustment with Georgiana until she was comfortable once again in playing with him in the room. Elizabeth looked on with pleasure. They were certainly a shy couple if they could be called such. Yes, she would call them a couple even if they were not ready to acknowledge it. In an effort to help them along, Elizabeth would leave them alone in the music room after a time so that, when Georgiana finished playing, they would have time alone.

On one of these occasions, Bingley had some news for her.

"Georgiana, I have been told by my solicitor that my inquiries into an estate in Derbyshire finally have been successful. Lord Beecham and his family have inherited property in Wales and will be removing hence almost immediately. They have offered Hillcock Manor for sale, and I have purchased it.

"Oh, Charles, that is wonderful. Is not this exactly what you were hoping for—a place here close to Fitzwilliam?"

"Yes, it had been my wish to live in the neighborhood since Darcy brought us here in the winter." He would not touch on Jane—only happy memories for Jane.

"When do you take possession of the house?" Georgiana ask hesitantly. She was not happy with the idea of his going—not happy at all.

"I can take possession from October 21st. On that day, I will have furniture and belongings moved from London to Hillcock, and my servants will move in. My housekeeper in London has agreed to take the post at Hillcock, and she will see about staffing the place and getting it ready for me. I would anticipate being able to move sometime in late November."

"I am very happy for you Charles," she said with a pout.

"You do not *seem* very happy."

"It is just that I am used to your company. I enjoy having you here—having us all together—and if you are to leave us, I would miss you and your company, your good humor, the way we all get along so well, that is all."

"Georgiana, come sit with me, please."

She joined him on the sofa. He surprised her by taking one of her hands in both of his.

"I know I have been something of an indifferent lover, giving you a variety of signs over the past several months. I confess it has been difficult for me to resolve myself to loving another after having loved Jane and then seeing her die, but I can say that I have done so. I did so back in June, and since then I have been trying to understand my feelings for you—what they are, what they should be, what they could be. I know that I have come to love you. I want to be with you, and I do not want to enter that huge mansion at Hillcock alone. It would not do for me for a minute. I bought that place for you, so that you would have a home, here, near those you love, near your brother and Elizabeth. I know it was presumptuous on my part. I had no assurance that you would accept me, but I thought if I showed you that I could provide you a home and could take care of you, that you would see that I did truly love you, that I did care for you, that I wanted to protect you and grant your wish of being near your family. I love Darcy and Elizabeth dearly. Marrying you is a selfish thing for me. Not only do I love you, but also I love your connections. Having Darcy for a brother and Elizabeth for a sister—there could not be greater happiness. The four of us, as friends and couples could always be together, and we would soon be joined, hopefully, by children who would increase our joy. Our homes are so close we could have daily intercourse with each other if we wanted and surely weekly visits. I offer to you every advantage I have. I will need your active help in running so large an estate. I need a partner, an equal."

Bingley paused for a moment, searching her face for some kind of encouragement.

"Georgiana, please, will you marry me?"

Georgiana thought for a moment. Her heart was admittedly confused. His declaration was not expected. He was right; he had not been a consistent lover, but he spoke well, and he made sense. She felt a bond between them, and all he said about their connections and friendship with Fitzwilliam and Elizabeth was true. After feeling dominated by her brother for so long, the offer of being Charles's equal and his helper was attractive. But most importantly, did she love him? Elizabeth told her to marry only for reasons of the deepest love and affection. She was not sure what that meant since Charles was the first man for whom she felt anything at all. But if she gauged it according to how she would feel if she said no and let him walk away, then she knew she loved him. She could not do without him. She would join him at Hillcock Manor. She would become his wife.

"Yes, Charles, I will marry you."

"Oh, Georgiana, I promise you that you will never regret it. I promise you that I shall love you and take care of you for the rest of my life."

"Charles, I am afraid."

"Of what, my love?"

She was surprised to hear him call her 'my love.' She admitted to herself that she liked it. It made her feel close to him, and she needed such security at that moment.

"Of leaving my brother and Lizzy—of growing up so fast. I do not know what to do—how to be a wife."

"I do not know how to be a husband. We shall learn together. If you like, we could take an extended honeymoon someplace to get to know each other better before we move to Hillcock and the duties that await us there."

"I would like that. Please hold me, Charles."

He stood, took her hand and raised her from the sofa. He stepped towards her, put an arm around her back and pulled her gently against his chest, his other arm around her waist. Slowly, hesitantly, she put her hands on his forearms, then around his shoulders. He pulled her closer to him. She responded in kind. They stood there for a time, which seemed like infinity to them, as their bodies became acquainted for the first time.

"Georgiana, may I kiss you?"

Shyly, she said, "Yes, Charles."

He released her back, but kept his arm around her waist. He raised his hand to her chin and stroked the skin below it. Holding her chin upwards, he lowered his lips to hers, touching them lightly, lingering for just a moment.

She leaned back against his chest, and stayed there for quite some time until a noise in the hall caused them to separate.

That noise was Elizabeth. She had come across them, and she was giving them privacy in what she knew must be the aftermath of a proposal as it reminded her of her own situation with Darcy. She was going to allow them as much time together as they required until she heard Darcy's footsteps on the staircase. She decided to interrupt them discreetly to avoid any embarrassment. No doubt, Mr. Bingley would have an errand shortly with his future brother.

IT HAD BEEN MANY DAYS since the ladies had separated from the gentleman after dinner. Darcy could see no reason to be away from Elizabeth; he did not like cigars, and Bingley had no objections. On this occasion, though, Bingley asked if they could remain behind, or preferably go into the library.

"Certainly, Bingley. What is on your mind?" Darcy had a pretty good idea of what Bingley wanted. He had been paying quite a bit of attention to Georgiana of late. His announcement of the purchase of Hillcock Manor and her sudden interest in it beyond what would be considered normal curiosity only led him to one conclusion. He was happy that this conclusion, the only logical one for both of them, had finally been reached. He would send a thank you note to his solicitor, whose wife was a friend of Lord Beecham's housekeeper, for letting him know in advance of the inheritance and of the sale of Hillcock so he could 'accidentally' tip off Bingley's solicitor. He would enjoy having Georgiana and him so close.

"May I have some brandy?"

"No."

"What?"

"No, Bingley, I would like you to get to the point. I would like to hear what you have to say so that I can join my betrothed in the drawing room."

"Well, sir, I —"

"Bingley, you never call me 'sir.'"

"Sorry, Darcy."

"Come on, Bingley; out with it."

"Very well. Today I asked your sister to marry me, and she agreed, and I am now seeking your consent."

"See? That was not so difficult, was it?"

"It was horrible, Darcy, and you are not making this easy for me. I thought you were my friend."

"The best one you have. Let me see. Do you love Georgiana?"

"With all my heart."

"Are you recovered from Jane's death and able to give that heart freely to Georgiana?"

"Yes. I realized in June that I must overcome those feelings if I were ever to be happy again. I will always hold fond memories of Jane, but my heart and my commitment belong to your sister."

"Are you able to provide for her?"

"You know I can."

"Will you be providing her with an appropriate settlement?"

"I will take your advice on this matter as I have no experience in such things, and I really do not know what to do. As far as taking care of her, I intend to be quite generous with her pin money. She deserves the opportunity to purchase what she wants for herself and what she feels the estate may need without worry of money. She will have a large apartment there with a bedchamber, dressing room, sitting room, nursery and a room for letter writing, all connected, where she may remain in privacy if she wishes as a refuge from the rest of the house. She will have a personal maid at her disposal. There will be a footman in waiting outside her door at all times. I intend to purchase another barouche and four as her personal means of transport so that she is not confined to Hillcock if I should be out. Whenever she feels capable, she will be responsible for the accounts, which my housekeeper currently manages. She will train Georgiana and relinquish that duty to her."

"Bingley, it sounds as though you plan to be very generous with her. She is young. Are not you worried about spoiling her?"

"I realize she is young, but I intend to treat her as an equal. She will learn what she needs to do; I am patient, and I will love her through it. Society in this neighborhood already loves her, and as mistress of Hillcock, she will be able to do no wrong in their eyes. I will be the one they watch for mistakes. Elizabeth will continue to love her and help her. We will depend on your society very much. No, I do not think she will be spoilt. Do you?"

"No, not if you do what you say you will." Darcy had to smile. Georgiana would be very happy. He knew she would be, but he was gratified to hear it spoken.

"Bingley, I can see no objections to the match. I see only advantages, both to Georgiana, Elizabeth and to myself. I will enjoy having you as a brother. You cannot imagine the gratitude I feel in the fact that you acquired Hillcock and will keep Georgiana and yourself, so close to us. I am sorry for all the questions, but I wanted to make sure you loved her, that is all. I can see that you do, and I give you my consent." Darcy paced the room a moment. "Do you think I should talk to Georgiana for a moment?"

"That might be nice to give her equal time, though perhaps you ought not question her as rigorously as you did me." Bingley laughed.

"Please go out and entertain Elizabeth for me, and ask my sister to join me here in the library."

Georgiana did not expect such a long interview between Darcy and Bingley. They were close friends and had been for years. What could her brother possibly want to know that he did not know already? Now he wanted to speak with her. Only one topic would interest him. She always felt that Fitzwilliam would be in favor of a match between her and Bingley. Perhaps she was wrong. Perhaps her brother felt she was too young. Perhaps he felt she was making a foolish decision like the one she did with Wickham, but it seemed so different this time. No one was trying to steal her away. She was not running away. Bingley was his best friend, for Heaven's sake.

She knocked on the door.

"Come in."

"You wanted to see me, Brother?"

"Sit down, Georgiana. I have a matter of great importance to discuss with you."

She sat down somewhat nervously.

"Bingley came to me just a few minutes ago and told me that he has asked for your hand in marriage and that you have accepted him. Is this true?"

"Yes, it is."

"Why?"

"Why? Because I love him, that is why. Because when I think of going on without him, I cannot bear the thought. I want to be with him. I want to go where he goes, do what he does, listen to the things he says, be his lover, be his friend, and his companion."

"What about Hillcock Manor?"

"What about it? That is where we shall be living. I have never been there except for the dance. The ballroom seemed nice enough. I have not seen the rest of the house, and it was dark both when we got there and when we left."

"Will it not be nice to live independently of me on all of Bingley's money and do whatever you want?"

"I do not know how much money Charles has. I have never even thought of it until now. He told me he had enough. I probably should have asked to make sure he was able to take care of me. I just assumed that, when he bought Hillcock Manor and offered it to me as my home, he would be able to support me. As for doing what I want, I will do what Charles wants me to do," she said angrily. She had never spoken to her brother like that before, but she considered herself fighting for her life with Charles.

"Please do not be upset."

"Fitzwilliam, I am upset. I do not know what you said to Charles, but as he is your best friend, it should not have taken so long for you to give him your consent to marry me, if you did give him consent. And you know the kind of man he is. I know that he may not love me as much as he should, but I know that he does love me, and as we spend our life together, he will come to love me even more. And that love will develop quickly. I do not fear for myself; I only fear your disapproval. I choose Charles of my own free will and choice. This is not a Wickham scandal. No one is trying to steal me away for my money. I am not trying to run off in the night. Our relationship has stood the test of time, his grief for Jane, and his dealings with Wickham himself. I beg of you, Brother, to let me have him. Do not deny me this happiness. Please, do not." Georgiana was crying.

"Georgiana, the reason I questioned you was to allow me to gauge the depth of your love for Bingley, your consciousness of the situation into which you are marrying, and your sincerity. I have already given Bingley my consent for your marriage, and now I give it to you. Please do not cry, and please forgive me if you felt I was harsh. I am only looking out for your happiness, and I suppose I am sad that I must pass that responsibility on to someone else, as much as I love and respect Bingley."

"Oh, Brother, everything will work out fine; you will see."

"Come, Georgiana, let us tell Elizabeth the good news."

They entered the drawing room. Elizabeth was at her work while Bingley pretended to read a book.

"Elizabeth."

"Yes, Fitzwilliam?"

"I would like to announce Georgiana's engagement to Bingley."

Elizabeth gasped. "Oh, that is so wonderful! I am so happy for you. You both deserve such happiness, and I am so grateful you found it in each other." She ran to Georgiana and gave her a hug. "You know what this means, do you not? We shall all be brothers and sisters. Is that not wonderful? Georgie, when and where shall you be married?"

"I am hoping that Charles will agree with me that we be married with Brother and you if you do not mind."

"Well, the soonest I can be married is November 28. We intend to be married at the Lambton church."

"Then we shall, too. Does that plan please you, Charles?"

"Yes, very much so."

The remainder of the evening was spent discussing wedding plans, trousseaux, honeymoons, new clothes, and all of the pleasures and enjoyments that are part of such a happy occasion. Darcy saw an occasional shade of darkness pass across Elizabeth's face from time to time. He knew she must be missing Jane most of all, and perhaps her father and her family. They likely would not be there for her wedding and certainly would have no part in the preparations. She was alone in the world. The three of them, and in part her aunt and uncle in Gracechurch Street, were all she had left.

Rather than travel to town again, Georgiana felt they could rely on the modiste in Lambton for their needs and send away to town for what could not be had in Lambton. Mrs. Gardiner volunteered her services as far as they would go. By the time they were finished, both ladies were very satisfied with their purchases.

Wednesday, August 5 from Pemberley

Dear Papa,

The day you left town last month, Mr. Darcy proposed marriage to me, and I accepted. I have to thank you for your matchmaking, which furthered our understanding of each other's feelings and led to our engagement. I am so happy, Papa. He loves me so dearly, and I love him. I cannot describe the freedom I feel in my heart, knowing I shall have a home at Pemberley. It is so beautiful here: the walks, the gardens and the park. The house itself is stately and fine, yet it is such a home. I have been allowed to redecorate some of the rooms that have not been used recently—namely the nursery, the large dining room, the large drawing room, the morning room—and I am going to have the entryway refinished as well. Mr. Darcy says he is grateful for the feminine taste I am adding to the rooms. I am so glad he lets me decide what to do without arguing with me. He is a wonderful man, Papa, and I am so lucky to have him.

I want you to know that I am now allowing him to support me financially in all my needs and wants, so I no longer require or desire you to send me any allowance money. Please tell Mama of my wedding. Perhaps she will accept me again when she knows I am to marry a man of £10,000 a year. The wedding will be as soon as possible after Jane's year of mourning, on Saturday, November 28, at the Lambton church. It will be a double wedding with Mr. Charles Bingley marrying Mr. Darcy's sister, Miss Georgiana Darcy. Mr. Darcy and I are very pleased with their attachment. Mr. Bingley has purchased a large estate not an hour's drive from here called Hillcock Manor; it is the former residence of Lord Beecham.

You are all invited to attend the wedding and to stay at Pemberley. This house has many guest rooms, quite enough to hold my entire family, and you are very welcome to stay for as long as you wish. Mr. Darcy and I will be hosting a wedding breakfast at Pemberley for the guests and the house servants. We shall only stay a short time before we leave for the London townhouse to spend a few days, then on to a trip to the sea resorts for two weeks before returning to Pemberley until Mary's wedding, which we plan to attend. Do you know the date?

Mrs. Reynolds, the housekeeper, has promised carefully to teach me my duties as mistress of such a large estate, and I promised to be an eager student. We shall also do our best to look after the new Mrs. Bingley in her efforts to learn her duties as mistress of Hillcock Manor. She seems quite uncertain and almost afraid. She and Mr. Bingley will be taking an extended honeymoon before returning to Hillcock.

I have spoken to Mr. Darcy, and if you wish, Kitty is invited to stay with us during the spring and summer. That would take away from you your last daughter.

Please let me know where I stand in the family.

Yours, &c. EB

What a letter to write, thought Elizabeth, having to beg her family to attend her own wedding. It was all wrong, of course. They should be eager to attend and demand that she be married from Longbourn church, which was her right. But Mr. Darcy would have none of it. There were to be no more disappointments in her life, which a marriage in that church would be if her family did not attend. Better to have them travel the two days to Pemberley and stay there. He was right of course, but it was still a disappointment. However, the real disappointment was not having Jane there, as she always imagined that Jane would stand up with her. That is what they had talked about for so many years, late at night in her room when Jane would sneak out of her bedchamber and they would talk until the early hours of the morning. But Jane was gone, and it was not to be. She still cried for Jane when she was alone and she was sure of not giving alarm. But now, at the writing desk in the drawing room, she could not stop the tears.

Mr. Darcy had been watching her write a letter, presumably to her father, though occasionally she wrote to her aunt. He had noticed her shoulders start to sag, her head lean forward, and then he saw her tears. It had to be her father, and it had to be about her wedding. He hated the fact that her marriage to him caused some sadness in her life, but it could not be helped. He knew she was missing Jane, and the breach in her family was now like a fresh wound. He walked over to her.

"Elizabeth."

He knelt down on the floor, to match her height as she sat in the chair, and took her in his arms. She rested her head on his shoulder and cried softly with the pain of a confused heart, both happy and sad at the same time. They stayed that way until Elizabeth raised her head.

"Thank you, Fitzwilliam. Thank you for coming to me and holding me."

She then kissed him — rather passionately, he thought, given the occasion. How he loved this woman. He was so grateful that she was willing to share her pain with him. He took the letter from her, folded it and posted it for express delivery.

"Fitzwilliam, it does not need to go by express."

"If it caused all that emotion to stir in your heart, it deserves the attention."

"You are very kind, sir."

And so the letter was off.

Mr. Bennet was surprised to receive an express from Pemberley. At first, he was worried that something might be wrong with his favorite daughter, but as he read the missive, he found that she was well and that there was cause for great joy. He would share the letter with her mother and see what kind of response he received from her.

"Mrs. Bennet, I have received an express letter from Elizabeth."

"I told you I do not want to hear her name mentioned in my presence, Mr. Bennet."

"She is to marry a man worth £10,000 a year. Is that not wonderful?"

"Who is this man?"

"Why, it is Mr. Darcy. You remember him, do you not?"

"I remember him as a proud, disgusting man. He slighted Lizzy at one of the assemblies. Well, if she wants to lower herself to marry such a man, I suppose she is getting what she deserves after her treatment of poor Jane. I shall never forgive her for killing Jane."

"Mr. Darcy loves her very much. I know him well. He is a kind, generous man. He will care for her very well. I think you should join Mary, Kitty and me at their wedding."

"They cannot get married; she is in mourning."

"They are to be wed on the first Saturday after her mourning is over. We are all invited to stay at Pemberley and to attend the wedding, which will be at the Lambton church. Her friend, Mr. Bingley, is going to wed Mr. Darcy's sister at the same time."

"WHAT!" cried Mrs. Bennet. "But he loves Jane! How can he do this to Jane and marry someone else? He ought to remain faithful to Jane."

"Mrs. Bennet, Jane is gone, and he must move on with his life—something you ought to do.

"Hmph!"

"Miss Darcy is a sweet, loving, kind girl, who in many ways is like Jane. He could not make a better choice of wife."

"I cannot believe it. Everyone is forgetting poor Jane as soon as they can."

"They will marry in a double ceremony with Mr. Darcy and Elizabeth. So, will you go with us?"

"I have a mind to go there right now and scold Mr. Darcy out of his plans to marry Elizabeth. She deserves no such attention. And Mr. Bingley, too."

"You will do no such thing, Mrs. Bennet. You will leave the young people alone."

"You are well aware, Mr. Bennet, that you cannot stop me, that I can do whatever I want, so please be careful how you speak to me. You and the girls go; I shall not. Mr. Bingley is a traitor, and Elizabeth sent Jane to her grave. She will have no attention from me. I am disappointed that you would even consider going, but I should have known better. You have always considered Elizabeth to be without fault, your darling girl, better than all the rest of us. You love her and hate me, your wife, whom you are bound to for the rest of your life. You see that your favorite will be married shortly and no longer yours. You will then be all alone. I shall have nothing to do with you. I hope you enjoy your library, Mr. Bennet."

"I enjoy it quite well and have for many years. Please excuse me."

Thursday, August 6, from Longbourn

My dear Elizabeth,

It was a pleasure to hear from you. I was surprised to receive your missive by express, but by so doing, you insured that it stayed out of the hands of

Dearly Beloved

Mrs. Bennet.

Thank you for your invitation to Pemberley and your wedding. Mary, Kitty and I will accept it. In order to visit with you just a little, since I know your time will be taken up with preparations for the wedding, I propose that we come on Tuesday, November 24th. We shall stay until the Monday following your wedding and then return to Longbourn. I need not say how excited we are to come and visit you.

I am sorry to say that your mother has no intentions of coming. She is still full of anger towards you and now directs some of it at Mr. Bingley for not remaining faithful to Jane's memory. I told her he has to move on with his life and that this is a wonderful match for both of them, but she will not listen to me.

Perhaps you will receive a visit from her. She threatened to go to Pemberley and scold some sense into Mr. Darcy so that he would not marry you. I do not for a minute believe that she would have the slightest chance of success. Perhaps relieving her anger may do her some good towards healing the breach. I do not know whether she will follow through on her threat, but I thought you should know. I can do nothing to stop her from her endeavor should she undertake it.

Congratulations on your engagement and upcoming wedding, my dear. You will be a very happy woman as you two are very suited for each other. You will be able to soften his manners and make him easier and more comfortable in the company of strangers. Because of his status in the world, his information and knowledge, he will teach you things you have not known or had access to and that will increase your importance in society. Be generous with your wealth. You have the power to do much good in the world. I do love you very much, my child. &c. Your father.

When Elizabeth received this letter, she immediately went to her sitting room upstairs for privacy. She was pleased to hear that her family would be attending her wedding. She was not surprised, though, that her mother was still angry with her. The question was: would she ever stop being angry? Would her mother ever recover from Jane's death and move on with her own life? She was shocked to learn that her mother even considered a visit to Pemberley to try to persuade the future bridegrooms out of the decision to marry their chosen lovers. It was laughable to consider that Darcy might be motivated by anything she had to say, but she was worried about Bingley. Elizabeth knew that her mother could say enough to make Bingley feel guilty if he was not as resolved to Jane's death as he appeared and not as in love with Georgiana as he claimed. Elizabeth hoped these things were not true. She hoped her mother would not come, but she resolved to talk to Darcy about it. Long ago, he had told her that she should trust him; she had for all this time, and he had helped her without fail. This seemed to be when she needed to trust him.

First, she must find him. She went through the house looking in all the usual places he might be: first, the library and the billiard room. Then she knocked on the door of his private sitting room with no answer; he was not in the drawing room or the kitchen. She asked Mrs. Annesley and Mrs. Reynolds, but they had not seen him. Puzzled, she went outside and circled the house, thinking that perhaps that he may have gone for a walk or even for a ride, though usually he told her if he went out riding. Then there he was, sitting on a little-used bench in an out-of-the-way alcove.

"Fitzwilliam, what are you doing out here all alone? Are you well?"

"Yes, Elizabeth, I am well."

"What is wrong?" She sat down next to him.

"I am thinking about all the changes that have occurred in my life during the past year, and I am feeling a little insecure, I suppose, and a little guilty for feeling this way."

"You should not have to suffer guilt because of feelings of insecurity."

"I suffer these feelings of guilt because there is one who has suffered far more than I have and I am ashamed to admit that my own mind is troubled."

"What troubles you, Fitzwilliam?"

"I am soon to be married to a woman I have loved for almost as long as I have known her."

"And does that trouble you?"

"No. I am just afraid that somehow I will disappoint her — that, as we become used to each other's company, the feelings of love will wear away and perhaps I may not love her as I do now, and she may not love me, and my heart breaks at the thought."

"I can see how that would upset you. I am sure that she would be concerned as well. What will you do?"

"I am trying to decide what to do. I do not know yet. But I cannot allow that to happen. I love her too much. I shall never take her for granted—never."

"I think that is a wonderful place to start. How will you do that?"

"I will renew the memory of our wedding day every day by greeting her each morning with a kiss and holding her close every night."

"What if she becomes angry with you? That might happen at some time. Then what will you do?"

"She is a very strong-willed woman. On the other hand, she is very intelligent. This combination creates someone who is determined to be right—and very likely is. I have my pride to worry about. Will I be willing to let her be right, especially when she is, especially when it matters, and even more so when it does not? I cannot, will not, let anger and bitterness ruin our love. I just hope she feels the same."

"I am sure she does." Elizabeth was both touched and amused by the conversation they were having, Darcy talking to her as if she were not there. That being the case, she could not help asking him,

"Fitzwilliam, tell me about this woman you love."

"Her name is Elizabeth Bennet, and she is from Hertfordshire. I met her when she was staying with her sister at my friend's house. Her sister was gravely ill. Elizabeth stayed with her night and day, loving her and nursing her. I could see in her eyes the desperation setting in as the end approached for her sister. What made it worse was that her mother blamed Elizabeth for her sister's ill health. When her sister died, Elizabeth's mother would have nothing further to do with her, would not even allow her to return to her home. Elizabeth is loving, caring and gentle. I have seen her with my sister, Georgiana, when she poured out her heart and soul and Elizabeth helped her unload a burden that had been weighing on her shoulders for months. No one else could have done that. She has made me smile when I never thought to smile again. She has made me love when I thought I would never have such a feeling again. She has also caused me to fear."

"How did she do that?" Elizabeth was quite concerned now. This was not at all what she had expected to hear from him.

"One day while her sister was ill, there was an assembly near my friend's home. While there, she was confronted by her mother, and she subsequently fled the room. She ran off in the direction of the house in the dark and cold. I went after her, finally catching up with her. She was frightened, cold and disoriented. I cannot bear to think what would have happened to her had I not found her. I knew I had strong feelings for her, but it was at that moment that I knew that I loved her, and it was also at that moment that I knew I could have lost her."

"Oh, Fitzwilliam."

"And in the spring, she became ill with some sort of nervous complaint. It was very serious. She could not speak, and I believed she could not understand. She could follow some instructions, but if left to herself, all she would do was sit and stare out the window. By then, I knew that I was just waiting for her mourning period for her sister to be completed before I asked her to be my wife, and suddenly, she was taken from me. I was afraid. How could this have happened? How could Elizabeth be inside that body but unable to talk, to act, to think, to be with me? But no matter. I was determined. I knew that I loved her, and so I would take care of her. She would stay with me for the rest of her life. I would sit with her and talk to her, and I told her all about my feelings for her. I thought she could not hear me, so I opened my heart. Then one day, she suddenly came back. She turned to me, touched my cheek and said, 'Thank you for finding me.' I almost cried."

By then, Elizabeth had tears running down her cheeks. She never knew this about Darcy. She had never imagined how he must have felt. Everything that had hurt her had hurt him. He had a kind, tender heart, easily affected — not like the hard image he sometimes showed to the world. How could she ever love him enough?

"So you see, she means the world to me. I cannot live without her. I do not know how to treat her well enough. I want her always to love me the way she does now." He looked at her with just the hint of a smile at the corner of his lips.

"Fitzwilliam, if you always tell her you love her, and kiss her every morning, and hold her close every night, I think you will do a lot towards having a lasting love affair with her."

"Thank you for listening to me and for your advice. May I ask one thing?"

"If it would be proper."

"May I kiss you?" He leaned towards her. She could feel his breath on her cheek.

"What would your lover say to that?" Her heart was pounding in anticipation of what was to come.

"I do not think she would mind." He took her chin, turned it towards him, and brought his lips to hers.

"Neither do I."

Her lips were taken by his mouth. All his worries for her were done away. All her concern was put behind her. Together they had faced one of the challenges they would encounter as man and wife, and together they had reached their own conclusion.

"Fitzwilliam," said his lady to him one day. "I find myself troubled regarding news I received recently from my father. I do not know what to do with it, or whether anything should be done."

"Would you care to share this news with me, my love?"

"Well, yes, I would. My father told my mother about our wedding. He accepted our invitation. He and two of my sisters will be coming."

"That is good news, Elizabeth. What can be wrong?"

"He told me that my mother may travel here to confront you with all the reasons you should not marry me in hopes of breaking off our engagement. She intends to speak to Bingley as well to accuse him of being unfaithful to Jane and fill him full of guilt in hopes of breaking off his engagement to Georgiana. I am afraid of the results."

Darcy stood and went to Elizabeth and took her in his arms.

"Elizabeth, nothing in the world that anybody can say will make me change my mind about loving you or wishing to marry you. Please do not fear. That ring you wear belonged to all of the Darcy wives for the past three generations and you will be the fourth. Do not be afraid on my account. She has treated you horribly. She should be worried that she may not gain admittance to the house. I will not allow her to hurt you continually in the manner that she does. If and when she does come, I will not let her see you. Is that agreed?"

"Yes, I will stay away and not come down unless you send for me. But what of Mr. Bingley? I fear he could be hurt by what she might say about Jane. I do not want anything to happen to disturb his happiness with Georgiana. They do not deserve this. They have dealt with Jane in their own way, but the topic is delicate, and they do not need it raised in such a harsh manner."

"I will not allow Georgiana to see your mother, either. Both of you will remain in your apartments if she comes. I will speak with Bingley. And remember, Elizabeth, my love," — he smiled at her and kissed her nose — "she may never come, you know."

Elizabeth crinkled up her nose and laughed. "Of course, Fitzwilliam, you are right. I suppose I am overreacting. It is just that I feel we—all of us—have found so much happiness here at Pemberley that I do not want it ruined by anyone, even if that person is my mother."

"Elizabeth, I will protect us and ensure that our peace of mind is not affected. She cannot be any worse than my Aunt Catherine, whom you have not met yet."

"Thank you, love."

Chapter 12

All worries regarding Mrs. Bennet had long been forgotten until one day in the middle of September she arrived. Since the problem with Mr. Tuesby, the servants had been instructed that any callers were to be asked to wait in a small drawing room that opened off the entryway until Mr. Darcy could be found, and that he alone would receive callers. But Mr. Darcy could not be found, and this woman insisted that she was Miss Bennet's mother, so the servant felt it would be harmless to show her into the room where Miss Bennet sat with Miss Darcy. Later that day, this servant had a new position in the stables.

"Mama!" cried a very surprised Elizabeth.

"Well, it is the proud Miss Lizzy, too good to take care of her own sister. And who do you have there with you, Miss Lizzy?" Mrs. Bennet asked with a sneer.

"Mama, this is Miss Georgiana Darcy."

"Ah, the little chit who is trying to steal Mr. Bingley from Jane. He will never love you! Never! His heart is lost to my daughter, Jane! For your own good, give him up. You are nothing to him." Mrs. Bennet could not believe her good fortune in having the opportunity so quickly to put that conniving Georgiana Darcy in her place before it was too late for Jane.

"Mama! Please do not speak to Miss Darcy is such a manner! None of that is true! Mr. Bingley loves her very much, and they are to be married in November. He loved Jane, but Jane is gone, Mama. He cannot love her forever."

"Mrs. Bennet, please... I... It is not my... I do not mean... If Jane..."

Georgiana stammered, looking at Mrs. Bennet as though she had seen a ghost. "Oh, Lizzy, it is true, is it not?" Tears began streaming down her pale cheeks. "He does not love me. He cannot love me." Georgiana sat back down on the sofa. "Oh, my life!" she whimpered.

Elizabeth moved to sit by her. How could she let Georgiana think such things, but how could she stop her mother? She felt wretched. Where was Fitzwilliam?

"Miss Lizzy, let her suffer. She deserves it."

"Mother, I insist that you leave this place at once. No one wants you here. I do not want you here. I shall call for your carriage immediately."

"Oh no, Miss Lizzy. Not until I have had some words with Mr. Darcy. I must warn him of the trouble he is inviting by this sham of a marriage to you. How dare you raise your eyes to him? He deserves a wife worthy of his admiration and respect. No one can respect you. You ignore the wishes of your family, allowing your sister to die while you are out dancing and shamelessly flirting with officers. If not for you, Lydia never would have thought to run off with Wickham, and now she is taken away from me because my Brother Gardiner arranged for their marriage and your father allowed it to happen. But, of course, you were always your father's favorite. But who gets the last laugh now? You are gone from the house, and he remains with no one now. He shall certainly receive no attention from me."

"Mother! You know that none of those things is true."

"Do I? Is Jane still alive? Is my Lydia still at home? Tell me that!" demanded Mrs. Bennet bitterly.

"Jane was too ill. I stayed with her night and day. I did everything for her. Lydia made her own choice with Mr. Wickham; you must see that."

"See that? I do not see that. All I see is a disobedient, disagreeable daughter living in undeserved luxury who should be turned out—"

"That will do, madam!" roared Mr. Darcy.

The room fell silent. Mrs. Bennet turned to face him with a triumphant look on her face. Elizabeth was shocked to see him. Georgiana stopped crying and looked at him expectantly, not knowing what to do or say.

"It is a pleasure to make your acquaintance again, Mrs. Bennet. If you have anything further to say, please direct it to me. My sister and Miss Bennet will not be able to hear any more of it, as they will be retiring to Miss Darcy's private sitting room. Ladies?" He motioned with his hand to

Elizabeth and Georgiana. They obediently and gratefully stood and walked quickly from the room, nearly running by the time they passed Mrs. Bennet, who was standing near the door of the drawing room.

"Please sit down, Mrs. Bennet. Let me call a servant for some tea." Mr. Darcy walked to the door and motioned to a footman. "Please ask Mrs. Reynolds to bring tea to the drawing room, and then find Mr. Bingley and summon him to the library. Tell him that I need him but cannot attend to him directly."

"Yes, sir."

He returned to the drawing room.

"Mrs. Bennet, I believe you were about to apologize for some unkind remarks you made to my sister. I have not seen her so distressed in quite some time. I am sure you did not mean it, but I would like to hear your explanation nonetheless."

"Your sister cannot marry Mr. Bingley. I told her so. He is in love with Jane and can never love her. She is nothing to him and never will be. He will always love Jane." Mrs. Bennet said, not quite so sure of herself in Mr. Darcy's presence.

"Mrs. Bennet, she is engaged to my friend. I have given my consent to their marriage after carefully interviewing both of them to determine that they are marrying because of affection for each other and no other reason. They are to be married on November 28 at the Lambton church. He loves her dearly. Yes, he did love Jane, and in his heart, I believe there is a part of him that still does, but unfortunately, your daughter has passed away, and life must go on without her. She would have wanted him to be happy. She was a happy person herself—one of the best people I have known. Do not take that memory from her by denying my friend his own happiness."

Mrs. Reynolds brought in tea and poured out a cup for each of them.

Mrs. Bennet continued on, but in a subdued tone. "You must know, sir, that Lizzy allowed Jane to die. She did not care for her. You will be marrying someone unworthy of you and undeserving of your attention. Please do not lower yourself. Please do not ruin your reputation. Please do not honor her. She did nothing I asked. She was out dancing when her sister was dying. How could she do such a thing? Tell me that, sir. How could any sister do such a thing? She killed Jane!" Mr. Darcy seemed to unnerve her, to confuse her. She was unable to remember all that she wanted to say to him. She was unable to preserve her anger. He charmed her, like a snake before it strikes its prey.

"Mrs. Bennet, in marrying your daughter Elizabeth, I will be marrying the best person I know. But please, Mrs. Bennet, sit back for a moment. I know this is distressing to you. I can tell you why my betrothed"—he stressed the word—"was dancing that night." Mr. Darcy paused, took some tea, and paused again, allowing Mrs. Bennet time to relax against the sofa and calm herself. She submitted to his silence and power; she was unable to speak.

"Miss Jane was being attended by a physician from town as well as the local apothecary. Miss Elizabeth was acting as their nurse. She was with Jane at all hours of the day and night, day after day, night after night. She was ceaseless in her efforts at helping and loving Miss Jane. At one point, there began to be concern over Miss Elizabeth's health, and the physician from London thought an evening out at the officers' ball would be beneficial for her. The physician, the apothecary and one of the housemaids sat up with Miss Jane all night.

"Miss Elizabeth was very hurt by the things you said to her that night, Mrs. Bennet. Distressed and appalled would be better words. When she ran from the assembly room, she was on her way back to Netherfield—on foot, cold, alone and in the dark. If I had not gone after her, I do not know what would have happened. She was not well when I eventually caught up to her. She was crying and screaming your name; her skin was cold to the touch, and she was disoriented. I do not think she would have made it back to Netherfield. I think you would have had two mourning rings to wear, and the first one would have been for Miss Elizabeth. You did a terrible thing that night, Mrs. Bennet."

Mrs. Bennet was discomfited. She was not used to being rebuked, let alone by a person younger than herself, but she held her tongue. Mr. Darcy was too intimidating to challenge, and Mrs. Bennet's conscience was beginning to be pricked.

"Miss Jane was very ill. The physician did all in his power to save her, but to no avail. He said her ailment was of a peculiar kind from which a person was not likely to recover. There was never any hope. Miss Elizabeth did all she could to make Jane comfortable. She loved her, cried with her and stayed with her. There was nothing more that Miss Elizabeth could do for her.

"Mrs. Bennet, I love your daughter very much. She is the kindest, gentlest, sweetest woman I know. All of this must be to your credit as a mother. I am grateful to you for raising such a daughter. It grieves me that you are alienated from each other, particularly at such a sad time. I know you both loved Jane very much. I have been a daily witness to what Miss Elizabeth has had to suffer as a result of Jane's death. I can imagine that as a mother it has been horrible for you and that words do not describe what you feel."

Mrs. Bennet began to weep. Darcy watched her in silence, allowing her to feel her pain and regret, knowing there was no other way for her heart to begin to heal.

"Oh, Mr. Darcy, I loved Jane so much," she said between sobs. "She was so beautiful. I am sure she was to marry Mr. Bingley. She always was so kind. Everyone loved her. I miss her so much." She continued crying. Darcy could not help but be touched at the feelings of a desperate mother. "Oh Mr. Darcy, what have I done?"

"Nothing that sincere conversation and true love cannot repair, Mrs. Bennet. Miss Elizabeth has equally grieved over her estrangement from you. She never has understood it. She has come to accept it, however."

"Do you think she would come back with me to Longbourn?"

"I will not allow it. She will remain with Miss Darcy and Mrs. Annesley until we are married. You are very welcome to attend our wedding. I am sorry, but I cannot part with her—not now. And frankly, I do not believe that you deserve her."

"I suppose you are right, Mr. Darcy. Please apologize to your sister for me. I do not think I should stay any longer. I shall return to Longbourn." With that, she left the house and entered her carriage, which had remained in front of the house.

"Georgie, please, sit down with me." Georgiana had been pacing the floor, crying. She had been overwrought with grief, and Elizabeth was shocked at her reaction. She seemed to be mourning Bingley. She sat down on the sofa with Elizabeth, who leaned over, gave her a hug, and then held her hands.

"Georgie, I remember you once told me that I should not listen to my mother—that she was only trying to hurt me—but that I should trust you, instead. Do you remember? You told me to trust you."

Georgiana nodded.

"Now, what does your heart tell you about Mr. Bingley?" asked Elizabeth, softly, slowly and carefully.

"That he loves me," Georgiana whispered.

"What about your brother? Do you trust him?"

"Yes."

"Your brother never would have consented to Mr. Bingley's proposal if he was unsure of Mr. Bingley's regard for you. Do you doubt that?"

"No."

"And what about me? Do you trust me?"

"Oh yes, Lizzy, you know I do."

"Very well. Then I want you to know that I am convinced of Mr. Bingley's love for you. He adores you." Elizabeth allowed this news to sink in. "And most importantly, do you trust Mr. Bingley? Be honest with yourself, because if you do not, you should not marry him."

"Oh, Lizzy..." Georgiana burst into fresh tears and ran off into her bedchamber.

Elizabeth did not go after her. She stayed where she was, and a tear trickled down her cheek as she began to fear for herself and Mr. Darcy. Why, oh, why had her mother come and ruined everything? Why was her family always taking away everything that was dear to her?

"BINGLEY, ELIZABETH'S MOTHER WAS JUST here. She confronted Elizabeth and Georgiana alone, and I am afraid she hurt them both deeply. When I finally found out that she was here, I hurried to intercept her, but it was too late. Georgiana was confounded, stunned and in tears. Elizabeth tried to comfort her, and Mrs. Bennet carried on about how Elizabeth was a disagreeable, disobedient daughter."

"Where is Mrs. Bennet now?"

"She is on her way back to Longbourn. I talked to her, and I think she softened her feelings somewhat. She has been overcome with sadness due to Jane's death, and she acknowledges that she has not acted reasonably with regard to Elizabeth. She asked me whether I thought Elizabeth would go back with her to Longbourn. I told her that I would not part with her, and that she, Mrs. Bennet, did not deserve her. Surprisingly, she agreed."

"Now that is a miracle! What about Georgiana and Miss Bennet?"

"I interrupted Mrs. Bennet's tirade and sent them off to Georgiana's sitting room. I am quite concerned for them both, more so for Georgiana than for

Elizabeth. Mrs. Bennet attempted to convince my sister that you were in love with Jane, that you could not possibly love her, and that you never would."

"But that is not true! I must see Georgiana. Would you send for her, please?"

"Very well. Be gentle with her, Bingley," Darcy warned.

Elizabeth opened the door and took the note from the tray. It was addressed to her and was written in Darcy's strong hand. She was relieved to see it; she shut the door and sat back down.

My dearest Elizabeth,

I want you to be reassured of my love for you. I also want you to know that nothing anyone might say will ever change that. You are precious to me above all the treasure of the earth.

Your mother has returned to Longbourn. Please know that you can move about the house safely and unmolested.

Bingley is heartsick for Georgiana. I have related to him some of what your mother said to her. He asks you to convince her of his love for her and begs her to join him in the library, where he will wait for her all night if he must.

I remain forever yours,
FD

Elizabeth felt relief upon reading his missive and felt a weight lift off her shoulders at this assurance of his love. She was secure in the knowledge that he had not been affected by her mother's words and that she was safe, her future happiness untarnished. Her loyalty for him increased at the thought of his confronting her mother and ignoring her accusations. She began to cry from sheer relief and joy.

Nevertheless, Georgiana remained devastated. Bingley wanted to see her, and Elizabeth knew that Georgiana must go to him. It was necessary that her faith in him be restored, that he disprove her mother's horrible words, and that Georgiana's troubled heart be eased. Elizabeth composed herself for the endeavor. Georgiana must not see her cry; she would interpret it the wrong way.

"Georgie, I have received a note from Fitzwilliam. My mother has left the house to return to Longbourn. She will not bother you again."

"I am glad she is gone, Elizabeth, but she has hurt me. Does my brother still love you?"

"He sent me a note with two purposes. One is to reassure me that he loves me, and the other to ask me to convince you that Mr. Bingley loves you and to tell you that he is in the library waiting for you, and that he will stay there all night if he must in order to see you."

"Lizzy, do you really think he does love me? How can he? Jane was so beautiful, so kind. Of course, he loves her. How can he possibly think of me?"

"Georgie, you once told me that you did not want to change Mr. Bingley's life but to share it. A small part of that life will include Jane, I imagine. He will not pine after her. He is committed and devoted to you. It is not worth wondering about what would have happened if Jane had not died. Both of our lives would be different. Sadly, she is gone, and now Mr. Bingley is yours.

"As for myself, I have to wonder whether Fitzwilliam would have noticed me long enough to have loved me and found me at Longbourn. What if he had not? Could I ever have loved another? But it is a question I must not try to face even though it requires me to ignore Jane's death. Jane is gone, and I am to marry your brother. There are no 'ifs.'"

"I suppose you are right, Lizzy. It just hurts. I wonder whether he would still love me if she were alive, or whether he regrets loving me, or whether or not I am as good a person as she was."

"Georgie, those are difficult feelings to deal with. The only thing that may help you is time—time spent with Mr. Bingley. You should not feel pressed to marry in November if you are not comfortable. Perhaps a longer engagement would be better to give you more time to know your heart. But I believe that, were you to search the rest of your life for love, you would not find it in such a loving, devoted man as Mr. Bingley."

"He is a wonderful man, Lizzy."

"He is waiting for you, Georgie. Would you like to see him?"

"Yes, I would."

BINGLEY PACED BETWEEN THE FIREPLACE, the door and the window. He had no idea how Darcy was able just to stand there and gaze out the window, as was his habit. Would she come? Had Mrs. Bennet ruined his best chance for love? Miss Bennet and Darcy were strong people. This disturbance would not upset their relationship. If anything, it would give them a chance to escape into a corner of a room, supposedly unnoticed, to 'talk' about it. But Georgiana was a delicate person, thoughtful and reflective. Bingley felt she had suffered much in her young life. He was worried that Mrs. Bennet had poisoned her against him.

There was a knock at the door.

"Come in," Bingley said.

A servant opened the door, and Georgiana timidly walked in, followed by Elizabeth. All four seemed rooted to the floor. Elizabeth looked at Bingley, and Darcy looked at his sister. Darcy broke the silence by walking over to Elizabeth. He took her hand, kissed it gently, opened the door, led her through it and then shut it quietly behind them.

"Georgiana, please know that I love you. Mrs. Bennet is wrong. She had no right to be here, no right to disturb our happiness."

"But Mr. Bingley, how can you love me after having loved Jane?"

He winced at her formal address. "Because I have committed my life to you, Miss Darcy. I cannot help you with what might have happened. All I can help you with is what is happening now."

"What is happening now, Mr. Bingley?"

"I am terrified that I am losing you—that somehow, you no longer love or trust me, that Miss Bennet's mother has come and ripped you from my side, and that through that means, two people who belong together will be alone. And it is a crime that this should happen."

Georgiana began to cry. It was a crime, and she felt like the victim. As he crossed the room to take her in his arms, she turned her back on him. She did not mean to. She had been rocking herself back and forth on the balls of her feet and had tripped on the hem of her gown. Her foot became twisted in the material, and she ended up facing the other way. It was to be a tragic mistake. He stopped his progress towards her.

"I thought you loved me, Miss Darcy." He spun on his heel, left the house, ran to the stables, saddled his horse and rode off without saying a word to anybody. When asked later, nobody knew where he had gone.

'I thought—?' What did he mean? "Charles, I *do* love—"

Then the door slammed shut, and Bingley was gone.

Georgiana ran to the door and threw it open, but he was nowhere to be seen. She ran down the hall to the entryway and asked the servant whether Mr. Bingley had passed by. He replied that he had, and Georgiana went outside but could see no one. She waited for a moment, and then from the far left of the house, a rider left the stables and went up the road towards Lambton. It had to be Mr. Bingley. What had happened? She sat on a bench and cried bitterly, swearing to herself she never would love again; the pain it brought was too great.

The good servant became alarmed. Miss Darcy never behaved in that manner. He left his post and went to the drawing room where he cleared his throat, and Miss Bennet and Mr. Darcy parted rather quickly from each other.

"Mr. Darcy, please forgive the interruption, but may I speak a moment with you in private, sir?"

"Yes, of course," said a flustered Darcy, still straightening his cravat.

As he moved through the door, he shut it behind him.

"Sir, your sister is on the bench in front of the house, crying. I believe it concerns Mr. Bingley, who took his leave without saying a word just prior to her coming outside. He did not ask for his horse or carriage, but went to the stables himself. I saw him riding off towards Lambton."

"Thank you."

Darcy walked quickly to the front of the house and moved toward Georgiana. She did not even notice him as he came near her, and he sat down on the opposite bench.

"Georgiana," he said softly.

Between sobs, Georgiana answered. "I do not know what happened. He suddenly left the library. I was going to tell him I loved him. He slammed the door and left. I saw him ride away."

"Did he say where he was going?"

"No, he just left. What have I done, Brother? Why did Mrs. Bennet ever have to come? Why is everything ruined?"

"Everything is not ruined. There is some kind of misunderstanding. It has been a day of high emotions. I will find Bingley. All will be well in a few days. Let me take you to Elizabeth."

Elizabeth was shocked to hear what happened, especially after seeing their reaction to each other when she entered the library. Eventually, Georgiana stopped crying, but there was little Elizabeth could say to comfort her. She just did not know what to think, and she was worried about Bingley. She was shocked that he would dare think of leaving in such a manner and not tell anyone where he went. Darcy immediately had gone towards Lambton after him , but it was getting dark. She hoped the cool air would clear his head. Of all the things that could have happened because of her mother's visit, she feared this one the most. She always felt that she and Darcy could weather any kind of opposition to their relationship that Mrs. Bennet could throw in their way, but Georgiana was not as strong. Neither was Bingley. Their relationship had not stood the test of time and struggles. This was just too much, too soon. Mrs. Annesley joined them in the music room while Elizabeth played the pianoforte. Georgiana was too shaken to do anything other than sit under a blanket. She refused to go to bed, saying that she did not want to be alone.

DARCY KNEW THAT BINGLEY HAD quite a head start on him, but it was getting dark. This was not at all like Bingley, but then, he had never seen Bingley in love before. He had no idea what had happened, but it had to do with Mrs. Bennet. He had never seen two people so happy together as Georgiana and Bingley. He remembered how she had fought for his consent when they were discussing her marriage. Yes, she loved him, and from the conversation of that same evening, he knew that Bingley loved her. Things could not continue like this, and they obviously were not going to be able to work it out alone. Curse Mrs. Bennet!

Darcy stopped at the Lambton inn, went inside and inquired after Mr. Bingley. He was lucky. Bingley was in a room upstairs. Darcy went up the stairs and knocked on the door.

"Go away, Darcy."

He ignored the request and opened the door to find a half-dressed Bingley sitting next to the fire, nursing a bottle of brandy. Nursing was not the right word. Half the bottle was gone.

"What happened, Bingley?"

"Why do you care? You have your Elizabeth. Nothing bothers you."

"I love you and my sister, and I want to see both of you happy. You will live close to us at Hillcock Manor."

"I am going to London tomorrow. I will find a new solicitor to sell the place. I am not coming back here, ever." Bingley was working very hard to hold back his tears.

"Bingley, tell me what happened."

"We were talking. She started crying. I started to go to her, and she turned her back on me. I told her, 'I thought you loved me, Miss Darcy.' And then I left as fast as I could."

"Well, when you were leaving, she was turning back to tell you that she loved you. She had tripped over the hem of her gown. You were so upset, Bingley, that you did not give her a chance."

"Oh, Darcy!" Bingley collapsed back in his chair. "I am so sorry. What have I done now?"

"What am I going to do with the two of you? How can you let Mrs. Bennet take away your happiness?"

"She will be happier without me. All I do is cause her pain."

"No, she will not. You have caused her pain this evening, but Mrs. Bennet is the source of all the problems. Put down that bottle and get dressed. I am taking you back to Pemberley right now."

"I cannot bear the thought of seeing her, Darcy."

"Well, you have to, because this misunderstanding must be cleared up. She is devastated, and so are you. She has come to realize that Jane is dead, and she also realizes that wondering what would have happened if Jane were alive is not an exercise that matters. I hope that you are going to learn to trust her and give her credit for being a mature woman, regardless of her youth. You are perfect for each other. You must maintain the 'each other' at all costs."

"IF FITZWILLIAM CAN BRING BACK Mr. Bingley tonight, will you agree to see him? I think you should. I think neither of you should go to bed with this hanging over your heads. I am so sorry about my mother, Georgie. I know you did not deserve it. Let us go to the drawing room and see what luck Fitzwilliam has."

"Very well, Lizzy."

DUE TO THE LATENESS OF the hour, it took the men an hour and a half to return to Pemberley. The ladies heard them come in, but their footsteps receded up the staircase. A servant brought a note to Georgiana.

Miss Darcy,

I beg you please to forgive my hasty departure earlier. I know I gave you great pain, and I know it was all a misunderstanding. Darcy found me in Lambton. We are cleaning up and will be down to you shortly unless you send me word that you do not wish to see me.

Georgiana, I apologize for my immature behavior. I am sorry for not loving you enough and causing you to doubt me today. I will do better. Please forgive me.

I promise to love you always.
Charles

Georgiana had tears in her eyes as she handed the note to Elizabeth. Elizabeth read it with a smile. Finally! She went over, hugged Georgiana and told her that everything would be well.

THE GENTLEMEN CAME DOWN TO the drawing room. Bingley decided that the fewer words spoken, the better. He walked over to Georgiana, put an arm around her waist, a hand on her face, and kissed her as if his life depended on it. She responded to him willingly, knowing her life depended on him. Darcy and Elizabeth left the two alone, satisfied that this struggle would soon be over.

Bingley broke away from her first. "Georgiana, you must let me—"

She put a finger over his lips. "Shhh. Please kiss me again, Charles."

Bingley leaned his head down to her willing lips and kissed her again. He felt her love course through his body, confirming what Darcy had told him: that she loved him and that she no longer entertained any thoughts of what things would be like if Jane were still alive. Her kiss told him that she thought only of him.

Georgiana wrapped her arms around his neck and pulled herself close to him. The sensations of being loved by him were so new, so wonderful. How could she ever have doubted him? As he ran his hands slowly over her shoulders and back, she resolved never to doubt his love again.

"Charles, I am so sorry. Please allow me to tell you this. Please allow me to stay how sorry I am that I confused you and made you angry with me. It was not my intention to hurt you. I am sorry I was uncertain about your love for me. I promise I shall never be again. Please forgive me; please do not leave me again."

He began to stroke her cheek.

"My love, it is my fault for becoming angry, for not being willing to listen to you, for not giving you a chance to talk to me. I did not realize the torment in your heart. I did not trust you. I did not love you enough. I will spend the rest of my life proving to you that I do love you and that I am worthy of your love."

"Charles, I do love you." She leaned into his arms. Her mind finally felt at peace. As for Bingley, his pride was humbled by the love and trust shown to him by the woman in his arms. He would ever be grateful to her brother, who with great patience, pulled him out of his selfishness and brought him back to his sister. Darcy trusted him with his sister. He would live up to that trust.

BOTH COUPLES WERE GRATEFUL THAT the rest of September passed quietly. October was to be an exciting month, for on the 21st, Bingley was to take possession of Hillcock Manor. Georgiana was familiar with the road between Hillcock and Pemberley since she and Bingley had taken Darcy's curricle there many times to look at the place from the outside. It was a new home, only 50 years old and built in the Palladian style. Henry Repton had left his touches on the house and grounds. It would be a pleasure to live there. Georgiana considered herself the most fortunate girl in the world. During one of these rides, Bingley asked her about the changes in her life.

"Do you think you will miss Pemberley? You have lived there all your life."

"Well, I have spent a considerable amount of time in London, but I will miss Pemberley. I have such memories there of my father and brother. I never knew my mother, you know, but my father would tell me about her."

"You will have no memories at Hillcock."

"I know, but I will have the chance to make new ones. There will be you, Charles, and all our children. There will be so many things that we shall do together, and I will strive to remember them all. I will tell the children about their grandparents. It is sad to think they will have no Grandpapa to hold them on his knee and tell them stories of his youth. Fitzwilliam will have to do the same with his children."

"Yes, I bring no grandparents to our marriage, either, and unfortunately, I am not too happy about their choice of aunts, at least on my side of the family. You should know that I have not invited either of them to the wedding."

"Charles, you did not!"

"It is true. I become ill watching Caroline fawn over Darcy, and I am not going to subject Miss Bennet to such treatment on her wedding day. I am sure we will all meet in London, and they will of course be invited for short stays at Hillcock along with the Darcys, but I am not going to tolerate that behavior from her any longer."

"Well, Charles, I have always been uncomfortable with her behavior towards Fitzwilliam. I know he does not like it."

OCTOBER 21ST FINALLY CAME, AND the four friends traveled by coach to Hillcock, where they were met by the housekeeper and several servants who had traveled from London. Bingley gave them a tour of the house, or at least as much as he could remember, then they explored the rest of it. There were plenty of guest rooms, and the master suite was wonderful. It appeared that it had not been redecorated in many years, and Georgiana and Bingley agreed it must be refinished before they could comfortably occupy the rooms. While they were drawing up their designs, Elizabeth and Darcy continued alone.

"Elizabeth, would you not like to have a new home?"

"Yes."

"You would?"

"Of course, I would not want to remain at Longbourn for the rest of my life."

"But you have not been at Longbourn for almost a year now."

"But it is still the only home I have. I have only remained other places as a guest—at the will of the owner without any rights or privileges. Yes, I would very much like a new home."

"I have never considered you as anything but the mistress of Pemberley since the day you arrived there."

"That is very generous of you, Fitzwilliam, but hardly the case."

"But still, that is the power you have had over me."

She walked over to him, put her arms around his neck and whispered in his ear, "Then I am glad of it, Mr. Darcy." He started to kiss her neck. She began to squirm a little until they heard Georgiana call their names.

"You will absolutely love our rooms when they are finished, Elizabeth. We decided to leave all the furniture and just do the walls and floors in lighter colors. Charles thinks they can have all the work done in a few weeks. We will find someone to help us while we are in London on our honeymoon.

Is that not wonderful?"

"Yes it is, Georgiana. How do you like your new home?"

"I like it very much. It will be a wonderful place to live. Oh, I shall miss Pemberley, but I shall like being Mrs. Bingley and living at Hillcock very much." She took Bingley's hand and kissed it, a gleam of love shining in her eyes.

Darcy just smiled at her. He was sad, though. His little sister had grown up.

BINGLEY TRAVELED DAILY TO HILLCOCK, usually with Georgiana. He had decided, at least for now, to retain the steward and principal staff members of the household. He met with them for hours to catch up with the affairs of the estate so he could assume his place as its master. Georgiana decided to be bold, and she began to visit the tenants in the parish. At first, she was shy and had to force herself to speak. Some people thought her proud but also found that a confusing idea, because if she were shy, why would she come to visit?

Gradually, with practice, she taught herself a series of questions to ask and responses to make to the anticipated answers. It was not the fluid conversation one would expect from a lady, but Georgiana attempted to enter the lives of the people for whom she felt she would be responsible, and she went to lengths to know them. Eventually, some of the tenants caught on to what she was doing, but the question remained: why did she come if she was not sincere? They could only attribute it to shyness. They pitied her and made efforts to help her feel comfortable. Georgiana understood this to mean that they were desirous of being her friends and immediately was able to relax in their presence.

From that time forth, her visits were anticipated with a true desire to see her, and when a tenant family stood in some sort of need, they felt comfortable asking her for help or direction. She would take no action on her own, but she would take their troubles to Mr. Bingley to let him decide what was appropriate. She decided early on not to interfere in the business of the estate, but she would rely on him and the goodness of his heart when she came to him with the personal matters of troubled tenants. The sweetness of her heart endeared her to these new friends; they found her a welcome change to the proud Lady Beecham, whom they did not miss at all.

"Bingley, I have something I would like to show you."

"I would love to see it, Darcy."

"Good. Please come with me to the library."

Darcy motioned for Bingley to sit down as he bolted the door. Darcy went to a set of books on a shelf, removed them to a table and opened a panel. Inside the panel were several boxes, which he brought out and set down before Bingley.

"These are my mother's jewels. They belong to Georgiana, except for this necklace and ring. My mother left them to me to be a gift from her to my wife, whoever she may be. I will give Elizabeth the necklace the night before we are married, so that she may wear it at our wedding. She already has the betrothal ring. This wedding ring matches it."

"They are beautiful, Darcy. I do not know what to say."

"These jewels have been in our family for many years. They came from my mother's father on her marriage and now they go with Georgiana on her marriage to you. These jewels are nothing compared to her, Bingley. Please take care of her."

"I will, Darcy. I will."

November passed quickly. The days were full of preparations for the wedding or assisting Bingley at Hillcock. Tuesday was to bring the arrival of Elizabeth's father, Mary and Kitty.

"Fitzwilliam, tonight is to be our last evening of peace and quiet until we are married. Do you not find it strange that we should be taken from each other by the demands of other people as we come close to our wedding instead of being allowed to spend more time together in preparation for the sacred state of matrimony?"

"It is strange when you say it that way. I am very selfish and have not had to share you with anyone for the past months; I am not looking forward to the demands other people will place on you, even if they are your family."

"I am so glad they are coming, Fitzwilliam; I have not seen them in so long. Please do not think I love you any less."

"Of course I will not," he said, drawing her close to him. "Let me show you." He kissed her with love, yearning and a little fear—fear that, somehow, she might disappear and all of this might be a dream. Every night he prayed it was real.

Chapter 13

The carriage that Elizabeth had been awaiting finally was heard approaching the house, and she hurried out to meet it. As it came to a stop, the door flung open, and Kitty flew out, then Mary, then her father.

"How wonderful it is not to be cooped up in that carriage! I thought we would never get here. Lizzy, what a wonderful house this is, and this is all to be yours?" asked Kitty.

"I am very glad you are all here. You are all very welcome."

"I am very proud of you, Lizzy," said her father.

"It is so good to see you again. Thank you for coming." She gave him a kiss on the cheek.

"How are you, Mary? Does your Mr. Collins still love you?"

"Yes, very well. I am looking forward to your wedding so I will know what to expect at my own."

"I know what you mean. I felt the same at Lydia's wedding."

"But you were not engaged to Mr. Darcy then."

"No, I was not, but I had great hopes that I would be. Let us all go in the house so I can show you to your rooms."

"Miss Georgiana Darcy, this is my family, Mr. Bennet, whom you have met, Miss Mary Bennet, and Miss Catherine Bennet. They will be staying at Pemberley through next Monday. They know that we will both be leaving on Saturday after the wedding breakfast."

"It is a pleasure to meet you. You are all welcome to Pemberley. I am so happy that you could come to attend Elizabeth's wedding and that you will be there for my wedding, also. Miss Mary, I understand you are to be married soon. I hope this is a special occasion for you as you anticipate your own wedding. Miss Catherine, I hope we can be friends. Elizabeth tells me you are to stay with her and Mr. Darcy during the spring and summer. I hope you will visit us often at Hillcock Manor."

"Thank you, Miss Darcy," responded Kitty.

As for Mary, she felt like she had peers in Elizabeth and Miss Darcy, as a bride-to-be in a short time. Her wedding was scheduled for mid-December.

"Mr. Darcy is out on estate business at present. Perhaps you would take pleasure in the library, Mr. Bennet. Let me take you there now," offered Georgiana.

"Thank you, Miss Darcy. I have heard a great deal about the Pemberley library."

HAVING DELIVERED MR. BENNET SAFELY to the library, Georgiana led the ladies into the drawing room, where she called for tea.

"Miss Mary, I understand that you will be marrying Mr. Collins, the rector of my Aunt Catherine's parish."

"Yes. He is very proud of his relation to your aunt. He is quite attentive to me and visits about once a month, from a Monday to a Saturday, so I see him as often as possible, though not as often as I would like. I have not yet been to Kent to his home in Hunsford, which is next to Rosings Park as you know. I will not see it until we are married. He tells me it is a nice parsonage and that he is making improvements for my comfort. He has said something of shelves in the closets for the rooms upstairs. I hardly know what he means, but I am grateful for the attention all the same."

"I am so glad you are marrying him for affection. There are so many who marry for convenience or who are forced into arranged marriages. I understand it is a good match for your family, also. I am pleased for you. To marry for love and make a good match as to fortune is the best there is. I congratulate you, and I am sure you will be very happy. My aunt can be a little overbearing, but she means well, and she will treat you kindly. I think you will be happy in your situation. It is a long way from Hertfordshire—fifty miles, I believe. But even that distance can be traveled from time to time."

"Thank you, Miss Darcy. Yes, we hope to be able to visit in Hertfordshire and hope that my family will visit us. The parsonage is not large, but it will admit one of my sisters and her husband at a time."

"Kitty, have you heard from Mrs. Wickham?" asked Elizabeth.

"Only on two occasions. She says that married women are too busy for much writing. She is always in a violent hurry to be off to this place or that. She did mention a dinner with General Rothwell. She said that it was rather dull, but she hoped that the officers would be more lively without the general around."

"Lydia is Lydia still, I see," commented Elizabeth.

"I am shocked that she would be chasing after officers now that she is married. I find it to be inappropriate behavior, Lizzy. When I look back at my own behavior of the past year, I am not satisfied with it."

"Well, Kitty, all of us have much to learn in our lives, and some lessons are harder than others. I am pleased to see you have changed, and I agree: Mrs. Wickham's behavior is not quite proper."

"How did the wedding go, Lizzy? I wish I had attended," said Georgiana.

"I believe it went well. I was very distracted with my own thoughts." Elizabeth smiled.

Georgiana looked at her with a confused expression on her face that quickly changed to understanding.

The week passed by in preparation for the wedding. Mary and Kitty assisted Mrs. Reynolds, leaving Elizabeth with as little to do as possible so that she could enjoy Mr. Darcy. To get away from all the noise of the preparations, they often joined Bingley and Georgiana on their daily excursion to Hillcock.

"Elizabeth," said Darcy, "Jane died one year ago today."

"I know. I cannot believe it was so long ago. So much has happened to me since then." She turned to face him. "Fitzwilliam, I could not have survived this year without you. I know that you have saved me on more than one occasion, and all my happiness is due to you. Thank you so much. Thank you for loving me. I do not deserve it."

"It has been a difficult year for you. I admit I am very much looking forward to seeing you in your new clothes. I think you will be very pretty in the light, colorful patterns. As far as having saved you, somehow I know you would have survived without me. You are a very courageous woman. What dependence you placed on me in the early days of our relationship is a testimony to me of your trust and affection even if you were unaware. I was extremely grateful to be able to help you in any way I could. I was so happy to be connected to you in the smallest way; to have shared a part of your life in any way possible brought me the greatest satisfaction. I loved you then, and all those things became, for me, endearments from you.

"It must have been horrible for you," cried Elizabeth.

"I love you enough to do anything for you. As far as your not deserving it, you are the most deserving woman there is. I could not imagine myself ever loving another. I feel bound and committed to you already. I took my vows for you at the Wickhams' wedding. I repeated the words of the ceremony but substituted our names instead of theirs. I remember looking at you the whole time."

"Fitzwilliam, I did that, too! In two days, we will have our second wedding, then. You are too good to me, Mr. Darcy—just too good. But I do not know what I would do without you."

However, she did know what she would do with him, and so did he. He gathered her up in his arms and began to kiss her ears and cheeks. She reached around his neck and pulled herself close to him.

Their lips met in a tender kiss that expressed their love and commitment and seemed to last…

…AND LAST. Finally, the pastor of the Lambton parish had to clear his throat to get their attention. With a final quick kiss, they parted, though still holding hands.

The pastor continued: "O Eternal God, Creator and Preserver of all mankind, Giver of all spiritual Grace, the Author of everlasting life; send thy blessing on these thy servants, this Man and this Woman, whom we bless in thy Name; that as Isaac and Rebecca lived faithfully together, so these persons may surely perform and keep the vow and covenant betwixt them made (whereof this Ring given and received is a token and a pledge,) and may ever remain in perfect love and peace together, and live according to thy laws; through Jesus Christ our Lord. Amen.

"Those whom God hath joined together let no man put asunder."

Then the pastor addressed the congregation: "Forasmuch as Fitzwilliam Darcy and Elizabeth Bennet, and Charles Bingley and Georgiana Darcy have consented together in holy wedlock, and witnessed the same before

God and this company, and thereto have given and pledged their troth either to the other, and have declared the same by giving and receiving of a Ring, and by joining of hands; I pronounce that they be man and wife together, in the Name of the Father, and of the Son, and of the Holy Ghost. Amen."

She was now his. The wait for her was over. He could bear with patience the prayers and scriptures of the remainder of the service.

Elizabeth never would have imagined that the joy that she felt now was possible a year ago. The day after Jane's death had been so black. It had seemed impossible, the pain so great. She had a new best friend now, someone who loved her even more than Jane ever could.

Mr. and Mrs. Bingley led the way down the center of the chapel to the doors. As she was walking behind them, she heard someone say to her,

"Congratulations, Mrs. Darcy!"

She reveled in the appellation. She was proud of her new name, of her new husband. How could she not be? He was the best man she knew.

Darcy handed her into the carriage waiting for them outside the church and sat next to her for the five-mile trip to Pemberley.

"Elizabeth, my love, thank you for marrying me," said her husband.

"Oh, Fitzwilliam, you have made me so happy." He put his arm around her, and she leaned her head against his shoulder. He took her hand and drew circles on the back of it with his fingers. She felt penetrating warmth from his touch, and her skin tingled where he touched her. Smiling, her thoughts took her to places that would formerly have been forbidden. She thought he did not notice her blush as they passed under the large trees marking the road to Pemberley.

"Mrs. Darcy, may I ask of what you are thinking?"

Elizabeth was caught. What could she say to him? She reached up and stroked his face with her hand.

He was hypnotized by her touch. All he could think of was the sensation of her fingers as they moved around his face and neck. Her skin was so white. He let his finger glide across her shoulders and along her collarbone, and up along her chin, and behind her ears. She looked up at him with absolute trust, willing to surrender herself completely to him. He was overwhelmed.

"Elizabeth, you are the greatest of all God's creations, and once again I say, thank you for marrying me."

She took his hand with both of hers and kissed it. She kissed each finger, gently and slowly, never taking her eyes off him. When he could stand it no more, he collected her in his arms and gently pressed his lips to hers, whispering to her how much he loved her and appreciated her. With a tear in her eye, she greeted his kiss with anticipation and gratitude — gratitude that he loved her despite her faults, gratitude that he would choose to marry her and accept her into his life, and gratitude for the passion he so willingly expressed for her and of which she could not get enough. She opened her lips, and he deepened the kiss as his hand freely roamed the curves of her body.

The ride to Pemberley had never seemed so short before.

Epilogue

The Darcys left the wedding breakfast as soon as they could. They were only interested in each other, and this interest could not be satisfied in the company of others. The ride to London passed like a dream. Mrs. Darcy entered the townhouse as its mistress. Somehow, it seemed different this time, not arriving as a displaced guest. The joy she felt in the embrace of her husband could not be described.

Mr. and Mrs. Bingley stayed in London for a month before returning to Hillcock Manor. Mrs. Bingley stepped into her role as its mistress with little difficulty. When Darcy had estate business that could not be put off, Elizabeth went to Hillcock to visit Georgiana, help her with her duties, and accompany her on visits. She was loved by everyone in the parish and soon excelled at her duties. The estate flourished under Mr. Bingley's careful attention.

The Darcys attended the wedding of her sister, Mary, in December. Elizabeth did not want to share Darcy with anyone, so they arrived at the inn at Meryton only the day before the wedding. Her mother said very little to her. Mrs. Bennet was quite wrapped up with the wedding, and Elizabeth was unsure of what to say. Darcy was determined to prevent a recurrence of anything like the scene that occurred at Pemberley in September, so he refused to allow them to be in the same room together without his presence. Elizabeth did not mind. She could hardly do without him. They returned to Pemberley after two days.

Elizabeth gave birth to a daughter the following year. Though her husband traveled to Pemberley for the occasion, Mrs. Bennet did not, and she died before Elizabeth's son was born. They never reconciled, and Elizabeth never again returned to Longbourn. Her father came to visit her and the children at Pemberley.

Elizabeth and Darcy kept their marriage fresh by remembering their wedding each morning with a kiss and holding each other close at night. For them, the magic of early love never wore off, and to each other, they always remained dearly beloved.

The End

Also by Lewis Whelchel

Rocks in the Stream

New Releases from Meryton Press

Echoes of Pemberley

The Journey

Find Wonder in All Things

Rainy Days

CPSIA information can be obtained at www.ICGtesting.com
Printed in the USA
LVOW090051171112

307573LV00002B/152/P